A Walrus in Oxford

by

Stella Stafford

A Walrus in Oxford is Little Wychwell Mystery Number Seven

It follows:

Did Anyone Die?,

A Very Quiet Guest,

All that Glisters is not Silver,

Speak of the Wolf,

Some People Go Both Ways

and

Walking Where the Willows Whisper

Dedicated to the real walruses
whose habitat is being destroyed by climate change

Walls, who is now a don at Kings, is seeing strange things in both his apartment and his college room. Is something sinister really occurring or has he just been devoting too much time to academic study and gone a little mad? Why has the Walrus, one of the college contemporaries of Barnabus and Walls, reappeared in Oxford? Is this just coincidence? Barnabus, Walls' best friend and also an indefatigable mystery investigator, springs in to help his friend uncover the truth.

This is a work of fiction and entirely the invention of the author's imagination except that Oxford, Oxfordshire and many of the places described in this book really do exist, others do not, most notably Kings and Coromandel Colleges and Little Wychwell.

Any resemblance between the characters in this book and real people, whether alive or dead, is entirely accidental.

Médecin sans Frontières is a genuine international independent medical and humanitarian organisation but Andy the Walrus is entirely fictional and thus does not work for them and never has.

Chapter 1

Elodea opened the door of the Old Vicarage in Little Wychwell.

It was Mr Shipman, the gamekeeper, beautifully dressed, as always, in tweed plus fours, jacket and cap.

"Good morning, Mrs Smith!" he said.

"Good morning, Mr Shipman!" said Elodea, wondering at his arrival and hoping that Evvie, his wife, who had various mental disorders, had not gone missing again.

"How are you? I hope you are well!" he said.

"Very well, thank you. And you?" said Elodea.

"Very well," replied Mr Shipman. "I am here to deliver something to you. Evvie has sent you a message," he announced.

He reached into the left-hand breast pocket of his jacket and pulled out a very folded piece of paper.

On the outside, in tiny letters, were the words "The Vicar's Wife" in red biro.

"Ah!" said Elodea. Evvie had called her that before. The much-loved vicar of Little Wychwell was, in fact, a single man and lived in a smaller house in the main street. Elodea and John had bought the rambling Old Vicarage when the church had sold it off, "in need of slight repair". But many of the previous church incumbent's activities had taken place in their rooms, such as coffee after church and parish meetings, and had been assumed by the villagers to go with the house.

Elodea and John had long ago become used to the notion of hosting all of these. So Evvie's confusion was less peculiar than it might have seemed, especially as the current vicar was also called Smith.

"I expect she's written some kind of funny joke out for you. She's such a card, my Evvie!" said Mr Shipman, but he had a slightly anxious look as he spoke.

"Ah!" said Elodea again, but this time in a way that suggested that Elodea understood and that if the note should happen to be a tirade about the cruelty of her husband, who was a very kind and loving husband who absolutely adored his erratic and troubled wife, then Elodea would ignore it.

She opened the folds, carefully, so the thin paper didn't tear.

"You mustn't show it to me. Strict orders. It's a secret just for you, she said," said Mr Shipman.

Elodea was struggling to read the tiny red handwriting placed right in the very middle of the page. She tilted the note towards the sun to see it better.

"I haven't got my reading glasses with me, Mr Shipman," she said. "Shall I pop in and get them?"

"If you would do me the honour to borrow mine," he said, producing an ancient and battered looking tin spectacle case from his inside pocket. "My father had these before me, and very good I find them."

Elodea gratefully perched the old-fashioned glasses on her nose. The lenses were much stronger than her own and the writing was now rather too large and still rather blurred, but she could read it.

"Beware of Satan and all his works. For the son of Belial has sought to have you in his claws. The Devil appears in many guises – man, woman, child or beast. But you will know Beelzebub when you see him, however he appears. For this is the sure sign. You will know him by his redding."

Elodea's mind ran back to last summer and Fran. Fran wore red. Was this a rather *belated* warning? Then she told herself off. It was not a true warning; it was meaningless rambling drivel, generated by a disturbed mind. She must pray especially hard for Mrs Shipman this evening, pray that the poor lady might get the medical help she needed.

She glanced up at Mr Shipman's anxious face. Then she pretended she was still reading the sheet and laughed loudly in the most convincing way she could when she 'finished'.

"*Such* a joke, Mr Shipman. I don't know where she gets her ideas from! Do you want to read it? Or shall I tell it to you?" Elodea asked, rifling through her mind to see if she could think of any suitable jokes that Mrs Shipman might have written in a letter and hoping he didn't actually read it himself. The poor man, he suffered so much already.

"No, no," said Mr Shipman. "If Evvie said it was a secret from me I had best not read it in case I forget and repeat the joke to *her* next. Then she *will* be vexed. Good day to you!"

And he touched his cap, turned, and walked smartly and quickly away.

Elodea was suddenly aware of riotous sounds behind her. She swivelled round just as there was a loud crash. Pippy, her aging Yorkshire terrier, shot out of the kitchen and fled into the quieter sanctuary of the drawing room where she curled up on a heap of books and newspapers, her nose between her paws and a wary look on her face.

Elodea dashed into the kitchen to discover Theodora standing on the draining board and throwing cups down at Amadeus, her big brother. He was catching them as well as he could but had clearly just missed one. Its shattered remains littered the stone-flagged floor.

"Playschool time!" Elodea yelled at the top of her voice, while grabbing Theodora and holding her firmly under one arm and, at one and the same time, picking up the pieces of china from the floor before anyone stood on them and cut their foot.

Breathlessly she dumped the pieces into the bin and turned to Amadeus.

"However did Theodora get onto the draining board?" she asked.

Amadeus considered for a few seconds.

"She *jumped,*" he said. "Like *Spiderman*!"

Amadeus was not good at lying and no one could possibly have believed this whopper.

"Don't be *silly*! How *could* she have?" asked Elodea. "Tell me how she *really* got up there!"

"She jumped, she jumped, she jumped, she jumped, she jumped, she jumped, she jumped!" sang Amadeus, jumping up and down on the spot himself to demonstrate.

Elodea considered the realistic possibilities. Surely Theodora couldn't have reached the draining board by clambering up the pile of books at the other end of the kitchen and toddling or crawling right round the work surfaces, negotiating the heaped debris that they contained, while Elodea was talking to Mr Shipman? *Could she*? In that short space of time?

Elodea sighed. For Theodora, unlike her quieter and better-behaved older brother, who seemed to take after his mother's side of the family, was unquestionably a *Smith*. She was over-intelligent, inventive, loud, rebellious, physically very able and always ready to experiment with a frightful new idea. It was all too possible that she *had* managed this feat.

"Wump!" Theodora pronounced at the top of her toddler voice, directly into Elodea's ear. "Me wump!"

Elodea glanced up at the clock. "Quickly, Amadeus, shoes on! Playschool! We are going to be late as it is! You will be starting nursery school soon, and then we really must get out on time."

Sometimes Elodea thought that having to bring up two of her grandchildren when she had already brought up four of her own children was a little much. Their parents, Barnabus and Angel, were taking an 'off-peak-pre-the-next-baby' holiday in Portugal for a week. Thank goodness, she said to herself, that Barnabus and Angel were back tomorrow. Elodea usually looked after the children in the daytime, while their parents were at work, but not for the whole twenty-four hours.

"Why don't *we* get to go to Portugal for a 'pre-the-next-baby' week while *they* have the children full time?" John, Elodea's husband, had asked when he had first heard about the trip. "*You* look after the children *all* the time as it is! They are taking you for Neddy!"

"I'm sure Barnabus could manage without me for a week if you want to take me to Portugal," Elodea replied. "Name the week!"

"You know I'm too busy to take a week off any time soon. Why can't Angel look after them more of the time?" demanded John.

"Oh, John dearest, you know she can't! You know about her post-natal depression. Poor dear; she would love to look after the children but you know she's never been able to cope with staying at home with them. And her wages are *vital* for the mortgage," Elodea replied.

"So why does she keep having another baby?" John persisted. "She didn't get on with the first one, so why not stop at that? She *must* like them really. I tell you, they are taking you for Neddy. The money *can't* be an issue. The amount she earns I could pay her the equivalent of her wages and she could stay at home! And then you could have your life back!"

John had never taken Angel's career at the Maitre Hotel seriously. He thought it was ridiculous for someone with an Oxford degree in Engineering to work as a waitress, and had never understood the graduate employment problem.

"Oh but, John, she's the deputy manager now, you know. She earns a lot more than you think," protested Elodea. "In any event who could resist having another baby like Amadeus and Theodora? They are *so* sweet! You know they are! And I don't mind looking after them. And you are away most of the time yourself. You are away in Switzerland next week so they won't bother *you* in the slightest. I shall enjoy the *company*!"

There was no answer to that. For John, Elodea's physicist husband, spent a lot of his time globetrotting to attend work collaborations, discussions, workshops, conferences, projects, and for many other reasons. Elodea imagined his rooms in

Oxford starting with surprise whenever he reappeared in them, the way little-used rooms are always startled when a human returns to them after a long absence.

For now Elodea resumed her surveillance of her kitchen for possible routes that a toddler could use to climb up to the draining board. Climbing up from the other end of the kitchen seemed the only possibility but how ever had Theodora managed to negotiate all the tottering piles of lost property, cookery books, bottles of tomato sauce, mugs, tins, bags and other kitchen accoutrements that littered the work surfaces?

Elodea suddenly remembered Mrs Shipman's note. Could Theodora have used satanically induced levitation as a method to raise herself to the draining board? She glanced at the children. No, neither of them were wearing red. Then Elodea giggled at her own silly thoughts. *Obvious*ly neither of the little angels could *possibly* be the Devil! Poor Mr Shipman! She did not know how he coped. Whatever jumbled and confused idea would Mrs Shipman come up with next?

Elodea forgot about both the draining board and Mrs Shipman as they moved into the next round of their regular early morning drama. Amadeus had failed to get one of his shoes on straight and this crisis had been enough to trigger the regular pre-playschool tantrum. Amadeus flung himself to the floor screaming.

"Won't go! Won't go! Won't go! Hate playschool! Won't! Want to stay with you and Theo! Waaaaaaaaaaaaaaaaaaahhhhhhhhh! Waaaaaaaaaaaaaaaaaaahhhhhhhhh! Waaaaaaaaaaaaaaaaaaahhhhhhhhh!"

Theodora, always ready to join in any screaming match, opened her mouth and delivered a succession of ear-splitting shrieks herself.

Elodea picked up the pair of sound-blocking earphones that she kept by the telephone especially for this purpose, jammed them on her head and smiled at the children. Then she yelled, at a volume to compete with theirs, "We are leaving! *Now*! *Immediately*!"

The sounds from the hall drifted into the drawing room but the dusty atmosphere, the piles of books and the collapsing sofas muffled and calmed them. Pippy was sharing the drawing room with the ghost of a long-dead vicar. Having decided that her refuge was a safe one Pippy had carefully rearranged her pile of books to make herself a comfortable nest. The vicar was roaming round examining his own ghostly bookshelves to find the book he needed to complete his sermon. They both felt at peace, glad that they were not in the hall. Pippy settled deeper into her nest and closed her eyes for a nap. The long-dead vicar patted the little dog on the head as he floated past.

In the distance the front door slammed shut.

Then Pippy realised they had forgotten to take her with them for her walk. She whimpered a little.

The long-dead vicar was just saying "Don't trouble yourself, little dog; they will notice and come back for…" when the front door burst open again and Elodea, disguised as a whirling dervish, shot into the drawing room, grabbed Pippy, and dashed out again.

The front door banged shut again. The ghostly vicar leaned back in a ghostly chair and gave a satisfied sigh as the clouds of dust straightened themselves out and settled down in layers again. He could now get on with his sermon uninterrupted but he thought that he would instead take a nap. The sunshine that filtered in through the threadbare curtains, still closed as no one had remembered to draw them back yet this morning, was very pleasant, subdued yet warm. He sighed and shut his eyes.

Chapter 2

Elodea, having safely deposited Amadeus, headed away from playgroup with the pushchair, looking neither to right nor left as she concentrated on keeping up a bruising pace. Theodora, tethered by her harness, jolted in the air occasionally as they hurtled onwards. "Through brush, through briar, through mud, through mire," thought Elodea to herself, waving a casual hand at two of her acquaintances as she shot past them.

"Ah!" said Mrs Wigley to Agnes Grey. "She be trying to get that child to sleep again."

If Elodea continued at this speed for long enough she knew that Theodora, over-stimulated by the jolting and the exciting number of scenes that were shooting past her eyes, would, eventually, be forced to let her eyelids droop, snap open, droop, snap open, and finally close. Then Elodea could slow down to a normal walking pace and, provided the pushchair did not actually stop, Theodora would take a nap and Elodea could spend some peaceful time with her own thoughts.

Pippy, lying on soft layers of towelling on the buggy parcel shelf, enjoyed the wild rides. She stuck her head out between Theodora's feet and pretended to be a dragon but eventually she too curled herself up and descended into a deep and happy doze.

As they thundered forwards Elodea's mind wandered back to Mrs Shipman's message. A thought had occurred to her: perhaps 'redding' did not mean the *colour* red but was a misspelling of the word 'reading'. That left her a wider field of possible devilish candidates. For a start, her *entire* family were avid readers and many of her friends were also very keen on literature. A rather wicked smile made her lips curve upwards. She was thinking of the person she knew who read most of all. Yes, a *definite* candidate! Priscilla, her friend from university and now a Classics don at Coromandel College.

Elodea's conscience immediately smote her. How could she possibly, even to herself, have suggested for one second that dear, good, well-behaved Priscilla was a manifestation of the Devil?

Her mind scanned backwards through her memory to those far off days when she had first met Priscilla. They were both freshers at Oxford at the same college. On her very first day there Elodea had arrived far too early and feeling nervous and misplaced. She unpacked a few things and then went and read the college noticeboards. She noted all the events which she was supposed to attend, both those for freshers in general and those particularly for PPE students. Then she wandered up and down the completely empty corridor near the noticeboards for a few minutes, still seeing no one else at all, and then, not quite knowing what to do, she went back to her room and unpacked some more things.

An hour later she heard the student in the room next door arrive. Parents were depositing her, saying goodbye, heading away. After leaving what she felt was a decent interval, Elodea popped round and knocked on the door.

A girl opened the door. Her rather plain looks were not improved by the quite unwelcoming frown on her face. She looked as if she had been interrupted in the middle of a most important task.

"*Ave!*" she said.

"*Ave!* I mean, hello! I'm in the room next door!" Elodea said.

The other girl stared at her as if this made no sense at all.

"My name's Elodea!" Elodea added.

"Ah!" said the other girl.

There was silence for a few moments and then the other girl, concluding that the conversation had finished said *"Vale!"* and shut the door again.

Elodea gave up. She decided to go and explore the rest of the college by herself until it was time for the college PPE freshers to attend a sherry reception with their tutors, where she found plenty of other people who *enjoyed* conversing.

The following morning, when Elodea entered Hall for breakfast, she saw her next-door neighbour sitting by herself with a cup of black coffee. Elodea headed over to the same table, with a full tray of porridge, cooked breakfast and a pile of toast.

"Ave!" said Elodea, deciding to appropriate the other's greeting.

"Don't interrupt me! I'm reading!" the girl replied.

Today it might be possible to conclude that Priscilla was wearing some form of Google glasses, Elodea reflected, but in those far-off days there was no such thing. There was nothing on the table but Priscilla's cup of black coffee. Elodea glanced round behind her – no writing on the wall behind, no visible writing anywhere that she could see. Elodea was a voracious reader who read whatever was available, including items such as the back of cereal packets, but there was clearly nothing with any form of lettering on it in the immediate vicinity.

Elodea, refusing to be defeated in her social outreach efforts, sat down opposite the girl and started to plough through her breakfast. By the time she reached her third slice of toast the other girl finally stopped staring into space and focussed on her.

"You have the room next door to me," she said.

"Yes," said Elodea. "I came round yesterday; do you remember? I was feeling a bit lost and lonely and I wondered if you were as well but you didn't seem to be so I went to the PPE sherry reception and then to meet the Principal and then I went to a freshers' disco with the rest of the PPE crowd at *Coromandel* because Elizabeth – she's one of the *other* PPE students – has a cousin there. There were lots of dreamy boys there as well as rather geeky ones and it was wonderful and we met..."

Elodea looked at her companion. Priscilla's eyes had a faraway look. She was no longer listening.

Elodea sighed and went to get some more toast and coffee. You seemed to be allowed to eat as much breakfast as you wanted and Elodea, despite being very thin, was permanently hungry.

She got back and put the toast and coffee down.

"More toast," the other girl said, suddenly and unexpectedly. It wasn't a question. It was a statement of fact.

"Yes," said Elodea. "I'm always hungry. People sometimes ask me if I have worms or something but I think it's really because I am never still. I move around all the time, or dance, or..."

Elodea looked at her companion. This conversation reminded her of the one between Alice and the caterpillar in Lewis Carroll's *Alice in Wonderland*. The other girl had vanished into her own mind again. Elodea gave up and instead ate three more pieces of toast. Priscilla's eyes came back into focus. She looked at the third piece of toast avidly as it vanished, and licked her lips.

"Could you get me one, too?" she said.

"One?" asked Elodea, jumping slightly.

"*Uno*," elaborated the other, thinking that it was strange that even for fluent speakers of their non-native languages it was often *numbers* that proved the sticking point. Even so, not to understand 'one' was *most unusual*. Elodea had seemed to speak English quite well on their previous day's encounter, but clearly it must be her *second* or even *third* language. *Italian* by the look of her. Priscilla looked at Elodea with a degree more interest: here was a possible case study for the difficulties experienced by those who spoke English as a non-native language. Clearly Elodea had some very basic linguistic difficulties despite apparent fluency. Then Priscilla looked at the butter dripping from the edge of Elodea's slice of toast and reconsidered the size of her order. "No! *Cinque!*"

Elodea was used to people mistaking her for an Italian but still sighed as she began to say "I'm not…" before she realised that she had lost the other's attention yet again.

Elodea, deducing correctly that Priscilla meant five pieces of toast, went to find a full rack of toast and butter and a plate and a knife, while muttering under her breath about some people's legs not seeming to work.

When she returned she held the toast at a slight distance till she had the other girl's full attention.

"I was just wondering," Elodea said, "what your name is and what you are reading."

"Priscilla, Herodotus, thank you!" replied Priscilla. She stood up, leant across the table, grabbed the toast and plate, and returned to her invisible book.

Elodea liked to recite passages of literature to herself, and she had a good visual memory so she usually also saw the entire page of print in her mind's eye. But never before had she met anyone who read entire chapters, or possibly entire books, from memory.

"Well," Elodea said, quite aware that she was talking only to herself, for Priscilla had returned to her 'book', "I'll, I'll see you later, I expect, bound to meet on the stairs or something. Come round to my room if you like, and we can have coffee. I have *biscuits*."

Even the word 'biscuits' did not register, which was strange as it had a magical attraction for most students. Elodea gave up, dashed off to her room to get her purse, and then took a trip to Blackwells to buy the books on her reading list – real solid books, with paper and print. Elodea felt more than a little freaked out. She supposed there might be lots of Priscillas at Oxford. Was she going to feel really stupid and insufficiently academic the whole time she was here due to requiring the use of printed paper as a normal reading medium? She thought of the other PPE students. They had seemed perfectly normal, not particularly studious, and very friendly. It was comforting to look around Blackwell's well-packed shelves and conclude that most people read books in the way she herself did: using actual solid books. It must be Priscilla who was the exception.

Elodea now reflected that most freshers at Oxford had a terrible revelation in their first week or so there, similar to hers with Priscilla. For all, save those actually destined to achieve very high firsts, discovered that they were not, as they had always been at school, in the top rank of academic brilliance but in fact had been demoted from 'promising officer' rank of academic achievement to 'cannon fodder. Most of us were and still are just remedial-level academics, I suppose, she thought to herself, it's not as if they don't make it quite clear with the academic gowns: for scholars those really large gowns with sleeves, for exhibitioners the shorter and sleeveless, for commoners the shortest and most sleeveless of all. Elodea sighed as she thought how stupid Oxford tutors must think nearly all of their students to be. However, she said to herself, it is really a good system, for the really academic-and-subject-brilliant become harmless academics and the rest of us who are destined to return to the real world have empathy for the less able and the underdog ever afterwards.

Elodea was awoken from her thoughts by the noise of a bicycle bell almost immediately behind her. She jumped a foot in the air and then swivelled round to see the Vicar beaming at her.

"Is dearest Theodora asleep?" he asked as he cycled along slowly beside the pushchair to keep Elodea company.

"I do hope so," Elodea replied. "I can't stop pushing to lean over and look at her face properly because if she is asleep, that will wake her up."

The Vicar leaned dangerously off his bicycle to see Theodora's face, making a gigantic wobble as he did so. Elodea snatched the pushchair out of the way just before he toppled into it. The Vicar slammed a foot down on the ground and rebalanced himself.

"Yes, yes, the little lamb is fast off. Good, because I wanted to discuss next Thursday's coffee morning with you. It is OK if we hold it at your house as always?" said the Vicar, quite unruffled by his near tumble.

Elodea knew that he only asked this as a formality. To begin with, when they first moved in, Elodea and John had thought it funny that parishioners arrived regularly on their doorstep to use their big downstairs rooms for meetings. They had even tried explaining that the house was no longer the vicarage *as such*, and been totally ignored. By now only the Vicar himself ever asked their permission and then in a way that suggested certainty of acceptance.

"Of course, of course!" she said.

"Excellent! Let's get down to the fine details then," said the Vicar.

"Just, just a moment! *Before* that," said Elodea, "I have a quick *theological* question. Do you think the *Devil* ever manifests himself in *apparently human form*?"

"I don't see why not. Do you?" replied the Vicar. "There are many references, both biblical and historic, suggesting such manifestations. Now, *the coffee morning*…"

Elodea thought it was just as well that he had his mind on the coffee morning, for as soon as she had asked the question she wished that she had not. It had been foolish in the extreme as it was entirely possible that he might have delivered an hour of carefully prepared and referenced sermon as a reply. Even worse was the possibility that very question had been the subject of one of his *recently* preached sermons and the Vicar might have been surprised and hurt that she could not remember it. The Vicar always preached long, abstruse and very academic sermons and his flock collectively, Elodea included, took the opportunity to reflect quietly on their own thoughts, enjoy a nap, or even surreptitiously read the Sunday paper or a book or complete a crossword puzzle.

Elodea thought she would look the subject of manifestations of the Devil up on Google next time she had any leisure time. There were bound to be some exciting references about it, even if most of them were suspect and untrue, especially as the suspect and untrue were bound to be the most satisfying.

The subject of the coffee morning did not take long as the Vicar himself had only the vaguest grasp of how such things worked. Elodea smiled politely as he explained that it would require both tables and chairs and, er, *things*, you know, ah yes, coffee probably and cakes and…. Then he told her a very interesting anecdote about golden eagles, reported on the current health of all the birds and animals in his little garden 'bird hospital' for injured wildlife, and pedalled away.

Elodea returned to thinking about her early days in Oxford. She had been far too busy with receptions and meetings and starting her study to attempt further acquaintance with her next-door neighbour over the next few days. But she had scanned the college lists on the main noticeboard and concluded that the Priscilla studying Classics was likely to be the correct one. Everyone else on their staircase soon had their name fixed on their door together with a little notebook and pencil in case callers came when you were out and wanted to leave a message. But Priscilla's door remained resolutely blank.

So Elodea was very surprised when there was a knock at her own door and she opened it to find that it was Priscilla standing outside.

"Hi!" Elodea said. "Would you like a cup of coffee?"

"No," said Priscilla. "It is time to go and join the Bodleian. *Tempus rerum imperator.* Shall we travel thither together?"

Elodea had entirely forgotten this important event.

"Goodness!" she cried. "So it is! I'll get my gown."

They walked down and back together and swore the correct solemn oath and joined the Bodleian. On their return, Priscilla consented to have coffee in Elodea's room and they had a little laugh together about the 'kindling fire' section of the oath, and then Elodea felt that they were definitely friends.

The ratio of male to female students at Oxford was five to one at that time. By the end of third week Elodea had already attracted all five of the male students to whom she was entitled, and also Priscilla's share and several more who should have belonged to other female students. As she never liked to hurt any of the young men's feelings by giving them the cold shoulder there was a constant stream of male visitors calling at Elodea's room for coffee or a chat. There were so many of them that this had even been noticed, rather sourly, by the very unobservant Priscilla. Elodea's diary was packed with social events to which she was being taken. In fact even Priscilla was beginning to wonder how Elodea could conceivably be fitting in her lectures, tutorials and essays. Elodea knew only too well how she was fitting in all the work and play as her hours of sleep grew shorter and shorter every day and she was a regular member of the 'essay crisis miscreants club', meeting in the college library between the hours of 2.00 am and breakfast on the night before tutorials. Every time Elodea staggered out of the library at 9.00 am she decided to forsake all social activities and become more organised. But somehow she never did.

Elodea was growing rapidly thinner and the black circles under her eyes were becoming daily more pronounced. If Priscilla had looked with any attention at her fellow humans she could hardly have failed to notice and be concerned. But as she never did, Elodea's physical state did not trouble Priscilla in the slightest.

In fourth week, as Elodea walked up to their rooms with Priscilla after dinner in Hall, Elodea sighed lugubriously – such a *very* loud and *very* sad sigh that it even penetrated to Priscilla's brain through her current thoughts about her own weekly essay, which was now in its third orderly and carefully referenced draft.

"*Lorem ipsum*?" Priscilla enquired.

"Just this *boy* who has asked me to go to the cinema this evening and I don't want to go with him but I was too weak-kneed to hurt his feelings by refusing, so now I *have* to go," replied her doleful friend. "He is going to be *so-o-o* boring! A *scientist*, Priscilla!"

"What *sort* of scientist?" asked her friend.

"A *physicist*!" wailed Elodea.

"A *physicist*!" exclaimed Priscilla, in the same intonation that she might have used if she had been told that a human-sized rat had asked Elodea to go and see a film with him. "What on *earth* were you *thinking*? I expect he had to have special coaching to take the *Latin* entrance paper and I doubt if he knows *any* Greek at all. Scientists! *Nanos gigantum humeris insidentes*!"

Leaping to the defence of the underdog, as she always did, Elodea protested, "But they have to learn *German* to study Physics; I remember that from school. German for Physicists. They had an extra course."

"What's that got to do with it?" demanded Priscilla. "German is *not* a classical language."

Elodea groaned a little at Priscilla's narrow view of life and said, "But I think they have to know about Latin and Greek for maths, surely, all those Greek letters in maths. Don't *physicists* do *maths*…?"

Elodea trailed off after looking at Priscilla's expression and then began again. "Anyway, I read Economics myself. *That's* a science."

"*Hardly!*" sniffed Priscilla. "In any case, it is tempered by Philosophy and Politics in your case."

"Very true," quoth Elodea, "but, you know, Pris, I don't know which of them I hate most. They are all three of them totally *dire*."

Priscilla ignored this comment as Elodea was always complaining about the dreadful nature of the subjects in her course and Priscilla had abandoned any hope of finding out why Elodea had taken PPE in the first place. She had even asked Elodea this question directly several times, and Elodea seemed quite unable to produce any form of adequate reply since Priscilla did not count "My school said it was a good choice for me" as any form of explanation.

"To get back to this evening," said Priscilla, "*whatever* are you going to *talk* to him about? You can't even discuss *literature* with *scientists* as far as *I* know."

"We're going to the cinema. We won't have to talk to each other. We can watch the film," said Elodea.

"Do you know what are you going to see? Is the film about science? Almost bound to be *entirely* scientific if he is a *scientist*," said Priscilla.

"I'm sure scientists watch *other* sorts of films," protested Elodea, "but actually it's *2001, A Space Odyssey*. Apparently they are having a special reshowing of it."

"So it *is* about *science*. *Quod erat demonstrandum*!" said Priscilla.

"It's not *really* about science," said Elodea. "It's science *fiction*, not science. It was a huge blockbuster when it first came out. But I *don't* want to go to it, especially not with *him*."

"There is only *one* solution," pronounced her heartless friend. "You cannot possibly go to *this* film with this *person*. *You'll have to go out somewhere else. Momento vivere*! He'll get the idea if he arrives and you are out, and that saves you from having to be cruel to his face, which you are clearly incapable of achieving. *Facta non verba*!"

Even now, so many years on, Elodea felt herself blushing red with shame at her readiness to take up Priscilla's suggestion rather than risk the horrors of *being bored*.

"But where could I possibly go?" she wailed, as if there was nothing else whatsoever that she could possibly do in the whole of Oxford that evening.

"You *sing*," Priscilla said, as a statement not a question.

"Yes, I know. I'm afraid I do sing a lot. I'm so sorry. Does it disturb you?" said Elodea, who thought that Priscilla had veered right off the subject and was about to complain about Elodea's continual warbling penetrating through the wall between their rooms.

"Problem solved!" said Priscilla. "Come and join Coromandel Choir this evening; Coromandel have a joint one with us and are short of first sopranos. *I* am going there myself, although not as a first soprano, *obviously*!"

At that time most people had to leave their own colleges in order to meet the opposite sex at all unless they were at one of the five mixed colleges. It must be *so* much simpler now, thought Elodea, but maybe people didn't get out of their own colleges nearly as much, which would be a bad thing. The idea that the whole world was encased in the walls of your own college and that the distance to any other college was almost insuperable was a strong enough belief even when she was at Oxford at a single-sex college. Consequently men's colleges at that time often combined with women's colleges to get the full range of voices for their student choirs.

Priscilla's suggestion seemed to give Elodea a brilliant escape from an evening of tedium with a physicist although it would hardly help with her other problem of getting on with her overdue essay before 2 o' clock tomorrow morning. Elodea convinced her conscience that the lack of first sopranos in Coromandel Choir was a disaster which it would be *wrong* of her to not immediately aid. She also told herself that this definitely excused her from either having to go to the film or from avoiding seeing her physicist by telling him that she had an essay crisis and then being forced by her conscience to go and work in the college library all evening. So she scribbled, hastily and carelessly, "So sorry. Had to go out. Back later" in a callous way on the pad of paper pinned to her door, and went off to Coromandel Choir practice with Priscilla.

But when the two of them reeled back up the stairs later, having followed choir practice with drinks in the bar at Coromandel College, Elodea was amazed to discover 'her' physicist still sitting outside her door, waiting patiently for her to return. He rose awkwardly from his crumpled heap on the floor and unfolded himself to his full height. In the restricted space of the corridor Elodea suddenly realised how very, *very* tall he was. He was also very muscular, not at all the style of male student that usually appealed to Elodea. She preferred the slighter, more artistic looking type, she thought to herself, not overgrown giants. But she raised her eyes to his and his eyes looked at her anxiously, and they were beautiful eyes, full of honesty and devotion and kindness and, yes, even *love*. She felt very wicked for abandoning him. She was also very nervous, for she had betrayed him *on purpose* and how terrible if he should ever find out and be dreadfully hurt. *What if Priscilla told him*?

"You were *rather* a while; I was so worried about what the emergency might have been," he said. "Did you have an accident and have to go to E and R? Are you OK?"

"Yes," gasped Elodea, "I'm, we're, yes, *very well*."

"Thank goodness for that! So glad they fixed you up OK!" he said.

"Actually I wasn't ill," said Elodea, honestly.

He turned to Priscilla. "Oh, it was you who was ill. Did you have a fall or something? I hope you are OK now!"

"Hmmph!" was all Priscilla said, for she refused to speak to scientists in general, them being, in her opinion, a lesser species. But the boy heard this as 'Yes!' for he was, naturally, looking at the far more beautiful Elodea again. Elodea decided not to refute the suggestion that Priscilla had had a medical emergency.

"I think we'll have to give the film up," he said. "I don't think we can even get there in time for the *late night* showing now. What a shame you missed it while you were looking after your friend! There might be something on at the Penultimate Picture Palace. We could find a Daily Info sheet somewhere and check."

Elodea had a dreadful thought. She looked at her watch.

"The college will *close* in a few minutes. You must *leave*!" she cried in alarm, for in those days her college had a curfew exit time for all but its own female members.

Her eyes grew even larger than usual and looked very serious. "Otherwise you will have to jump the back wall to get out and the Principal or the Dean might be hanging around and you will get into terrible trouble, and me too probably! Fined or rusticated or even – "

He interrupted her, quietly but firmly, looking untroubled at these dire suggestions and thinking how much he would like to kiss her.

"I think I can run faster than your Dean or Principal," he said, calmly, "but come out *with* me instead. Come for a *walk*! I love walking at night. Sometimes I go *roof* walking. Have you ever done that?"

"Actually," said Priscilla, magisterially, "Elodea is going to have coffee with *me* next. Perhaps you could call back to visit at a more suitable time, tomorrow, say, or even next week. *Perfer et obdura; dolor hic tibi proderit olim*."

Priscilla thought she was rescuing Elodea from an unwanted visitor. But to her surprise neither of the others were even listening to her carefully composed speech of rebuff. Instead the boy reached out his hand and took Elodea's, and Elodea said to him, "What a wonderful idea! Although perhaps *not* up on the roofs: a little tiring, don't you think, and not really allowed, so…"

"Will your friend be OK now?!" he asked, suddenly remembering Priscilla's supposed illness.

"What?" said Elodea. "Oh yes, *yes*, she'll be *fine*! Bye, Pris!"

They both headed off together and vanished from view around the bend in the stairs.

"Not at all to *my* taste! But *entirely* up to her! *Ut sementem feceris ita metes*," said Priscilla to herself, and she wandered off to her own room to study in peace without Elodea crashing about next door.

Now Elodea sighed with happiness at the far-distant memory, for she had abandoned all of her other admirers from that day. She had been going out with John ever since, and had, of course, married him too. Since John was a model student Elodea's social life shrank to a more manageable proportion of her time and she became a model student as well, although her wails about the stupidity of all three of her subjects continued for the entire three years of the course.

Elodea never did 'roof walk' while at Oxford. She was not afraid of heights and quite nimble enough to scale the routes up to the roofs, but her conscience stopped her. She knew that roof walking was illegal and therefore wrong, and so she could not bring herself to do it. Not even to have the thrill of dancing by star- and moonlight high among the beautiful Oxford spires with the man she loved. She imagined what it must have been like up there, looking down on a dreaming city while balanced on a medieval turret or clinging to a gargoyle. John had continued to roof walk for the whole of his undergraduate and postgraduate time, only abandoning the practice when he became a junior don. Perhaps it was not too late, Elodea thought. Maybe she should suggest a trip round the roofs with him to John, say, for next weekend. She laughed out loud at the absurdity of her own idea.

Theodora jerked awake at the unexpected noise, looked around, saw she was trapped in the pushchair, with no opportunity for mischief, and began to yell with the full force of both lungs.

Bother! thought Elodea, accelerating. She forced the pushchair forwards at top speed until Theodora was joggled back to sleep again.

Then Elodea turned a corner and through an open gateway saw old Mr Wheatley sitting on a chair with a double-barrelled shotgun across his knees, in a field that was otherwise empty save for gigantic plastic-wrapped cylindrical bales of silage. She waved at him.

"Hello there!" he roared to Elodea at a volume that woke Theodora again.

Elodea stopped the pushchair for she might as well give up now and let Theodora scream while she talked to the deaf old man, and then she could try the high-speed sleeping method again.

"After pigeons, Mr Wheatley?" she yelled back.

"Some young varmints have been rolling my bales around. Split a couple of they open and landed one right down in Gibbett's Wood. I'm watching them now, I am. If I gets my hands on those little varmints they'll soon stop playing 'roll the bale', I'm telling 'ee!"

"Super!" yelled Elodea, not being able to think of any more suitable adjectives. She wondered about Mr Wheatley as a possible human manifestation of the Devil. He *could* be diabolical, she supposed, but she had never seen him *reading* anything other than the very respectable *Farmer's Weekly* and he *never* wore *red* to the best of her recollection. Then she told herself off: he was a sweet old man and his liking for activities like the boggart dancers was purely due to his respect for village traditions. His current activities seemed perfectly reasonable to her, as a long-term inhabitant of Little Wychwell, for, in Elodea's view, if someone was vandalising the bales they deserved to get chased by Mr Wheatley with a shotgun. Some people never understood that farmers' crops were valuable and that damaging them was just as bad as shoplifting or robbery. Old Mr Wheatley would never *actually* shoot someone, at least, not on *purpose*, she added to herself.

Elodea continued onwards between the high hedges on either side of the narrow road, the buggy still emitting ear-splitting shrieks, and on the next corner they nearly collided with Lady Wilmington, who was riding a huge black hunter, his sides burnished so well that you could almost see your face in them.

Her Ladyship waved to Elodea and pulled her horse up. Elodea did not even have to consider if Lady Wilmington could be in any way satanic. She was a very upright pillar of the community, despite once having been married to a master criminal, and also extremely kind and good, Elodea said to herself.

Ignoring the noise that Theodora was making, Lady Wilmington bellowed at Elodea, "Can YOU read the SECond READing in MORNing SERvice on SUNday? Mrs ATHell is having her HIP done!"

"Yes, yes, of course!" Elodea replied, nodding her head to help to get the point across and hoping Lady Wilmington could lip-read over Theodora's yells.

Lady Wilmington looked at the screaming infant and fished in one capacious tweed pocket. Eventually she extracted an old and quite unhygienic looking paper bag from which she removed a dubious unwrapped golden sweet of huge dimensions.

"BarLEY suGAR!" Lady Wilmington announced, leaning sideways from the saddle to give it to Elodea. "Pop IT in HER mouth. Soon HAVE her QUIet."

Elodea took the suspicious morsel. It had bits of paper and fluff attached to it and did not look at all wholesome. Once upon a time she would never have given an infant such a thing. She looked at Theodora, mouth wide open so that she could scream better. Elodea leant over and put the sticky object directly into Theodora's gaping pink maw.

Theodora choked slightly. She glared at Elodea. Then she sucked. Then she smiled. She continued sucking.

"KNEW it WOULD work!" said Lady Wilmington. "I keep them for the VERy SKITtish HORses; they LIKE them TOO. She'll SOON be TRAINED with that to HELP. Always MAKES them QUIet as a DOVE on the LEADing REIN."

Elodea hoped that Lady Wilmington would never tell Angel and Barnabus that Elodea had used Her Ladyship's horse training methods on their precious daughter.

"Yes, YOU may HAVE one TOO!" said Her Ladyship, opening the mouth of the bag a little wider and waving it in mid-air.

Elodea was just composing a polite denial when she realised that Lady Wilmington was addressing the horse. He swung his gigantic head around, slobbering with anticipation, and put his muzzle into the bag. Then he took it out – one sweet held daintily between two huge teeth.

"Good BOY, RaJAH! So CLEver," said Lady Wilmington, "the WAY he CAN pick ONE up so DAINTiLY!"

The horse had somehow managed to negotiate the sweetie past his bit and was crunching it with evident satisfaction.

"Would you like ONE, ELoDEa?" asked Lady Wilmington, reaching down with the bag again.

"No, thank you, Lady Wilmington. So kind of you to offer!" said Elodea, politely.

"It's OK; I've GOT plenty!" said Lady Wilmington. "Go ON, have ONE!"

Elodea took one gingerly between her fingers. "Thank you so much!" she said. Rajah did not seem pleased. He rolled the white of his nearest eye at her.

Lady Wilmington tossed a barley sugar casually towards her own mouth, caught it neatly, started sucking, restored the bag to her pocket and said, in a slightly muffled way due to the sweet, "MUST go! MUSTn't let RAJah GET cold!"

"No, of course not. Bye!" called Elodea to thin air, for they had vanished around the bend.

She looked at Theodora, still sucking contentedly and quietly, her eyelids beginning to droop again, and wondered if they sold these really huge barley sugar sweets at the local village shop and whether keeping them in a paper bag in a tweed jacket and adding some horse saliva was important, or whether the standard sweet would be just as soothing.

She looked at the sticky object she was holding between her own fingers. Pippy looked out at it and licked her lips but Elodea said "No!" very firmly as she was quite sure that so much sugar would be very bad for very small dogs. She was momentarily tempted to save the sweet for when Theodora's first sweet was finished but, firmly resisting this notion, she looked around to make sure no one was watching her and then slid it quietly into the ditch, making sure she posted it through a gap between brambles that went right down into the water. Elodea did not want the sweet to catch on the undergrowth so that Lady Wilmington noticed it, suspended there in glowing orange, next time she rode past

Elodea looked at Theodora, who looked wholly blissful, and then had a terrible smiting of conscience about feeding Theodora a combination of sugar, paper and horse saliva just in order to keep the little angel quiet. How could she have done such a thing? It must have been the hypnotic effect of Lady Wilmington's air of command. No wonder she controlled horses so well! Elodea began to panic in case the poor child was food poisoned and then decided Theodora had already sucked off the top layer so that worry was too late. Then she remembered that Theodora might choke, and decided there was no alternative but to remove the remainder of the sweet as soon as possible. She leant over to do so but Theodora, sensing the thought, clamped her lips firmly shut, sucked more avidly and glared at Elodea so fiercely that Elodea stepped back. Elodea was left to weakly reassure herself that if Theodora *should* choke she would certainly *hear* her and could whip her out of the buggy and turn her upside down at once. Elodea told her conscience that she was sure she had read somewhere that animal saliva was *very* hygienic, which was why all animals licked their wounds, and that she knew for *sure* that *paper* was *perfectly edible*. Elodea had a rather uneasy feeling that these saliva facts were probably from that very reliable source known as a Facebook posting, but managed to convince herself that even so it was *definitely true*. In the long term Theodora suffered no ill effects at all and it must be admitted that Elodea acquired a large bag of outsize barley sugars from the village shop and put it in her coat pocket 'for emergencies', and that following this purchase her walks with Theodora became far quieter and more leisurely.

Having tucked her conscience back into bed and soothed it to sleep, Elodea's mind turned back to Mrs Shipman's warning, and then again into the long-ago past at Oxford. She smiled as she thought of John as he once had been – a gawky and nervous young man. Then she wondered whether Mrs Shipman have possibly have meant *John*. If 'redding' *was* reading, John's literary diet consisted almost entirely of scientific papers in journals and even occasionally whole scientific textbooks. There were religious fundamentalists who thought that "science is the Devil's work". However, reasoned Elodea, rather illogically, the note had said that *she*, Elodea, would know the Devil by his or her 'redding', and Elodea herself did not think that the papers that John read were in *any* way devilish. She found John's preferred reading material *incomprehensibly boring and dull* but not *satanic*. So, no, *and*, she added hastily to herself, she would in any event definitely discount her own beloved angel husband.

Who else was there? There was, of course, Charles, Priscilla's mainly completely absent husband. Charles was nearly always either in Canada, where he had taken a Professorship soon after his marriage, or climbing in the Himalayas. Not that she could possibly have really thought of Charles as the Devil either, she told herself firmly. Elodea had never been particularly fond of Charles because she always felt that his marriage to Priscilla had simply been a cynical ploy to get a larger 'married' flat in Wolfson College, and Charles' subsequent behaviour in rushing off to take a job far away from Priscilla had not persuaded Elodea otherwise. But Charles and Priscilla had *stayed* married and Priscilla also seemed very happy with their long-distance relationship, so Elodea scarcely thought Charles could be labelled as *actually evil*. Elodea considered Charles' leisure pursuits: being an avid mountaineer hardly seemed like the work of Beelzebub. A nonsensical phrase "Does the Devil climb mountains?" shot across her mind, in the form of a black-and-white tabloid headline. She giggled and decided to Google that phrase later, just for fun to see what came out. Then she looked at the time and hastened onwards.

Chapter 3

Elodea was now on the homeward stretch of her walk, travelling up the main street of the village. She was now considering the rest of her family in relation to Mrs Shipman's warning. However she pulled herself up quickly from this activity as she was perfectly sure that none of her own darling angel *children* or *grandchildren* could *possibly* have any Satanic qualities whatsoever, and then graciously extended this exeat to her children's partners as well.

So, that left her friends and acquaintances. Elodea began to run through her entire list of these. To which of them could Mrs Shipman *conceivably* be referring?

If gossip- and rumour-spreading ladies were the devil in disguise then Elodea had to admit that she had quite a choice among the ladies she knew in Little Wychwell. Beginning, naturally, with Mrs Wigley, the fastest gossip and rumour spreader in the entire village.

Elodea had a momentary vision of Mrs Wigley garbed in a traditional red devil suit together with horns sprouting from her head and a pitchfork in her hand. It was a fearsome, if hilarious, thought.

Then Elodea felt dreadfully, sinkingly guilty. Dear, *good* Mrs Wigley, always doing kind things for other people in the village, always ready to help anyone in distress, even if it was by appearing and talking to them when they might prefer to be alone. Elodea whispered a short prayer to ask God for forgiveness, barely audibly but nonetheless quite carelessly out-loud. Then she realised the possible and terrible magnitude of this error. First she glanced over her shoulder and then stopped entirely so that she could revolve on the spot and look in all directions.

She had been quite sure that the street was entirely empty before she spoke but one never knew where Mrs Wigley might pop up next.

Perhaps the Devil was hiding in plain sight. Could Mrs Shipman be referring to the Vicar of Little Wychwell himself? He did like hanging around in the churchyard at midnight, supposedly to observe the bats and barn owls. However that reason was extremely likely to be true in his case. The Vicar was a passionate naturalist, especially in the field of ornithology. This was such an important part of his life that he tended to neglect his vicarly duties in favour of his ornithological ones, but he was a dear, good man too. Elodea gasped at her own temerity and wickedness at even considering him as a candidate.

Another whispered prayer for forgiveness. Another hasty look round to make sure no one else was there to hear it. The Vicar also tended to pop up without warning, frequently bobbing up from behind a hedge due to the fact that he had been bird watching.

But, due to this furtive glance behind, Elodea had failed to look ahead, and she nearly collided with Miss Starbuck and her bicycle. Elodea jammed the brake on the buggy and yanked hard with both arms to bring it to a halt. The bicycle swerved across the front of the buggy and then stopped, neatly and precisely. Miss Starbuck slid from the seat, feet astride the crossbar, still holding the handlebars.

"So glad to *catch* you," said Miss Starbuck. "I was hoping to find you somewhere about. We need *extra helpers* at the pensioners' social evening on *Wednesday*. Can I put you down for washing-up duty? How *kind*! I always know I can rely on you!"

She hitched herself back on to the bicycle seat and, very upright, pedalled furiously away.

Elodea, good as she was, sulked for the next hundred yards. She *hated* washing up, and thought most of the pensioners were more than capable of doing it for themselves after their social evening., The same pensioners usually took did this job after other church functions. Of course 'pensioner' in the sense of those who counted as pensioners for a Little Wychwell pensioners' social evening, did not refer to those over sixty, but only those over eighty five or ninety. Even so, thought Elodea morosely, most of them seemed to be much bouncier than she was herself. "It must be the air," she said. "I didn't move into the village young enough myself. If I had always lived here I might be as healthy as they are." She pushed onwards, grumpily, turning up the lane to the Old Vicarage and the Church.

When she reached her own little lychgate, a smaller model of the one in front of the church itself, she had to pause to heave the pushchair up over the brick steps, and Theodora instantly awoke.

"Nonna!" Theo said, smiling up at her.

"Soon be inside, Theo, and then we can have our milk and biscuits and get you cleaned up and then play for a while before we get Amadeus back!" replied Elodea, somewhat mechanically, for she was staring dismally at the front lawn which bore a sad sight on its patchy green turf. A rook was lying on its back with a single red-splashed stab wound through its chest.

"Poor thing!" said Elodea aloud, while rushing Theo past before she saw it herself.

The rook must have had an aerial fight with a red kite and lost. This was not the first time Elodea had seen such injuries: she had witnessed these battles herself –

a red kite approaching the rookeries too closely, and one or two of the biggest rooks bravely flying out to drive the intruder away. Usually the rooks escaped but every now and then the kites were too fast at twisting and diving. Elodea admired the daring and courage of the rooks, charging out without hesitation to face such a huge opponent, but, she supposed, to be fair, the red kites did not like being attacked.

Elodea decided to clear up the dead body later. Maybe, she thought hopefully, if she was *lucky*, a scavenger might eat it for her or at least drag it off somewhere else. The bird was long past saving. There was absolutely no point in ringing the Vicar to ask him to take it to his bird hospital. At the thought of the Vicar, Mrs Shipman's words bounced back into her mind. She thought of the red splash of blood and Mrs Shipman's 'redding'. *Red kites*? Red in name and red in nature? They looked beautiful when they were soaring in the air but their faces seemed cruel to Elodea. Then Elodea told herself firmly that the eagle was a symbol of God and that no works of nature belonged to the Devil. Then she giggled at the thought of the Vicar's face if she ever asked him if any of his so well-beloved wild birds could *possibly* be *instruments of Satan*.

No sooner had Theodora been released from the buggy than Elodea's mobile began to buzz. It was deep inside the carrier bag, full of essential expedition items, that was slung over the buggy handles. Theodora was speeding away from her at a very fast toddle and Elodea knew she should follow her. However careful you were about moving things upwards or into locked cupboards, there were so many dangers lying in wait in a house for an inquisitive and strong minded toddler. But Elodea decided she *must* answer the phone in case another family member was ringing because they had an emergency at the other end. Elodea fished quickly and hopefully in the bag with one hand, while keeping her eyes on Theodora, but nothing in it felt like a phone. Where on earth had it got to? She started to fling everything out of the bag at random: feeder cups, nappies, tissues, purse, all hitting the floor and rolling in all directions.

Elodea unearthed the phone just before it switched to voicemail, and looked at the screen. *Walls*? *Walls* was ringing her? He *never* rang her. Something must have happened to Barnabus and Angel and they or someone else had rung Walls and not her and he was going to have to break the terrible news to her and…

She pressed 'answer' and screamed down the phone, "Walls, *what's happened*?"

 "Not too desperate, Elodea; don't panic. But there is a *bit* of a problem," his voice answered. But his voice sounded a little frantic. Its tone was not reassuring to an anxious parent.

"Angel! Barnabus! *What's happened*?" she yelled at an ear splitting frequency.

Walls winced as the noise hit his ear drum. "No, no, not Angel and Barnabus, nothing wrong with *them* as far as *I* know!" he soothed, "It is not *them* having a problem; it is *I*, me, *Walls, you know*. Buffy is *away*, as you know, and Yvette is *away* on a conference, and you are the first person I could think would be able to *help* me. I was hopeful that you could come *straight round*?"

Elodea's heart returned to its normal position and resumed its normal beat. Angel and Barnabus were *fine*. Even Walls could not be in too dire a strait for he was able to speak to her on the phone. But Elodea was caring for Theodora and Amadeus. Walls must know someone else in Oxford who could help him, surely? Walls had a pleading note in his voice. Elodea, who counted all Barnabus' friends as extra children of her own, did not like to refuse. Walls' own parents were far away in Boston. Yvette's parents similarly distant. But she could hardly abandon Theodora and Amadeus at the drop of a hat.

"Walls, darling," she replied, "I *would* be straight round – you know I would – but I have Theodora here and I have to collect Amadeus from playgroup later. I couldn't even *get* to Oxford and *back* before I have to collect him, even if I turned round and came straight back."

"*I beg you*!" Walls replied "Can't Mrs Wriggly look after them or something? It's really, really vital! I need assistance! *Right now*!"

"OK, I can *try* to find someone," replied Elodea, suddenly feeling brighter as she realised she had found a cast iron excuse to get someone else to look after the little horrors, no, no, the little *angels*, for a few hours, "but I'll be a *while*. I can't get there immediately; you know I can't! Half an hour driving would be *optimistic* at this time of day, so I could easily be an hour, you know, the traffic, and I have to get Theodora and Amadeus sorted out first. Will you be Ok for at least an hour because if not you absolutely have to find someone else."

"That's OK; I'll be fine till then. I'll just tarry where I am till you turn up. I'm right outside the apartments – not our apartment, that is, right outside the apartment block. I'll just set myself down right here on the pavement till you reach me," he answered.

He rang off.

How very odd, thought Elodea. The only scenario she could imagine in which he would wait outside the apartments was one in which he had forgotten his key and didn't want to disturb the caretaker of the apartments. But *she* couldn't help with that. Nothing about this made any sense.

Then Elodea remembered Theo! Where was she? Elodea dashed into the drawing room, which was the direction in which Theo had last been heading, and grabbed the protesting toddler from a one-legged balance on the top of a sofa back.

Theodora wasn't at all pleased about being removed as she had almost reached the high shelf of ornaments which she had been climbing towards for some time. She was even less pleased about being strapped back into the buggy again just when she thought she had escaped from it. She opened her mouth to its widest limit and expressed this opinion in screams that might have carried over a jet engine.

Elodea put her headphones on and retrieved the contents of the buggy's carrier bag from around the floor or the hall. Then she threw many more useful things into a *second* carrier bag and added it to the buggy handles. She closed the front door firmly on Pippy and ran with the buggy round to Agnes Gray's. Agnes was such a kind lady that she would certainly take care of the children for Elodea if only she was in. She was almost guaranteed to be in. Elodea's hopes were not dashed. Agnes agreed cheerfully to the imposition of Theodora and the later collection of Amadeus, and did not ask further questions about the "Oxford friend who is having an emergency". Agnes had simply assumed it to be Priscilla. Agnes, like most Little Wychwell inhabitants who had ever met Priscilla, were of the opinion that it was a wonder anyone so ignorant about the countryside could survive one day by themselves without help. Although, after Walls' kindness to her son, Marius, Agnes would have been even more eager to look after the children if she had realised that the true identity of the person needing help.

Thus it was only a record breaking ten minutes later that Elodea was turning her car onto the main road outside the Little Wychwell and heading for North Oxford, where Walls and Yvette lived in a very exclusive apartment block.

As Elodea drove past the front of this building she could see Walls near the main entrance. Being such an exercise fanatic, Walls had clearly got tired of sitting still on the pavement and was currently engaged in exciting stretching exercises.

Nothing much wrong with him *physically* then, thought Elodea to herself. He was wearing a striking bright scarlet tracksuit. *Red*, she thought and then mentally slapped herself on the wrist for accusing another of her friends of being diabolical. But it was Mrs Shipman's fault, Elodea felt, and now she had started this analysis she didn't seem able to stop herself.

As she turned into the private car park and pulled up in a visitor's parking space she found she was still considering the possibility of Walls being Satan in disguise. For a start he was astonishingly rich but then it was *love* of money that was the root of all evil and not money itself. There was no denying that Walls definitely *enjoyed* being rich but he had cast aside a business career to devote his life to academic study. On the whole, she thought, he loved academia *more* than money. For a second point he had most certainly been a Lothario before he settled down and married the staunchly feminist academic Yvette. Possibly some of his conquests, once rumoured to be every woman under thirty in Oxford, would consider him to be devilish. But, Elodea thought to herself, he was only really playing games. No one could surely ever consider him evil. She had never met anyone else either who did not just see his behaviour as somehow cute rather than dastardly. She smiled the indulgent smile of a mother with a slightly wayward offspring as she thought about this. It was no good, Walls was utterly sweet and innocent somehow, in a way not shared by many adults. He was a devout and practising Catholic, a diligent and hard working research fellow in Modern History and, and – here she gave a quite different smile even though it was still indulgent – one of the best looking men she had ever met.

She trotted round to the front of the building.

"Elodea!" he cried, giving her a devastating smile and a huge bear hug. "You are here! I knew you would come. You are so *reliable*! Everyone always says that. Elodea, so *reliable*!"

Elodea felt suddenly sad. Of all the adjectives to be thought to be by everyone else, *reliable* was very disappointing. She thought that it sounded like stout brown shoes, brown paper, brown tweed suits. In fact it denoted an all-over dull brown life. She considered words she might have preferred: successful, beautiful, fun, charming, intelligent… She sighed aloud.

"What *is* wrong?" asked Walls, all concern, for however bad his problems were he was always, even post-marriage, only too ready to rush gallantly to rescue a woman in distress.

"*Reliable*, Walls," squeaked Elodea, indignantly. "That's what's *wrong*! You said I was reliable! Reliable! And it's so true! Everyone else I know does important things and goes on conferences and to meetings and workshops and abroad and out to dinner and things, and here I am, always in Little Wychwell, always *reliable*! Always there to look after the children! Always there to come and rescue people! That's me! *Old and reliable, like a pair of slippers*!"

"Oh, Elodea, my angel! You are neither old nor in the least like a pair of slippers! You are glamorous and charming and intelligent and very sweet *as well* as being reliable! There! Is that all good now? Show me your glorious smile!"

He bestowed a kiss upon her hand and then one on each of her cheeks.

She beamed up at him. It took a hard woman not to smile after being kissed by Walls.

"Well," she said, "explain why I am here. What is this emergency which the reliable are required to fix?"

She had a terrible fear that it was probably something to do with plumbing. In her experience men were much less likely to know what to do with domestic plumbing like blocked U-bends or, even worse, overflowing lavatories, than women, unless they were trained plumbers, naturally.

He suddenly stopped looking confident. He looked behind, he looked in front, he looked behind again.

Then he whispered, very fast and very quietly, "*Casi no me atrevo decir, pero es mejor saber antes de ir arriba. Hay un cadáver en el apartamento.*"

"I'm so sorry, I'm afraid I didn't quite catch that," said Elodea, having not understood a word of the first half of the sentence and feeling that her dreadful conviction that the speech had ended with the information that he had a cadaver in his flat, which must surely be wrong.

He looked at her, disappointed.

"*Hablas espagnol*?" he asked.

She beamed confidently. She had *thought* it was Spanish he was speaking and she was not only right but she knew the answer to this particular question. The conversation so far had been *very* strange but she was very used to talking to academics and found that it was always best to humour them.

"No," she said, very firmly.

"Ah!" he said. This had ruined his whole tactic for using a method of communication that a chance person who passed by would not understand, unless they passer by happened to speak fluent Spanish. Walls had only learnt Spanish and English at school and found many of his polyglot Oxford friends very annoying when they conversed fluently in multiple languages. His Spanish was not *good* but it was *serviceable*. He had assumed that Elodea spoke Spanish because Barnabus did, although Barnabus seemed to speak most languages without ever having apparently learnt them. Clearly Elodea didn't. Walls felt a moment's superiority: at last, a language that *he* knew and *one* of his friends *didn't*!

Then he felt crestfallen at the failure of his plan to convey the message secretly. He only had one other language option available. He had once boarded with Priscilla for a while and, shocked at his linguistic ignorance, she had forced him to learn at least rudimentary Latin. Elodea must, *surely*, understand Latin. Priscilla would never have a close friend who didn't, would she? Walls frowned with concentration as he tackled the task of translating his problem into Latin. Yes, that would do it!

"*Problemata. Corpus in domum,*" he achieved.

"*Ah, je comprends! C'est un jeu! Nous devons announcer ça dans une autre langue! Le premier qui ne le fait pas, il perdra! Je peux jouer!*" replied Elodea, confidently, using French that might have confused a native speaker of the language but seemed excellent to her. "*Bon! Je le dites ça en française! Ecoutes…! Il y a un cadaver dans la maison!*"

Walls had no idea what Elodea had said up to her final phrase. However, he could recognise enough French to conclude that she had got the hang of what he had said and had confirmed this by repeating it to him.

"So, you've got that much, but there's more!" he said, "Wait till you hear this."

There was a pause while he realised that the Latin he wanted was entirely beyond him. He whipped out his smartphone and found Google Translate.

"There's more!" he repeated. "Listen! *Quod indutus esset*…"

"*Ah, je comprends!*" she cried delightedly. "*Tu connais quelque chose, je pense que je serais en mesure de gagner! Moi, je ne gagner pas les jeux chez moi parce que ma famille sont trop competitive. Et voila, je comprends! Je dois ajouter des mots à la phrase! 'Il y a un cadaver dans la maison et il porte un chapeau*!"

Walls had no idea what Elodea was trying to convey; he had again only grasped the gist of the final phrase. But he now had the definite impression that somewhere in his transfer of information things seemed to have gone seriously wrong. Elodea's demeanour seemed far too happy and bouncy for someone who had just fully comprehended that he, Walls, had a corpse in his apartment.

"*Non!*" he said, firmly, exercising the only word in French of which he was quite sure and then returning to English, "Except the guy *was* wearing a hat. You are dead right there."

Elodea switched to English.

"Have I got the rules of this game wrong *again*? Are we not changing languages and adding a garment each time? Is it more complicated than that? You must think I am *very* stupid!" she sighed. "It is a good job I am not playing this game with Priscilla. I'm not sure my French is entirely correct and she would be so cross with me about that and definitely angry because I was so stupid that I had not grasped the rules by now!"

Walls now understood Elodea's misapprehension but, with his mind firmly fixed on the chance of his mythical passer-by overhearing them, he decided to persist in

Latin. She seemed to understand Latin, after all. He must explain that this *wasn't a game*. What was the word for 'true' in Latin? Ah yes, the word true was in *this* phrase!

"*In vino veritas*" he said aloud.

"You're not *drunk* are you, Walls?" asked Elodea, rather anxiously. She knew that Walls never drank alcohol because of preserving his body for his many athletic pursuits but she was also beginning to think this was the only possible explanation for his behaviour. Perhaps he had just been to an academic event and decided to join in with everyone else or drunk some champagne by mistake for lemonade or some such accident?

"*Non!*" Walls said again, very firmly. He was still thinking about how to say exactly what he wanted in Latin.

He finally remembered that the Latin word for game matched a well known board game, and achieved a relevant phrase, "*In veritas. Non vino. Sed in veritas. Problemata. Non ludo. Corpus in domum meum!*"

"It *isn't* a game! Oh, that's so disappointing! I thought I was bound to win because I still have Ancient Greek *and* Italian *and* German to go, and I know languages aren't your strongest point! I never win word games in our house! I was so pleased to think I might win *just for once!*" Elodea cried, sounding so disappointed that Walls felt quite guilty.

"May I offer my deepest and sincerest sympathy for your sadness, I did not mean to cause you distress" he said, and kissed her hand again. Then he resumed his attempts to communicate the actual situation.

By now he also wished he had rung someone else up for help – someone less irrational. What to do? He finally decided to just repeat his last phrase more slowly and clearly and hope she got the full import of it and realised the gravity of the situation.

"*Non!*" he said again. "*In veritas. Problemata. Non ludo. Corpus in domum meum!*"

"You mean there's *really a corpse in your flat*? Really and truly!" exclaimed Elodea, very loud and on a note somewhere near top A, for Elodea was a first soprano with a voice which glissando-ed rapidly up the scale when startled.

"Shush!" said Walls, looking round nervously again.

"*Whose body* is it?" hissed Elodea. "*Who* is dead? What are they doing in your apartment? It isn't Yvette is it? She really is away isn't she?"

"No, definitely not Yvette. Why would it be Yvette? I don't know who this guy is!" answered Walls, *sotto voce*, abandoning Latin as a hopeless cause and reverting to stage whispers in English. "I just popped back from college – I've been sleeping over in college while Yvette is away on this conference, in my college room, you understand. More accessible for my research – but I was running out of a few essentials so I just called back here to restock. I went upstairs and the apartment door *was* unlocked but, Elodea, I never remember to lock it mainly because I tend to forget to carry my own key. Frankly it doesn't seem worth it, no one can get in here without the door code for the building. Yvette is always telling me not to do that and now I'm thinking that maybe she was right all along. Anyways, the door was not only unlocked but just a bit ajar, which seemed kinda strange because I usually remember to close it. So I thought I might not have actually closed it to if I *was* hurrying, you know. Well, I shoved the door open a fraction wider with my foot. I didn't enter the place because as soon as the door had shifted a bitty I saw... *it*! And what I saw with my own eyes simply *wasn't possible*. That's why I asked you to come here. I want you to come there with me right now and then we can both cast an eye in and then we can realise it's a trick of the light and I just need my eyes testing. Then we can have a good belly laugh together and then you can go straight home without too much disruption to your schedule."

"Shouldn't you have rung the police straight away? Or an ambulance? What if whoever it is isn't dead? Or what if they weren't dead when you looked in and then they went and died while you were waiting for me? What are the police going to say about all this delay? You'll be on the CCTV! What did you actually do next?" said Elodea, using as quiet a voice as she could under the circumstances of her extreme agitation at this appalling news but also using a note that was now the C above top A.

"I don't know! I don't know!" replied Walls, sotto voce, "Consider how you would have felt if you had found that! I was just hoping it was all false. Still am! You know, maybe the floor just happened to look like a corpse was right there on it because of the way the light falls? Maybe I have never looked at that section of the flooring before with the light at that angle? I can't even remember what I did next. I guess I pulled the door to, got down the stairs and out of the building, and then rang you. That must all be on CCTV as well so the cops'll know I didn't enter the apartment. I could make the claim that I didn't even notice it. I got to the door and then hastened back down because I remembered you were paying a visit and couldn't access the building through the main door because I had omitted to give you the code."

"That won't wash with the police; they'll have a recording of all your mobile calls somewhere or other. You'll just have to tell the *truth* and say you *panicked*. Anyone might have gone into a bit of spin if they found a dead body in their doorway. We'd better go up *right away* and find out exactly what *is* going on," announced Elodea. "Personally I am most sincerely hoping that it *was* a trick of the light, *that's all*!"

"You don't know all the facts about what I saw. I ought to explain the details," said Walls, to thin air, for Elodea, ignoring the lift, was already running up the stairs. He, feeling quite queasy about returning to the scene of his ghastly experience, decided she could go and have a look all by herself if she really must. He stood there feeling determined not to go back upstairs for thirty seconds and then, seized with guilt because he decided she might be in danger, dashed after her at full tilt.

But, due to her early lead, she still reached the apartment door first. Walls had left the latch down on the lock despite having closed the door, for, when she pushed the door it swung open easily. She stopped and considered the scene in front of her.

"Don't go in! It might be *evidence*!" Walls suddenly hissed in her ear.

"Where *was* it?" she hissed back, jumping a little because she had not heard his approach along the thickly carpeted service corridor.

"*Was*? Where *was* it? You can't see it?" asked Walls.

She turned round towards him and realised he had his eyes tight shut and his hands in front of them. He reminded her of a scared toddler with fingers over their eyes because what you can't see isn't there.

"Don't be *silly*!" she said. "For goodness sake, *how old are you, Walls*? Open your eyes!"

"*I don't want to never ever ever see it again*!" he whimpered.

"Well, you *won't* see it!" she said, bracingly. "There is *nothing here* except a view of your apartment. And," she ended on a wail of despair, "it's so beautifully furnished and decorated and so *tidy* and so *dust free*! I wish my house looked like this!"

"Oh, but that's easy for us because we have a *cleaner*, you know, and we only moved in recently so the décor is all brand new!" said Walls, comfortingly. He had taken his hands from his face now but still not opened his eyes.

"Walls!" she said in her best 'terrifying the children into behaving' voice. "Just look in yourself and tell me what you see!"

His eyelids shot upward. He looked in.

"Thank God!" he said. "It really has *gone*!"

"Yes, *nothing there*! You *must* have imagined it!" she said, brightly.

"No, no," he replied. "Not *just* 'thank God it's not there'. Thank God *I can't see it either*! I thought perhaps it had never been there and it was just me who imagined I could see it so that I was just seeing my own imaginings. But it's all good, I can't see anything either. *You can't see it. I can't see it.. Celebration!*"

"What *did* you see *exactly*, Walls?" demanded Elodea, deciding that trying to untangle his last statement was impossible.

"That's what I wanted to tell you *before* you bounced up here. So you would be prepared before you saw it. It wasn't an *ordinary* corpse. It was a *dead soldier. A dead World War II soldier.*"

"Your specialist area of study, Walls, *World War II*," said Elodea.

"Affirmative!" said Walls. "If not entirely correct. I specialise in the whole of twentieth-century warfare –but I guess World War II comes bang in the middle."

There was a long pause. Elodea looked at the floor. Was there any rational explanation for why the body of a World War II soldier might appear in Walls' apartment and then vanish again? She feared that Walls might have been *overworking*. He didn't seem to be drunk or drugged and it was very unlikely that he would be when his avoidance of alcohol or illegal drugs as part of his fitness regime had always been most faithful.

"You, you aren't taking any form of *medication* at the minute, are you, Walls, dear? Prescribed painkillers or antibiotics or anything of that nature? *Are* you?" she asked.

"No, I'm not! Elodea, be honest with me. *Do you think I'm loops*? Was I suffering a hallucination?" asked Walls

Elodea was about to say "I don't know", but then she looked at his frightened face and changed her reply to "Of *course* not! You are one of the *sanest* people I know!"

"Which," she added to herself, after making a quick review of her family, friends and acquaintances, "is *true* since nearly everyone I know is at the very least somewhat eccentric and many of them are completely barking mad, so I didn't tell a lie."

"*Tell me all about it, everything*," she said, holding his hand and patting it, for she realised he was shaking.

"It was just *there*. Just past the door and right across it, if you follow me. Face upwards. With blood all over, *dead*," answered Walls, leaning against the wall of the corridor and closing his eyes again at the recollection. "It was *ghastly, vomit inducing, hideous*!"

"But how could it possibly have got there? ….How about this? Maybe," said Elodea, "someone was walking down the corridor carrying a body, heard you coming, shoved it through the first open door they found and dashed off before you saw them. Then, when you had gone away they came back and picked it up again and took it off."

"Why," said Walls, "would anyone have been wandering down *the corridors of this apartment block* carrying a dead body that looked like a soldier from World War II?"

"*Why not*?" said Elodea, bracingly. "As likely to be doing that *here* as *anywhere else*. I'm sure it happens *all* the time. You know these re-enactment societies are very popular. Perhaps some of your neighbours belong to one? Ah! Yes! Maybe one of the local re-enactment society who happens to live in your apartment block killed another one of the re-enacters by mistake and brought the body back here to conceal it or get a spade or something and then heard you coming and had to stuff the body somewhere?"

"*Good* suggestion, good *suggestion*!" said Walls, feeling at the time that this explanation was *utterly* reasonable and also extremely likely. It was so much preferable as an explanation to himself being mad. Then an awful idea gripped him. He clutched Elodea's hand again. "Perhaps they've not removed it, perhaps they just moved it *further into the apartment*!"

"Oh, Walls, *of course* they haven't," said Elodea. "That just wouldn't be *logical*!"

"Whereas walking about the apartment block with a dead World War II soldier would be?" demanded Walls.

"*Yes!*" said Elodea, firmly. "And I am sticking to that because I am *not* stepping through that door to search your entire apartment for a body. *What if we found one?*"

Elodea shivered. So did Walls. The view through the door no longer presented itself as a charming, expensively furnished, very well kept apartment. The room seemed to have become filled with imaginary dark shadows, it looked gloomy and sinister. *Anything* could be lurking inside. Elodea and Walls both hastily averted their gaze and looked at each other with eyes grown huge with fear.

"We are *sillies*," she said to him. "There is *nothing* here. There is nothing to be afraid of. We are quite safe. Bodies can't harm us. But I do wish Barnabus wasn't *away*; he would have just leapt straight in and had a good look round by himself. *Walls*, I've just had a truly, truly terrible thought! What if the person you saw wasn't quite dead but very badly *wounded* and had crawled into your apartment to escape their attacker and then, after you saw them they *revived a bit* and crawled *further* in and they have now *died in one of the other rooms*?"

She finished this speech on a sepulchral whisper. They clutched each other's hands.

"So, it would still be there? A *corpse*? Still be lying there inside? Have died there?" squeaked Walls, "If that is so I can never live here again! I have to *vacate*!"

They stood there for a few moments, hands gripped tightly together in terror.

"OK," said Walls, finally, trying to get a grip on his emotions but with a voice that was still tremulous, "what next?"

"I suppose we ring the police?" quavered Elodea, dubiously.

"I guess we *have* to," said Walls, equally doubtfully, "but it's going to sound pretty off the wall, don't you think? And what if it *was* all in my head? What if my studies *are* driving me loops?"

They stood and pondered the problem.

"I think we really *should* ring them!" announced Elodea. "Because what if it was a dead body that someone *stuffed* into your apartment and then *retrieved*? If we don't tell the police, that makes us *complicit* in the crime or something like that. We could get charged with being accomplices or co-conspirators or something. I don't want to go to jail, I really don't."

"Agreed," said Walls. "But what exactly are we going to say to the cops?"

"The truth, the whole truth and nothing but the truth, so help us God, Amen, *naturally*," replied Elodea.

Walls groaned. "But the facts are going to sound so *dumb*!"

Elodea considered 'the truth'. It sounded pretty odd, even to her. The police might well suggest that a psychiatrist would be a more relevant expert to call than themselves.

Then she had a bright alternative idea.

"Of course!" she said, "You have CCTV in your apartment?"

"Yes!" said Walls.

"It's simple then! We watch that *first*, *before* we call the police? Don't you have it streamed live to your iPhone? You are an *idiot*, you should have thought of that yourself and already checked it!" said Elodea, knowing that Walls' security system would be bound to do that sort of thing; it would hardly be a cheap or out of date one.

"Yes, but I *also* have an intruder alarm that talks to my iPhone and that never said *anything* to me about anyone putting a body in my flat" he answered.

"So that means there definitely *wasn't* anyone *real* here? Nobody could possibly have entered or left?" she asked.

"No. It doesn't mean anything of the sort, unfortunately. See, Elodea, they're such a nuisance, don't you know? Security systems, they whine at you all the time, always panicking if I leave the door unlocked myself, setting off false alarms for no reason, sending me messages about nothing and everything else – so as soon as Yvette goes away I, er...I mean there's really no likelihood of crime in this area and these apartments, it's just silly having all these stupid alarms and so, as I said, in consequence, when Yvette's away, I , er...."

"You *switch the security systems off*!" Elodea finished his sentence for him.

She started to laugh – the apartment was covered with sophisticated security systems and they were such a bother that Walls had switched them all off.

"If I'd been *anticipating* this occurring I'd have switched it all back *on*, clearly," said Walls, very annoyed. "Can you just try to view this *seriously*?"

Elodea reduced herself to the odd giggle.

"*I know*!" she said. "The *building*! CCTV, internal and external! Who has that? Surely they should have noticed someone heaving a body dressed in WWII clothes around the corridors and dumping it into your apartment? Shouldn't they have *already* reported it? Who keeps the tapes?"

"The caretaker keeps it all. He's supposed to watch it all the time, not just view the videos later, but I bet he doesn't. I expect he doses off in front of the TV with a good old fashioned cup of English black tea. I'll go and beg him to let me view them. He's a nice old boy. He'll do that for me. I'll be back pronto."

"I'm not standing here waiting in this corridor till you get back," said Elodea. "The *body snatchers* might *reappear*! I'm coming *with* you!"

They pulled the door to the apartment firmly shut, making sure it was locked this time, and headed down to the caretaker's flat in the basement. Mr Brown, the caretaker obligingly let them use his computer to look at all the CCTV footage from the previous week, but it was to no avail. After a whole hour scanning photos at high speed they both had to admit there was no evidence of any unusual activity in Walls' corridor.

"Just a minute!" said Walls. "Have you noticed something odd about this? There's no sign of *us* either, me *or* you!"

Walls checked the numbers on the apartment door in case the Mr Brown had given them the records for the wrong floor but it was definitely the right corridor and the right apartment. Then he studied the times at the top of the video. The recording had stopped at ten o'clock that morning.

"Has the CCTV been working properly today?" Walls called out to Mr Brown, who was in the room next door to them. As Walls had correctly predicted he was seated in an armchair in front of his wide screen TV, feet resting on a foot stool and well supplied with a huge mug of tea.

"Lord love you, I wouldn't know!" replied Mr Brown. "This system always takes *at least* an hour off a day. Too fancy, you see, too fancy. Always going wrong! It keeps getting its storage full. Too many pictures, you see. They didn't pay for the storage upgrade. It's a wonder there's anything on it at all."

Walls and Elodea looked despairingly at each other. Then they thanked Mr Brown and repaired to the big front lobby to consider what to do next.

"No choice!" Elodea said firmly. "You *have* to ring the police. *Somebody* has to *search the apartment*, and neither of us want to do that. Perhaps…" She shivered again. "Perhaps what you saw was an *apparition*, a shadow of the past. Someone who lived in the big house that was here before they built the apartments, the son of the house, tragically killed during the war. Or someone you have been researching, you have called them, summoned them back…"

They clutched each other's hands again.

"I don't believe in ghosts" said Walls, stoutly, if rather unconvincingly, "So I'll ring the cops right now."

* * *

The interview with the police went very much as Walls had expected. They did not attempt to conceal the fact that they thought Walls was losing his academic mind and followed this opinion with a lecture on his stupidity at leaving his door unlocked and his security alarms off. But they took some samples from the carpet where he had said the body was lying, and said they would get forensics to analyse them, *just to be sure*.

Elodea's interview with the police went a little more smoothly, partly because she had very little evidence to contribute but mainly because she was inclined to agree that the police view of the case might very well be right.

"Never mind," Elodea soothed Walls, after the police left. "We *did the right thing*. If it does turn out to have *really* been a *body* they will be laughing on the other side of their faces *next* time they see us! I'm so sorry, Walls, darling, I must go now. I *have* to get back for Amadeus and Theodora. You are going *back to college*, aren't you? You aren't going to *stay* here?"

Walls felt miserable. He was now a marked man – the "man who imagined he saw dead soldiers". He was very aware that, despite her sympathy, this was what Elodea thought too even if she did not say it to him. It was also clear that she was now worried about what might happen if she left him alone here. Maybe I *am* losing it, Walls reflected sadly. Maybe I did conjure it all from my own mind. But, deep inside, he didn't believe this. There were things you saw that were *not* there and things you saw that *were* there, and this thing had been as *real* as it could possibly have been.

"Yes, yes," he said, "I'll go directly to college. I won't return till Yvette gets back."

She beamed at him. "That's a *good* boy!"

She stood on tiptoes and gave him a kiss.

"I'll come down the stairs with you," she said.

He got the impression she thought that he might attempt to re-enter the flat and then see another body there if she didn't escort him right out of the building.

"It's OK. I am heading directly back to college," he assured her. "Wild horses would not persuade me to stay in that apartment alone. But I must just reactivate the alarm system and make quite sure the door *is* locked."

He leant cautiously in through the door without putting his feet over the threshold and reset the alarm. They both tested the door to make sure it was closed and locked properly. Then they walked down the stairs together. She insisted on giving him a lift in her car right to the centre of Oxford and then seeing him jog away in the direction of Kings College before she went home.

"He'll be safe there!" she said to herself, as she left Oxford and headed towards her own safe haven of Little Wychwell. "Colleges are always such caring places! The other staff will look after him there. When Yvette gets back he will be fine. She is so *sensible* and *well balanced*. Walls needs a holiday – that is what is wrong – a proper holiday away from Oxford. Not a conference. He needs a real change, a real rest, somewhere different Bother! I should have invited him back to the Old Vicarage. That would have done him so much good."

Then she remembered the rook. "Double bother!" she said, aloud. "I should have brought Walls back here with me, then he could have buried the poor rook for me! I shall have to do it myself as it is. Maybe," she said, with more optimism than certainty, "maybe Cyril will have called round to see how Philomena is getting on and then he will have picked it up for me?"

Cyril Blomfeld was Lady Wilmington's pig farm manager and Philomena was Elodea's pet pig. Unfortunately he hadn't called, and Elodea had to commit the rook to the earth in a rather hasty way before collecting the children from Agnes Gray.

Walls was unaware of the narrow escape from rook-undertaking that he had had. He hated rural life even more heartily than Priscilla did. If he had been 'kidnapped' by Elodea and taken to Little Wychwell for a 'rest' until Yvette returned he would most certainly have *run* back to Oxford rather than remain in a place that Elodea thought was a beautiful countryside idyll and he thought was an awful backwater with no interest and nothing to do. Furthermore burying dead wildlife would definitely not have been an activity which the squeamish Walls would have enjoyed in the slightest.

 * * *

Meanwhile, in the police station, Sergeant Amos was making a note to ring Forensics and explain to them that Inspector Bryant wanted them to file the samples from Walls and Yvette's apartment safely but not to waste time, effort or money on analysis unless they received further instructions.

 For, as Inspector Bryant had said, if they wasted money on forensic investigations every time some mad academic had hallucinations about their own research topic the police would be even more overstretched than they were at present. In any case, the young man, er, this *Sebastian*, had said that they had held a party in the flat on the previous week, and how were they to tell the difference between skin and blood traces from an unknown captain in the Oxfordshire and Buckinghamshire Light Infantry in World War II and a set of random partygoers from the twenty-first century? He added that it was a shame that this *Sebastian* had not been able to give him *the name* of the corpse as well as its *regiment and rank* because then he could have traced one of its living relatives and checked the samples against their DNA. Sergeant Amos smiled slightly, in a polite way, as he was never sure, even after several years of working with him, as to whether Inspector Bryant was being sarcastic or serious.

Sergeant Amos ventured to mention that said academic had also been one of the young men involved in an earlier investigation of theirs, if Inspector Bryant recalled it – the rotting corpse found in a wood in Little Wychwell? Inspector Bryant said he was not likely to forget that particular case, especially the subsequent cover-up of the true facts by the *entire* population of the village resulting in all the prosecutions being so unsuccessful. Perhaps, Inspector Bryant added, the shock of discovering a body on that occasion was what had addled said academic's brain. Undoubtedly a psychoanalysis was required rather than police investigations.

Sergeant Amos then coughed, a little nervously, and added that Walls was *also* one of the two young men who had discovered the body of a tramp in the River Thames quite recently.

Inspector Bryant said, "Ah yes, again with a Little Wychwell *Smith* – Barnabus Smith, was it not? Said Smith was also involved in the discovery of the rotting body in the wood near Little Wychwell. And you need not bother to remind me, Sergeant, that Mrs Elodea Smith from this afternoon is, in fact, the discoverer of the 'scarecrow suicide' in Little Wychwell as well as being the mother of the aforesaid Barnabus Smith. I thought I might be hallucinating myself when we first reached the apartment building and discovered the identity of the witnesses. When I first took this post, Inspector McCleod mentioned the Little Wychwell Smith family to me as being a one-family *crime discovery wave* involved in several previous cases. At the time I thought Inspector McCleod was losing it. I apologise to his absent self; I understand entirely why he retired. The corpse discovery virus appears virulent among the family and all their acquaintance. Evidently highly infectious."

Sergeant Amos coughed again, *very* nervously. "Or the *non*-corpse-discovering virus in this case, perhaps, Sir?"

Inspector Bryant concurred with this view. He then said that next time he took a post he would make sure it was nowhere near any **** dreaming spires, although attempting to find a post with no one named Smith in the vicinity might prove impossible. He then gave a bitter laugh and announced he was going home.

Once Sergeant Amos had finished entering the case notes on the computer and completed his call to Forensics he consulted the clock and decided that he too was going home. "Academics!" he said to himself as he left, "All as mad as hatters!"

Chapter 4

After Elodea had left him Walls began to jog through the centre of Oxford towards Kings. He would run down to college and just go and get on with some of his research work in his college room, he told himself. There could not be any problem with his college room. It could not *possibly* have a corpse in it, real or imaginary.

But then he thought of his empty college room, on the dark staircase, and changed his mind. He told himself that *first* he would go to the college boathouse and take a single scull out for a turn up the river and back. Then he added, to fool and comfort himself, that the reason for this was because he felt he was back sliding in his training schedule. He then amplified this reason, to avoid the suggestion from himself that he was funking the idea of even going into his college room alone, by reminding himself that he had *intended* to put in a lot of work on his sculling technique this week, to take advantage of the spare time he had because of Yvette being away. When his inner self suggested that this was unconvincing, because the presence of Yvette had never yet stopped him from doing as many hours of rowing practice as he liked, he told it to hold its tongue and shut its mouth.

When he arrived at the boathouse he found that Podgy was there too. Podgy was number five in the Kings Senior Common Room Eight, in which Walls was number two, and thus it was the natural thing for them both to take a pair out together up the Isis and back. They strove and sweated companionably enough, criticised each other's technique and tried a few experimental improvements. On returning they went to the Bear, which was the nearest pub to Kings, for the rest of the evening, Walls ordering orange juice, for his devotion to exercise including eschewing all forms of alcohol and always had, and Podgy ordering a pint of bitter.

"You don't want to drink that poisonous stuff, Podgy, old fellow," Walls said, very seriously, as he always did. "Look at how toned I am. You don't want to be all flabby and beer-stomached when you get to my age."

Podgy was three years younger than Walls.

"Well, I'm going to *risk* it," said Podgy, as he always did. "Hasn't done me any harm *so* far!"

They added a large and calorie laden meal to their drinks and were both content. Due to being oversized rowers they rather overwhelmed the tiny pub garden, but they were accustomed to having to jam themselves into small spaces meant for people one or two feet shorter than themselves and did not notice the effect.

At midnight Walls parted from his friend, to whom he had not even mentioned the terrors of the day. By now Walls was definite that he had just had a silly attack of megrims and that the corpse was pure imagination. "A trick of the light," he told himself. "A shadow on the carpet. I must have projected some photo of a dead WW II soldier that I had in my memory onto the shadow somehow." Walls turned towards college. Podgy headed in the opposite direction to his own dwelling, as he did not 'live in'.

The narrow medieval backstreet that led to Kings was full of patches of deepest darkness and drifting shadows all filled with the spirits of the past. Walls had to stop himself from continually glancing back over his shoulder. There was no one else in the street, and yet he was sure that he could definitely hear someone following him. He told himself that this sound was simply the echo of his own feet and that he had been startled by it on previous occasions. He laughed heartily, in a deliberately careless way, to show himself how nonsensical he was being, and his own laughter echoed around the ancient stone walls in a very creepy way. He hurried on, breaking into a fast run, and swerved breathlessly into the Lodge and the reassuring greeting of the solid and worthy porter, Mr Biggs.

"Good evening, Mr Sebastian. Pleasant evening, Sir!" said Mr Biggs.

"Yes, yes, indeed. I will be staying in college overnight *again* tonight," replied Walls.

"Very good, Sir. Your good lady still on a conference, isn't she?" said Mr Biggs.

"Yes, indeed, Biggs, yes," said Walls. "Florida, I believe," he added conversationally. For Walls did not want to continue into college. For some inexplicable reason his feet seemed to be firmly rooted to the cobbles of the Lodge entrance.

"Very nice, Sir. Good night, Sir. See you in the morning when you go out on your run, then, Sir" said Biggs, in a way that suggested this conversation had reached its conclusion. Biggs was hoping to get back to his newspaper and cup of tea as soon as possible and also taking the opportunity to tactfully remind Walls that it was late and that Walls always got up to go running at five am.

"Yes, yes," said Walls, rather absently, as he leaned forward and peered ahead to try to see if that the first quadrangle was empty. "Er, so long! Er, see you again soon!"

Walls added "I hope" to himself following the 'see you again soon' and then told himself not to be so melodramatic and brainlessly idiotic. Walls headed boldly into the first and biggest quad. The moonlight was shining down now, making the shadows of the buildings stand out sharp and dark on the central grass square. The arches that marked the entrances to the tunnelled corridors into the other quads were jet black and seemed very sinister.

Walls no longer had his room in a bright modern block, he now owned a grander room in a much older staircase in college, suited to his more senior position. His 'room' was huge. In actuality it was several rooms: a sitting room, a bedroom and a recently added modern bathroom. But to reach it he must negotiate the dark walkways and cross several tiny quadrangles overhung with leaning dark buildings and the occasional tree. The trees would be ghastly silhouettes in the moonlight, casting sepulchral shadows. He knew that.

What if the door to his room turned out to be ajar? Had he *locked* it when he left? Had he even *shut* it when he left? If the door was ajar, or even if he opened it himself with a key, would he have the strength and courage to look in? When the moonlight was shining down through the little casement windows and making shapes and patterns and imaginary horrors on the walls and the door and the stairs themselves?

Walls stood there, staring at the first quadrangle. After a minute's pause he forced himself onwards. But as he got closer to his own room the drifting shadows seemed to be calling a warning to him, 'Go back, go back, go back!'. He ignored them, telling them that such warnings meant nothing but nonsense for those from *the land of the free and the home of the brave* who knew very well that shadows could not talk. He began to climb the ancient and worn stairs of his own staircase sideways, leaning his back against the comforting stone of the wall, taking a careful leap past each of the other doors with his eyes shut. His breathing was fast and shallow; his eyes were bulging with fear. At last he could see his own door. It was *not* shut. It *was* slightly ajar.

Walls advanced no further. He gave a little gasp, turned, and fled down the stairs, through the covered walkways, across the quadrangles. The sound of his fleeing feet ringing on the flagstones startled several other residents in their rooms. Those who looked out realised, however, that it was just Walls, evidently *taking some exercise*. One ancient don turned to his companion, with whom he was enjoying a late 'nightcap', "*Quite* mad! *Total* exercise freak! Must ask him to run more quietly at this time of night. Damned anti-social. I shall bring the matter of running in the quadrangles at night up at the next SCR meeting."

Walls reached the Lodge and just before entering remembered to slow his pace to a dignified walk.

"I've changed my mind," he said, as airily as possible, trying to make sure his breathing sounded even and relaxed, "I think perhaps I will sleep *out* of college tonight *after all*."

"Very good, Sir," said Mr Biggs, and let him back out of the gates again. "I guess he had a better offer," he added to himself.

Biggs thought that Walls must have just received a phone message from some female. All the porters knew of Walls' philandering behaviour before his marriage, and since they also knew Yvette many of them found it hard to believe he had entirely abandoned his previous licentious behaviour for such a plain-looking dumpy woman.

"While the cat's away the mice will play," said Mr Biggs to his newspaper crossword puzzle.

Walls stood on the cobbles outside Kings and reviewed a list of people whom he knew in Oxford who would be likely to be still up and also be happy to take him in for the night. He stopped at a name and smiled. Of course! Obvious.

Walls, the indefatigable athlete, began running at a fast but regular and unbroken pace towards a certain street in Jericho. He was no longer afraid. He was happy to have thought of such a brilliant solution to his problem. Walls had an inner conviction that everyone in the world was always glad to see him, especially female people, and thus never doubted that he would be welcomed when he arrived. She would be *delighted*, no question of that. He hadn't popped round to visit for ages. She was probably feeling neglected.

He ran through the city centre which was now mostly deserted and looked empty and forlorn without the crowds of shoppers and tourists. Then he headed onwards north and west to the maze of streets that was Jericho, once a poor area but gentrified in the nineteen seventies and eighties. The houses could now command premium prices despite being tiny with tiny gardens and originally very poorly built. It was, thought Walls, amazing what an estate agent could palm off on people. In his own view his modern apartment was, while equally expensive, *far* preferable to this kind of thing. The houses had no quaint charm for Walls, they were, in his view, unhealthy and inconvenient carbuncles that needed demolition.

Walls reached the correct door and was temporarily stymied to find the house in darkness. It was early yet for her to be abed, so he did hope she had not gone away for the night. He tried an experimental ring of the bell but nothing happened. Unlike Barnabus and Elodea he did not continue to press the bell repeatedly with a conviction that this must produce an effect eventually. If she wasn't there she wasn't there. He considered what to do next. Was she likely to return shortly? That was the question. He looked at his watch: half past midnight. So, if she was out for the evening where could she be? A college or university function was most likely, in which case it was worth waiting a few minutes to see if she returned.

Walls leant casually against her front door and waited. The street was deserted. The minutes passed very slowly. Somewhere on his key ring he still had a key to this door because he had once boarded here, but, tempting as it was to use it, he felt it was rude to enter without permission.

A few minutes of tedium later and Walls, who was beginning to feel a little oppressed by the shadows in *this* street now, managed to convince himself that letting himself in and making her some black coffee so it would be ready when she arrived would be kind and correct. But just before he put his key into the door he caught sight something very strange at the other end of the street. Aa large round yellow globe was wobbling around above the roofs of the parked cars. He stepped into the street to see what it was. The globe wobbled to the right, then to the left, tipped slightly and righted itself, wobbled again and, just as he realised what it was, finally crashed on to the tarmac with a clatter of metal.

He ran towards it.

"Are you OK, Pris?" he asked it. "Let me help you up!"

"Perfectly OK," her voice replied calmly from the tangled heap of yellow fluorescent jacket, overweight don and bicycle. "It is just that this road decided to rise upwards *just* when I wasn't expecting it. *Deus ex machina*! Very mean of it."

"Probably undamaged; she must be perfectly relaxed," said Walls to himself as he righted her and the bicycle, for Priscilla's breath seemed to be 99 per cent alcohol and 1 per cent air.

"Been out to Founder's Dinner," said Priscilla, conversationally, attempting to get back onto her bicycle. "Splendid evening. Uncorked some of the best from the cellars. *Cura fugit multo diluiturque mero*."

Walls removed the bicycle firmly from her and took her arm.

"I thought Coromandel *Founder's* Dinner was in Trinity." he said.

"Ah, yes, the *other* Founder's Dinner – that one is on Founder's *Day*, you know, old Thomas's birthday, whole college thing. This one is quite different. This is the Founder's Memento Mori Dinner, *exclusively* for the SCR, to celebrate the anniversary of his death Not *at all* suitable for the *younger* members of college: it's really rather gothic, lots of morbid references to death," replied Priscilla, and then added, "But we all thoroughly enjoy it. The best vintage wine is always served, and the food is particularly excellent!"

"But it isn't the 22nd August today. Didn't Thomas Coromandel die at Bosworth?" protested Walls, thinking to himself that a Memento Mori Dinner was not at all suitable for the older members of the college either, given the average age of most SCR members.   When he considered the matter further he also felt that celebrating the death of one whose life was so unholy that he was supposed to be doomed to walk the earth as a spectre eternally.

"Yes, but you can't have the dinner *that* far out of term," said Priscilla. "*No one* would go to it. *Auctoritas non veritas facit legem*."

 "How *typically* eccentric of *Coromandel*: celebrating someone's death on a day they didn't die on!" said Walls, losing his grammar entirely.

"Well *you* can't talk, given that *Kings* his so eccentric that it has a whole *set* of Founder's Dinners!" replied Priscilla.

"*Naturall*y we do," replied Walls. "One for *each* of our majestic and revered founders. *Obviously*! Many founders, many dinners!"

The air between them seemed to reverberate with tense memories of the old, old feud between the two colleges.

"*A diabolo, qui est simia dei*," said Priscilla, very rudely.

Walls had absolutely no idea what this phrase meant so he capped it with the only Latin phrase he could think of at that moment and said, "*In vino veritas!*"

"I'm so glad you agree that what I said was true," said Priscilla, somewhat belligerently since Walls' phrase implied that she might have *over-imbibed*. What a cheek to even *suggest* such a thing, she thought.

"I *did*?" said Walls, wondering what on earth he had agreed to. He hoped it wasn't too damaging. He gave up and swept her a charming bow, a surprisingly good bow given that he was still holding her up by one arm. "Er, *if you say so!*"

Priscilla felt the pleasure of victory and smiled on him magnanimously. Then she lost track of what they had been discussing entirely as something else floated into the back of her mind. Walls... yes, Walls, *standing in her kitchen cooking,* Walls cooking *delicious* food, food entirely suitable for someone who had recently downed a *few* beakers of *true and blushful Hippocrene*. Ah *yes!*

"Have you come to make *bacon sandwiches*?" she asked hopefully, as they reached her door. "I tell you what: *you* go and get some bacon and bread, and *I'll* put the coffee on. Then you can make me some bacon sandwiches as soon as you get back. *Duas tantum res anxius optat, panem et lardum.*"

Walls considered this suggestion. He was feeling a little peckish himself after all his running about and fright.

"OK," he said, not attempting to supply his originally carefully planned explanation for his presence at her door. "I'll go and get them as soon as you are in the house."

He removed her key from her hand, courteously, after her third attempt to make it line up with the keyhole, opened the door himself, helped her over the doorstep, put her bicycle in the hall with her, ignoring her command to him to take it round the back and into the garden, and steered her into the kitchen.

"You sit *there!*" he said, setting her firmly on the kitchen stool. He put the kettle on and made some black coffee. Then he put a large mug of it by her elbow. She had begun singing the alto part of the whole of Bach's *St Matthew Passion* and ignored him. Walls thought what a good thing it was that he still had a key to the front door. "I'll go and get the bread and bacon," he announced, loudly. She lifted a hand and waved it rather regally at him without ceasing to warble. When it came down to it, thought Walls, he might as well spend the night making bacon sandwiches for Priscilla rather than sitting up awake all alone, imagining all kinds of horrors in his own apartment or his college room. Since Priscilla had mentioned bacon sandwiches he really did not feel he could go to sleep before he had eaten one anyway. He could almost taste the luscious crispy bacon, the fried bread. He was salivating just thinking about it. Pancakes too. He could make *pancakes* as well as bacon sandwiches. Nothing, he felt, was more likely to restore sanity to his mind than a post-midnight feast of bacon sandwiches, up-and-over eggs, pancakes and maple syrup.

Knowing the distance he had to cover to reach the nearest 24/7, he collected her bicycle as he passed through the hall and, although it was much too small for him, pedalled off. When he eventually returned, laden with all the necessary ingredients, Priscilla was still sitting where he had left her, singing to herself, apparently oblivious of his presence in the kitchen. She had moved on to all the solo arias in Bizet's *Carmen*, transcribing them to the alto voice range. Was she working through composers alphabetically, he wondered. He started to cook *around* the stationary obstacle that was Priscilla. Why, he wondered, had he not thought to sit her down in *the lounge* instead.

But Priscilla was reviving. The smell of bacon was working magically. As soon as the first bacon sandwich appeared she appropriated it.

"*Ecce panis angelorum*," she said. After she had chewed and swallowed her first bite she then continued, magisterially, "I will conduct your Latin tutorial at 9.00 am prompt tomorrow. I hope you have brought your essay with you."

"Naturally I have," he replied, thinking it best to humour her and hoping she did not ask him to hand it in now so she could look at it before the tutorial.

"I have deferred your tutorial till then due to the Founder's Dinner this evening," she continued. "But you have been slacking in your studies lately and we cannot leave it beyond 9.00 am tomorrow. I am most displeased at your recent progress. *Tempus volat hora fugit.*"

Clearly any hopes Walls might have cherished of telling Priscilla about the awful corpse and asking for her advice about it were in vain. That would have to wait for tomorrow when she had recovered. Or, possibly, possibly he might never have to tell her about his reason for materialising in her house at all. That would be better.

Tomorrow he would be quite safe again. For Yvette was back tomorrow and so were Buffy and Angel, and the day after that Buffy would meet him for their regular weekly lunch by the river. No corpses would appear in the apartment once Yvette was there: she was far too sensible and severe to tolerate them appearing there all unasked. He loved his wife very much but he also found himself thinking, with gratitude, "If a corpse should materialise while Yvette was there she would yell at it, ask it what it thought it was doing in our apartment, and tell it to get out at once… And it would get out of there as well. She is *so* good at keeping order."

He thought that he wouldn't be able to use his college room *tomorrow*, but Buffy would come and check it out with him after work the day *afterwards*, and he didn't need to go in there *at all* till then. So there was no need to involve Priscilla in the problem loop at all. Being Priscilla, she would never ask him why he was there even if she met him in her house in the morning, as she would just assume she had not been paying attention when the reason was originally explained.

He also saw an opportunity in Priscilla's last speech to get her permission for him to stay overnight. Admittedly she was so alcohol loaded that she didn't know what she was saying but he still preferred to receive an invitation from his hostess before becoming her overnight house guest. So he replied "Absolutely!" and then continued, "If we are going to have a 9.00 am tutorial I had better stay here and sleep in the lounge, don't you think, so that I am not late for it?"

"A good idea!" Priscilla replied. "I am going to sleep *right here* on this lovely soft grass myself. *Astra castra, numen lumen*."

Priscilla got off the stool and began to lie down on the floor.

"No, no!" said Walls, who could see his cooking becoming completely impossible if the entire floor of the tiny kitchen was covered with a slumbering Priscilla. "Let 's get you up the stairs first, up we get!"

He put his arm under hers and around her back and heaved her upright and then guided her unsteady feet across the hall and up the stairs, laying her as gently as possible on her bed. Snores resounded in his ear before he had closed the bedroom door.

He returned downstairs, cooked himself a massive pile of pancakes and bacon, threw an egg on top and retired to the lounge to watch Priscilla's television. When he had finished eating he felt full and pleasantly weary, so weary that he no longer cared if a body should materialise on the floor of the lounge or not. Then he slept as deeply and soundly as his host upstairs.

But at 5.00 am he awoke promptly, sprang up, crept upstairs and had a quick wash and brush-up in Priscilla's bathroom, making as little noise as he possibly could since it was opposite her bedroom door. Then he considered the terrible silence from her room and was seized by a dreadful thought: he had not rolled her over onto her side in bed. What if she had vomited and choked overnight? So he pushed her bedroom door open just a fraction, as gently and quietly as possible, and listened carefully to make sure she was still breathing. Calm, even, contented breathing rang in his relieved ears. He tiptoed back down the stairs and went out for his morning run.

He was smiling naughtily to himself, for it had occurred to him that Priscilla would never remember that he had been there, never know he had been there at all. It would be such fun *never* to tell her and then see if she ever realised. He had very generously left her *all* his washing-up to do. She never usually cooked at all, either eating in College Hall or in restaurants. He thought how surprised she *would* be to find out what she had been doing during the small hours of the night and laughed as he ran towards the tow path for his usual five mile run.

Chapter 5

"Do you *have* to do that?" Barnabus asked Walls.

"Why not? It's better for thinking. The blood rushes to the head," Walls replied.

"But I'm not sure the back of the bench is strong enough to take your weight," protested Barnabus. "Besides which, if *I* stand up the bench will most definitely be so unbalanced that it will tip over backwards and take you with it."

"But you wouldn't *do* that, Buffy; I'm sure you wouldn't be so *mean spirited*," Walls answered.

Barnabus, in his work suit, was just licking his fingers after a particularly tasty chicken mayo baguette and fastidiously folding up the rather greasy paper it had been wrapped in. He was sitting on their usual 'weekly lunch bench' by the Isis. Walls, tracksuited and looking fit, had been poised in a handstand on the back of the bench for at least two minutes, and was showing no signs of righting himself.

Barnabus glared at Walls. "That's what *you* think. But you being upside down like that makes *me* feel giddy just from looking at you, and that's *very* bad for my digestion, so I might be tempted to rise from the bench simply to stop you."

"OK, if you *insist*!" Walls sighed and righted himself, then flung himself down on the grass beside the bench and started doing push-ups.

"I can't help laughing at the thought of Aunt Pris's face when she discovered she had been *cooking* while she was dead drunk!" giggled Barnabus.

"She surely would have realised that I must have paid her a call," said Walls.

"Why ever would she realise that?" said Barnabus. "Unless she has met Mama for coffee and Mama has told her what happened earlier in the day. Then she might have leapt to the correct conclusion. It's not likely though; Mama and Pris don't meet up very often these days."

"That, Buffy, is because your mama is too house-tied with *your* kids," answered Walls. "Because of *them* it was a close call as to whether she was able to extend succour and salvation to *me*!"

"I've told you before, Walls, Mama *loves* having the children at her house, and she doesn't always look after them, she isn't occupied with them at all *this* week. Angel has this week off as well as last week, and she and the children have all gone to visit Angel's parents for the *whole* week. So Mama has a week of perfect peace! Anyway, to return to *your*, er, *little problem*. I don't think it's as bad as *all* that. There seem to me to be *three possible rational explanations* for your apparent apparition."

"Three *rational* explanations? I am all ears!" said Walls. "Speak on!"

"Well, the first one is pretty obvious and I'm surprised you haven't thought of it yourself!" said Barnabus.

"What, what, Buffy?" replied Walls. "Believe me; I am desperate, desperate, for a rational explanation!"

"It was a ghost," said Barnabus. "Q.E.D."

"A *ghost*?" said Walls. "A spirit? A spectre? A spook? You call *that* a *rational* explanation?"

"Why not?" said Barnabus, blithely.

"Because there are *no such things as ghosts*. I do not *believe* in ghosts. No *sane* person could. And surely even people who do believe they exist can hardly call ghosts *rational beings*?" protested Walls.

"Whether you like it or not," pronounced Barnabus, firmly, "*ghosts exist*. I've seen them myself!"

"Don't talk such ****!" said Walls, equally firmly. "You cannot count imagining that you saw a long-dead baron of Little Wychwell, whose actual earthly existence has never been proven historically and whom even *you* cannot believe was ever a *werewolf*! I cannot, Buffy, believe for one second that even *you* consider the existence of werewolves to be actual. It was *evident*ly Tristram, either for fun, just horsing around on a horse with a set of wolves because he could, or else as part of a remarkably devious plot to kill his cousin due to scaring him into a heart attack. If he hadn't been beaten to it by an owl it would have worked out just fine. I entirely corroborate Angel's hypothesis on this matter. Totally."

"I don't in the *slightest* agree with you that there is any evidence that what I saw on that night was *not* a ghost. You may remember that the *Vicar* not only agreed with me but that he said he had seen the same vision himself! But I was *not* referencing the Evil Baron episode in my last speech," Barnabus responded, with a degree of hauteur.

"So what other spectral apparitions *were* you referring to?" demanded Walls.

"We have ghosts all over our house – not mine and Angel's house – Mama and Dad's house - the Old Vicarage. They are always wandering about in there," answered Barnabus.

Walls gave a derisive and disbelieving snort.

"And *clearly*," said Barnabus, ignoring Walls and pressing his point home, "if this is a ghost then this particular ghost has chosen to materialise in front of *you* because you are an expert on the Second World War, and thus he believes you can clear up the mystery of his fate, or avenge his death or some such similar idea. Or maybe just record his story for him? Yes, that seems good. *He wants you to research and record his story so he isn't forgotten.*"

"All I can say is that if that is why he is appearing in my life and if he is listening right now, I would like to tell him to abandon any hope of that idea. Go and haunt someone else. Point 1: I am not going to attempt to communicate with anyone who isn't alive and kicking. Point 2: I particularly abhor *corpses* so I'm absolutely not discussing any matters with *them*, whether they are actual or spectral. Point 3: I don't do 'research on demand'; I have quite enough work as it is. Point 4: I am not seeing any likelihood of the deceased offering me a large research grant or a prize or whatever for doing said research and I don't yet believe in spending hours of effort without financial or academic reward," replied Walls.

There was a brief pause. Barnabus wondered if *he* could track down the identity of the 'ghost' himself. Could it be someone who inhabited whatever was once there on the same site as the flats? That would be a good *starting* point for an investigation. If he could find out which families lived there, which of them served in World War II, find photographs of them in uniform, show them to Walls and then triumphantly prove his own point when Walls had to admit that he recognized that person as being the corpse on his floor.

Walls was feeling ruffled both by Buffy's irrational and disordered logic and by Buffy's persistent belief in supernatural beings. Walls argued that he himself might not like looking at corpses but that was because they were distressingly dead, *not* because he thought they were spirit laden.

So Walls sighed loudly and sadly and interrupted his friend's reverie, "OK, rational explanation number one rejected by me as impossible. *Rational* explanation number two?" he finished on a hopeful note. Maybe Buffy's next suggestion would be more sensible.

"Rational explanation number two. And I'm glad you accept the ghost theory as rational explanation number one. Otherwise this explanation would be number one. *See*, I told you it was *rational*."

"Do you know how vexatiously annoying you are sometimes?" asked Walls.

"Say I am not annoying or I'm not going to tell you rational explanations two and three," retorted Barnabus.

"OK, OK. I am sufficiently desperate to hear your theories in the vain hope that they might restore my peace of mind. You are not *ever* annoying, *ever*, honest!" replied Walls, spoiling this by adding, "I have my fingers crossed to avert that lie."

"Thank you for nothing!" said Barnabus, "All the same I will tell you number two. Someone hates you and is playing silly games to frighten you, *pretending* to be a corpse or getting someone else to pretend to be a corpse, or using a model corpse or something like that," said Barnabus, ticking off the point on his second finger as he said it.

"That," said Walls, "is *just* as *absurd*. No, not *quite* as absurd; it doesn't involve non-existent beings. But, Buffy, be *serious*! It's totally ridiculous."

"Why?" demanded Barnabus.

"Is that not obvious? Because, Buffy, no one, *no one* in the entire world hates *me*. Everyone I know *adores* me!" replied Walls, with a deep exhaled breath of total satisfaction in his own loveliness and adorability.

"Super egotist! You have the biggest ego I know! How can you possibly say that?" expostulated Barnabus. "Think about all those abandoned women, *years and years* of them! One night with you and then instantly dumped!"

"But I was engaged to Flic at that time! I couldn't have a *serious* relationship with *other* women! Anyway they don't *hate* me, Buffy; I always, always sent them a big bunch of red roses. No woman can hate you if you send her a big bunch of roses," replied Walls.

"And *after* you were engaged to Flic and *before* you were engaged to Yvette? Huh?" said Barnabus. "In any case you shouldn't have been *dating* other people when you were engaged to Flic! Damn it all! I like your interesting hypothesis about roses too, but I fear it may not hold water. And you know what else is really annoying. You don't know *anything* at all about this so-called corpse, do you? You didn't make notes, you didn't look at it carefully enough to get a clear memory of it. You are a *hopeless* investigator! I bet you aren't even sure it was a person and not a shop dummy!"

"The red roses are not just a hypothesis, you know; they are a tested and proven theory. You should send Angel some on a regular basis. When did you last send her any? I assure you it would improve your marriage no end. As to the corpse, you are right. I'll admit, I'm not sure of *anything* about it. As you know, I don't *like* corpses. I hardly *glanced* at the thing. Other than to register as a general impression that it was a dead soldier from World War II and that said dead soldier from World War II had absolutely no business being where it was. Other than that, as I told you, it was a captain in the Oxfordshire and Buckinghamshire Light Infantry. I did notice the stripes and the hat badge, but only because I saw those things automatically without even thinking, because of my research. I notice things like that" was Walls lengthy riposte.

"I don't *need* to send red roses to Angel! I don't have *any* reason to *apologise* to Angel! But I'll bear the red roses in mind in case I ever do have one. Right, let's run past what we do know again. How did you know it was dead?" said Barnabus.

"You don't need a reason to send red roses. Red roses are romantic. Women adore them. Angel deserves them from you! I am shocked that you do not send them to her at least once a week. You should have a regular order with the florist. I don't know why I know it was dead. I just know it *was*. Visualize my *shock*, you know, Buffy, my staggered amazement. Can you imagine opening one's own front door and discovering a dead Second World War soldier paying a visit? Dressed in full combat uniform? With blood all over it. I did notice *that* bit. It was lying on the floor. It was a Second World War soldier. A captain in the Oxfordshire and Buckinghamshire Light Infantry, to be more accurate. It looked pretty dead to me. I mean a soldier from World War II is *hardly going to be alive*, is he?" replied Walls.

"So," said Barnabus, sighing at his friend's failure to collect any useful evidence or examine the body properly or even look at it properly, "let's run back past what we know for certain actually happened *again*. You saw something that looked like a body dressed in World War II combat gear lying on your floor, it was wearing the uniform of a Captain in the Oxfordshire and Buckinghamshire Light Infantry. Then you screamed and shut the door. The whole process took under five seconds. That's it."

"A fair summary," admitted Walls.

"Colour of eyes?" asked Barnabus, but without much hope of getting a sensible answer.

"*No idea!*" said Walls, without sounding abashed in the slightest, "Um, probably shut? You know, dead sort of thing."

"Colour of hair?" demanded Barnabus with exasperation "You must have seen their hair, surely?"

"They had it very short in those days, in the military" said Walls.

"You didn't *look*, did you?" said Barnabus.

"I didn't exactly *not* look" Walls, excused himself, "But I didn't dash in and poke the thing around to see what its hair looked like either. I suppose you are going to claim you *would* have! . Its head was tilted back with its hat over its face. So you could only see the chin and the hat," then he added, with an air of triumph, "I say, I'll know something!"

"Go on, surprise me" said Barnabus.

"It *didn't* have any facial hair!" said Walls, looking very pleased with himself, "See, I noticed *that*!"

"I suppose you want a prize for observation now!" sighed Barnabus, "Did World War II soldiers have beards? Weren't they banned?"

"Well, yes, yes, they were, for British and American soldiers at least. But don't you see, this means that this soldier clearly wasn't a deserter or a prison camp escapee on the run who couldn't get access to a razor. Allow me *that*! And if it *was* a 21st century still-alive imposter *it wasn't someone with facial hair*! Allow me *that* as well!"

"Give me strength!" said Barnabus, turning his eyes up to heaven. Then he laughed and continued, "You know *what?* I have just thought of something! You are catching with me up on *finding bodies*! Three now! And I have only found five myself, and *you* found *two* of those *as well*!" He gave a whooping laugh.

"Are you *sure* you have only found *five*? It seems like *more*. But otherwise, I am prepared to not deny that fact. I am aware of that dismal reckoning on my part, and the gap closing with you had already occurred to me" said Walls. "Don't rub it in! Note, Buffy, however, that I have *so far restrained* myself from saying that it couldn't have been a *real* corpse because it was *me* who found it and not *you*. However, I will make use of that phrase if you mention the body count figures *ever again*. For you must admit that if this one isn't a bona fide corpse I might still have only found two and, as you just said, you were with me for *both* of those so I think we can count those as *yours*, not *mine*! Especially as I never actually *really* looked at either of them, you will recall that I had my eyes firmly closed after we fished one out of the river and I didn't see the other at all as it was behind a set of trees, I only had your live action report about that one. My corpse finding count might, therefore, still be at *zero*!"

"No, Walls, you cannot wriggle out of that score, it is *three*, definitely *three* for you," sang Barnabus, gleefully.

"With reference to the number three, I believe *you* claimed to have a *third rational explanation*. Your first two have been entirely irrational, so let's hear number three!" said Walls.

"Ah yes!" said Barnabus. "Rational explanation number three. Easy. You have roaming around the ivory towers for far too long, Walls. You've been researching and studying and teaching and what not in oxygen deprived heights of academia for too many years. You have, in fact, gone as bonkers as all the other long serving dons. You've started having your research topics materialise in front of you. I bet you Aunt Pris sees Trojan and Roman and Greek soldiers *all the time*, dead *or* alive. You should ask her for advice on this topic."

"For ****'s sake, Buffy! Not one of those explanations has been at all rational! You need to get back into academia and get your logical deduction and evidence related research skills back into gear! And if Pris does talk to Trojans and Romans and Greeks I feel the amount of alcohol she had just imbibed might be a major factor in their manifestation. I don't drink alcohol, you know I don't" quoth Walls, giving Barnabus a friendly punch in the ribs, "Now, I need some *real* practical help from you, not a load of tosspot theories!"

"My hypotheses are *all* perfectly rationally valid, even if none of them is yet proven," said Barnabus, with dignity, "and I am perfectly sure that *one* of them is the truth. I think we should start by unearthing your little black book. I bet you haven't thrown it away. Then we can go through it, decide which are the most likely females to be carrying out revenge attacks on you, and start investigating them."

"Even if I had ever owned a 'little black book' I would have thrown it away when I became engaged to Yvette," said Walls, in a stately way.

"I bet you *didn't*!" said Barnabus. "*Liar*! People never *ever* do that. They keep them somewhere, secretly for ever. I bet it's in your college room. I bet that's why you keep your college room as well as having the apartment. Your college room is stuffed with the evidence of your dissolute years, well hidden from Yvette's eyes! Speaking of which, what does Yvette say about this whole corpse in apartment affair?"

"I haven't told her anything about it and *you aren't to tell her either*! *Or* Angel!" said Walls. "You must not breathe a single syllable of this to Angel because Angel will go and tell Yvette. Yvette is my dearest love but I can see what the results of her discovering this would be. Seriously, Buffy, I don't want her to start socio-psycho-analysing me!"

"*I see your point!*" said Barnabus. "But don't you think *Priscilla* might tell Yvette?"

"Priscilla doesn't *know*!" said Walls.

"But Priscilla *will* know if she has been talking to Mama," pointed out Barnabus.

"As you said, Elodea and Pris don't meet very often any more. Let's hope they don't meet up before this is all sorted out and explained and pigeon holed and finished. Mind though, if they do meet it won't matter because Pris never listens to a word your mama says!"

"*That*," agreed Barnabus, "is *true*. But the way Mama runs on, on and on and on, one could have a bit of sympathy with Aunt Pris. Mama can talk the hind leg off a donkey. Did I tell you about when I didn't listen to her properly because she had gone on for so long about Agnes Gray's hens and then she put an important bit about Amadeus in on the end somewhere and I just hadn't heard her, and the consequence was that…"

"Whoa! Hold your horses, Buffy! How come Elodea hadn't told *you* about this corpse, *before* I did?" interrupted Walls, while thinking that Buffy's mama was not the only member of their family who could talk the hind leg off a donkey.

"Er, well, actually, she *had*, Walls, old boy. Only we had agreed that if you didn't tell me I'd pretend I didn't know, you know, in case it was *definitely* hallucinations and you would rather not talk about it," Barnabus answered. "But it's OK, Mama definitely hasn't told Angel because we agreed that Angel might think you weren't a safe person to have around Ama and Theo if she thought you were experiencing mental problems. Mothers, you know: overanxious and fussy."

"*Not safe round your children?*" exclaimed Walls. "Of *course* I'm *safe!*"

"Yes, yes," soothed Barnabus, "I know, Walls. You are the safest person I know. Safe as a fortress!"

They gave each other a quick bear hug and Barnabus continued, "But all the same, we thought it was better not to tell Angel. She isn't keen on the concept of ghosts, not at all. And supposing it's a *real* body it would be just as bad. Because, as you know, she gets sort of worked up about me getting involved with those as well, and with any sort of crime and things like that in general, especially me investigating things, you know, and she might tell me to keep my nose right out of it. Then I would have to, see? Then I couldn't help you. You know how angry she gets about the number of bodies and things I have already got tangled up in, anyone would think I was walking round looking for them instead of just happening to fall over them by accident; *you* know that."

"I read you," said Walls, "Quite so."

Walls remembered that he had not yet told Buffy about the practical help which he needed immediately, so continued, "Hold on though, Buffy, with all these, er, *rational* explanations, we are getting distracted from the main immediate issue. *My college room! I need real practical aid with that little matter*, right away! I need *you* to go there *with me so* we can both go into it together and check that it is completely free from any possible pollution by dead bodies, imaginary or real. I can't use it till someone else checks it out with me. This is becoming a bit inconvenient. Since Angel and the children are on vacation you can surely meet me after work tonight, and we can journey there together."

"How have you been managing without going into your college room till now? All that *important state of the art research* and the whole world waiting for you to get on with it?" teased Barnabus.

"I can manage to do my *research* without my *room* perfectly well. I have everything I need online and I can always take a wander to the libraries. And it's out of term so I haven't got any tutorials to take. Leastways I've only been out of it for two days!" protested Walls.

"OK, so you *need* me. I *can* meet you after work. But I expect you to treat me to dinner at the Bear afterwards," said Barnabus. "I get hungry at work and money is low after our little pre-number-three holiday. Hey, I haven't told you *anything* about our *holiday*. Or how exciting it is to be expecting number three. So thrilled. We dashed off on holiday as soon as we knew about the new Bump so that we didn't have a problem with getting away when Angel is more pregnant, as you know."

Walls made a huge effort to try to look thrilled himself at the prospect of hearing all about Angel's pregnancy, the expectations Barnabus had about his third child and the joyful details of someone else's vacation. He managed to achieve an enthusiastic response "Great! I'll surely enjoy hearing all that. You *must* tell me *all* the details this evening!"

Barnabus glanced at his watch. "I'd tell you now but it's too late now. I must run!"

"Treating you to dinner will be my pleasure!" called Walls, after Barnabus' retreating form.. Then he yelled, much louder, so Barnabus could not fail to hear him, "I'll be outside your office at 5.30."

Barnabus groaned. He had been met outside work by Walls before. Walls was such an exhibitionist. Everyone in Barnabus' office could recognise Walls by sight by now, they all knew he was waiting for Barnabus. He shuddered as he realised that a whole set of people would once again be reporting that "your *friend* is outside the front door doing flip flops" or "doing press-ups" or "standing on his head" or whatever physical jerks Walls might be using to pass the time. Barnabus was too late for work to go back and plan to meet somewhere else. Why ever hadn't he thought to say they would meet at the lodge of Kings College? Barnabus glanced at his watch again and increased his speed to a faster jog. He would barely make it back before the end of the lunch hour and he was going to be all sweaty for the whole afternoon now. Bother Walls and his imaginary bodies! Barnabus didn't want to have to go crawling round poking about in college rooms after work; he wanted to go home and have a lovely quiet evening on his own, taking an opportunity to relax while the rest of his family were away. But Walls unquestionably needed support and help. He could not desert his friend in his hour of great need. For Barnabus was more than a little inclined to Rational Explanation Three. I mean, he told himself, all that *study* even without being *married to Yvette*, and if you added in being married to Yvette *anyone* might start seeing things that weren't there. He would *certainly* see things that weren't there if he was married to Yvette. He set his jaw, a man on a mission. He couldn't abandon Walls. Walls had always been there for him. "No man left behind" he announced, loudly, to the surprise of the receptionist in the lobby of his offices.

* * *

At that very moment, in the Ashmolean Museum Café, Flodea and Priscilla were very busy disproving the theory that they hardly ever met any more. They were just assembling themselves and their trays of refreshment at a large table in the emptiest part of the café, at the far end from the servery, where they could have an extended chat in peace.

Priscilla took very little time to transfer her cup of espresso from her tray to the table but Elodea had a muffin, two t large slices of cake, "I couldn't decide which to have so I thought I might as well have both, and I'd already picked up the muffin before I thought I would prefer cake so it seemed a shame to put it back", and *two* large lattes "because, Priscilla, *one* is simply not enough to last through a reasonable conversation".

Then Elodea kept jumping up and down like an ill sitting hen in order to make several trips back to the serving area to get first a teaspoon, then a knife, and then several serviettes. Finally she settled into her seat and said, "Well, *we're* all ready *now*."

Priscilla restrained herself from pointing out sourly that she herself had been ready about ten minutes ago and that furthermore she was a very busy person who had had to fit a meeting with Elodea into her already crowded day, unlike those who were not in paid employment. As it was Priscilla contented herself with a sort of hrmph sound followed by "Yes, absolutely, one should fill up as much as possible while one can, Elodea. *Non semper erit aestas*."

"Such a kerfuffle!" said Elodea, ignoring Priscilla's remark mainly because she had entirely failed to realise it was sarcastic, "It reminds me of the other day when Theodora and Amadeus and I were dancing on the lawn in the rain and – "

Priscilla was, for once, actually listening properly to Elodea, she re-ran the remark through her head, surely she must have misheard it?

"I'm sorry, Elodea, I didn't *quite* catch that last bit," she interrupted. "I thought for a moment you said that you and, er, your *grandchildren*, were dancing on the lawn in the rain."

"Oh yes, we *were*, Priscilla! Such *fun*! It's why grandchildren are such super things to have! My children are all too old and grown-up for dancing on the lawn in the rain these days, so I've been dancing *by myself* for years. John doesn't enjoy dancing, especially not on the lawn in the rain. Anyway, to get back to what I was about to say, Amadeus suddenly said to me while we were dancing about, all wet, that…"

Priscilla sipped her espresso, put her 'I am paying full attention in a meeting' face on and escaped into her own highly academic thoughts. Elodea was quite used to talking *at* Priscilla about her children and grandchildren *without* Priscilla listening, so she ignored the lack of attention from her friend. This acceptance of each other's foibles was, after all, how they had remained friends for so long.

After about ten minutes Priscilla, who had been pondering and reanalysing a few tricky points in Chapter 10 of her latest book, suddenly interrupted a particularly thrilling story about Theodora and Pippy to announce, magisterially, "Before I *forget*, Elodea, I am *composing* a new book: *A Feminist Standpoint on Bacchanalia.*"

"How, how, *wonderful*!" said Elodea, stopped in full flight with her story, feeling appalled at the prospect of another book by Priscilla but nonetheless sounding as sincere and pleased as she could. Being a good and true friend, Elodea had so far waded womanfully through every single book that Priscilla had written. This had not been an easy task. "I shall look forward to reading it so much!" she added, crossing her fingers under the table.

Priscilla smiled in a self-satisfied way. She had no difficulty in believing the sincerity of Elodea's assertions because she was absolutely confident that no one could fail to both enjoy and be thoroughly well educated and enlightened by her books.

"Of course," Priscilla said, "you will have to be *patient*; it is only in *very draft* form yet. You will not have the pleasure of reading it for *at least* two years. *Cuivis dolori remedium est patientia*."

Elodea beamed with relief at this news, feeling that her suffering was much alleviated *right now* by the news of the anticipated date of publication. Then she hastily put in a speech to explain away the fact she looked quite so blissful. "I am *so* happy that you have a new book *in the pipeline*!" she cried. "It will be such *fun* to read it as soon as it *is* in print!"

Elodea looked at Priscilla's face. The word 'fun' had slid out of her mouth by mistake and it had very clearly been an error.

Elodea plunged on, "Because, as you know, learning new concepts and ideas is *such* fun and your books are full of so many exciting ones!"

Priscilla returned to smiling in a smug and self-congratulatory way.

"So," said Elodea, changing the subject before Priscilla began discussing either her future book or any of her past books any further, "you'll be wondering why I *had* to have coffee with you today! Such a weird thing happened the other day and I thought you might have some ideas on what to do, because I am *so worried* about Walls."

"*Walls*!" said Priscilla, who was accidentally listening to Elodea in the middle of recomposing her thoughts on Chapter 10, "It's an odd thing you should mention Walls because I was reminded of him only the other day!"

"You *were*?" said Elodea.

"Yes. It was after Founder's Dinner. You know Memorial one for dons alone. Our latest Prevaricator, as you know, is very keen on 'authentic' medieval re-enactment despite not bothering to check if his medieval concepts are in *any* way correct. You should hear *Frederick* on the subject. Frederick calls our Prevaricator "*Dare Pondus Idonea Fumo*'. However, under our aforesaid glorious leader's guidance the feast was particularly, er, *amazing* this year. The staff managed to make Hall look truly sepulchral, black and purple hangings everywhere. The whole dinner was accompanied by the gloomiest funereal music played by a medieval quartet with authentic replica instruments. The food was all *supposedly* recreated from a medieval funeral feast menu. To top it all off there was a magnificent subtlety composed of the figures of Death looming over the mangled and disfigured body of Thomas Coromandel while the Devil waited to take Thomas's soul. *Corpora lente augescent cito extinguuntur*"

Priscilla paused, both for breath and for effect.

"Super!" said Elodea, weakly, while wondering if Frederick was the Professor of Medieval History, having a horrible vision of the repulsive sugar sculpture in her mind's eye, and wishing that her friend could have at least found a more cheerful quotation to finish off the description of what sounded to Elodea like an extremely depressing meal.

"And" Priscilla continued, "as always, to *accompany* the meal, some of the *finest* vintage wines and port from the college cellar! At least the Prevaricator has had the sense not to change that aspect of the feast."

"*Ah!*" said Elodea, feeling this last phrase entirely explained Priscilla's enthusiasm for this perfectly ghastly event.

Priscilla took another sip of espresso and then continued, "I seem to have wandered away from the main theme of this lecture, the next slide should put us back in line. I mean, er, I must return to the main theme of this lecture, I mean *conversation"*

Priscilla looked at Elodea in a hopeful way. But Elodea was amusing herself by pretending not to remember what Priscilla had been discussing earlier either.

"*Do* go on, Pris" said Elodea, naughtily, "I am all agog for the next part!"

Priscilla paused for a moment, Coromandel College, medieval banquet, something to do with the decoration at the banquet, the hangings perhaps, the hangings on the…ah, yes, *Walls*!

"*After* the dinner I remembered how *Walls* used to cook me bacon sandwiches when he was staying with me if I got in, er, rather, er, *late*. The dinner had been a few hours ago by the time I got home, you know, naturally we had, er, *coffee* afterwards and, yes, *some* of the folk had some very good liqueurs too. But I had cycled all the way home. *Dum satur est venter, gaudet caput inde libenter*. So I cooked my own bacon sandwiches! They are *so* good after a celebratory event; they seem to entirely prevent any risk of a hangover due to the, er, *port*. They will hand it round at these things and it is so impolite not to take it. *One* glass of port can affect the liver *so much*, especially fine old vintage port, don't you agree, and I had also taken just *one small* glass of red wine with dinner. *Vinum est dulcia venena*. I was *vexed* with myself in the morning though. I found I had left *all* the washing-up till morning instead of doing it before I went to bed because, naturally, I was very tired by then. So *greasy*! Walls always used to do the washing-up himself when he stayed with me, and I had *no idea* what *congealed bacon fat* was like on a pan. *Now*," she added, apparently talking to herself in an very absent tone, "I think page five hundred and twenty five would be much improved if…"

Priscilla stopped speaking and wandered back into her own thoughts. She had even forgotten to put on her 'attentive' face and Elodea gave a wry smile at her friend's glazed and absent look. There was no point in continuing to try to transmit any information about Walls to Priscilla.

Instead Elodea embarked on her second slice of cake, savouring each sweet mouthful while musing to herself a little. What *was* the date for Founder's Memorial Dinner at Coromandel? Yes, *that figured*. It *did* match 'Walls Finding a Corpse' Day. Priscilla would have heavily over-imbibed at the dinner, *one small glass of wine indeed*! More likely to be at least ten large ones! Yes, Walls had clearly decided not to return to his college room after all. Priscilla must have been so surprised in the morning to find she had apparently been doing so much cooking. Elodea giggled and then began to laugh.

Priscilla subconscious ear-radar picked up the laughter. She laughed politely as well.

"*That story*," she said to Elodea, "was utterly *hilarious*! How *very* entertaining your *grandchildren* are!"

"*Absolutely!*" said Elodea without batting an eyelid.

Then Priscilla's phone made a bleeping noise. She picked it up from her bag and looked at the screen.

"Dear me!" she cried. "Important college planning meeting! I must go! Must dash! *Tarde venientibus ossa*."

"What a *shame!*" said Elodea, in soothing tones." Never mind!"

Priscilla leapt up and rushed from the café.

Elodea managed to keep a straight face till Priscilla had vanished from view. Then she chuckled to herself. Priscilla, bless her, was *so* transparent. This phone alarm with an invented important event that Priscilla must attend immediately was now the way that all their coffee sessions always ended. Priscilla really must think that Elodea was stupid.

Perhaps it was just as well that she had left in this case, for Elodea had also realised there was really no point in discussing her original purpose with Priscilla. Walls' hallucinations would probably mean very little to Priscilla. For when Elodea considered the matter Priscilla probably talked to dead Romans and Greeks all the time, especially after a few glassfuls of 'blushful Hippocrene', and would think such things were entirely normal. She seemed to recall that Priscilla had admitted to seeing the founder of Coromandel, the aforementioned Thomas, himself in the quad after a well-lubricated Founder's Dinner previously.

Elodea was also now perfectly sure that Walls, not wanting to be alone for the night, must have visited Priscilla on the night of the Founder's Dinner. Even if Priscilla had been *very* drunk Elodea thought it most unlikely that her non-cooking friend would suddenly have bothered to make bacon sandwiches. Naughty Walls – he must have realised Priscilla would not know he had been there.

But she told herself firmly, it was as well she had not mentioned the corpse in the flat incident. For if Walls had *wanted* Priscilla to know about the 'dead soldier' he would have stayed in the morning till Priscilla got up, and then told her all about it. So Walls must have thought of some reason *not* to tell Priscilla. What could it be? Naturally! Yvette! Of course, Priscilla was friends with Yvette, and Walls had decided not to tell Yvette so he couldn't tell Priscilla either in case she let it slip out. Ah, Elodea reasoned to herself, he did not want to tell Yvette in case she was scared about going into their apartment herself. What a good husband he was!

So caring! What a mercy that Elodea had not made the mistake of telling Priscilla about the incident.

Elodea sighed with satisfaction that the vagaries of fate combined with the eccentricities of Priscilla had prevented her disclosure. She then embarked happily on the muffin and her second cup of latte. She wished she had started with three cups now, these mugs were really very small, but there was a queue at the server now and she didn't want to queue up.

She had plenty of time before she needed to return to Little Wychwell. She thought she would take a quick tour of the Ashmolean and then browse through some shops. Priscilla was really *very* mean to dash off like that but Elodea didn't need her company. She could find plenty to amuse herself with in Oxford, especially as was not in charge of two or more small children for once. It was so lovely to get a week free from grandchild-care, even if she did love them very much.

A man was walking towards her down the length of the café. He had a loaded lunch tray. There were still lots of empty tables elsewhere but he seemed to be making straight for hers. She looked at him. She didn't recognise him but he looked to be about the same age as one of her sons, Barnabus, Paris or Tony, so maybe he was one of their friends? He definitely wasn't from Little Wychwell. No one she recognised from there at all.

As he approached her table he confirmed that his approach was intentional by waving to her. He was wearing jeans and a red T-shirt which was adorned with a black logo of a hand making a sign of the horns. He must clearly be a hard rock enthusiast. This didn't give her much of a clue about which of her sons was his acquaintance. They all had friends who were fans of this musical genre.

"Greetings, Elodea! Enchanted to find you here!" said the stranger.

He knew her name. No possibility that he had mistaken her for someone else. He also had a very posh Oxford accent which almost certainly meant he was one of Barnabus' friends and had been to Kings College with him.

"Hi there!" she said, trying to look and sound as if *she* knew who *he was* as well. But he had already seen her confused look.

"The Walrus!" he said, helpfully, balancing his tray on one hand and holding out the other to shake hers while bowing slightly.

"Ah, yes, of course! The *Walrus*!" she said, trying to sound even *more* confident. Clearly from the nickname he must be one of Barnabus' rowing friends, probably from the first eight. At least that narrowed his identity down.

He was not fooled by her tone this time either. "Real name *Andy"* he continued, "Andy *de Ville*! How are you?"

"Very well, thank you," she said, as her brain gave a sigh of relief. She had managed to make his face look younger, and finally remembered him. "And *you*? I do hope you are well. But *I* thought your surname was *Beaven*."

She carefully pronounced the 'beave' as in beaver because she remembered that he had always been *very* sensitive about his surname being mispronounced and how to pronounce it too. But, while remembering the pronunciation, she had managed to get the actual surname wrong.

"Not *Bea*ven, Elodea!" he said, in a slightly patronising way – he had the easy assurance of those with a high position in society, a splendid education and ancestral millions – "*Hea*ven!"

He pronounced the word Heaven as Heave- en. Then he continued.

"I changed it to my partner's name when we married. Heaven's such an *awkward* name. People *will* pronounce it like the celestial paradise and then if you correct that they start thinking it's *'Heathen'* instead. Not the sort of name to inflict on another mortal, better to lose it yourself. So I'm Andy de Ville now."

Elodea laughed politely at the possible confusion between heaven and heathen.

Elodea now had another reason to be nervous. Not only was she still struggling to remember exactly who the man himself was, but the word 'partner' was bothering her. Had he *really* wanted to get rid of his *own* surname; or had he married a feminist woman who wanted her man to take her surname rather than her his; or had he married *another man*, who wanted him to take his surname?

She couldn't remember Barnabus saying *anything* about Andy getting married, but then why would he have, and even if he had, why would Elodea have bothered to remember it? Andy was not one of Barnabus' *close* friends and she couldn't remember everything about all his wide circle of acquaintances. She must be very careful to only refer to Andy's partner in a gender neutral way unless he gave her some further information. But she didn't feel she could change the subject completely, she must say *something* about his marriage since she was sure that she hadn't seen him since he got married. She thought of a suitable statement.

"Congratulations! Have you been married long?" she asked. "I don't remember Barnabus telling me about it but I must have forgotten. You know, once round the goldfish bowl these days and I've forgotten everything!"

"We married *five* years ago," he said, "and divorced *four* years ago. I couldn't be bothered changing my surname *again*. Such a bother changing all my bank accounts and things the first time. So I kept the married version."

"Oh dear!" she said. "I'm so *sorry*! I do apologise, *most insensitive* of me, I didn't mean to give you pain!"

"That's quite all right," he said. "I assure you I have recovered. Water under the bridge. Pray do not worry about it."

He winced at the word 'bridge' as if he had remembered something. She noticed his full tray, still balanced on one hand with the soup going cold. Poor man, he must be *lonel*y. He clearly had *no one* with whom to take luncheon.

"Do join me, er, Andy. I'll, I'll just go and get another coffee for myself! And some soup too! It looks very good. It will take me a minute or two, if that's all right with you?"

"Super! Utterly charmed!" he said and sat down at the table.

Elodea dashed away to get another cup of coffee and the soup. She had suddenly remembered Mrs Shipman's prophecy and the desire to laugh was difficult to get under control. His name! De Ville... *Devil*! Being cast out from Heaven to become a de Ville when he married! The red T-shirt! The sign of the horns! He was the prophesy incarnate, the poor man!

"Really!" she chided herself. "I must stop taking any notice of the daft things Mrs Shipman says or writes. He is just a lonely divorced young man who doesn't like eating alone and was so happy to see me in the café so that he had someone else to sit with! I will go back and have a really friendly conversation with him and then perhaps we can go and look at one of the galleries *together*!"

Elodea finally set off for home a full two hours later, having had a most pleasant time with the Walrus. He hadn't had anything particular to do either so they had conversed about various topics over lunch and then they had gone to study the Dutch paintings together, and Elodea had thought how pleasant it had been to be looking at the exhibits while talking to another adult instead of a small child. Particularly since the Walrus had turned out to be another grown-up who was also very knowledgeable about art. She had promised to remember to tell Barnabus that the Walrus was around in Oxford for the next few weeks. They had avoided mentioning the Walrus's sad marriage failure again, and Elodea thought that she really must remember to ask Barnabus about that. It would be so awkward not knowing what had happened, just in case she happened to ever run into Andy de Ville again.

So Elodea rang Barnabus that evening, wanting to tell him that his friend was back in Oxford as soon as she could. Barnabus would certainly want to meet up with him and he would have time to do so while Angel and the children were away this week. But she was surprised by Barnabus' reaction.

"That lazy tosser! Thank you for warning me that he is about the place" he said, "I'll make sure to hide if I see him coming towards me."

"But, Barnabus, he seemed quite *charming* to me!" Elodea protested.

"Oh, he's *charming* all right. A proper *smooth talker*. That's how he got away with his idle behaviour for so long. Skipping training *all the time*! He *nearly got us bumped* in the Head of the River. The shame if we had been! Kings College First Eight *bumped*! He was demoted to the Second Eight, and personally if I had been the Head of Boats I would have chucked him out of the Boat Club entirely. *Useless drunkard*!" Barnabus said.

"He wasn't drunk today," said Elodea, "and I'm sure rather a lot of your rowing friends drank heavily."

"*None* of them were as bad as *the Walrus*! Complete alcoholic. It's a wonder he didn't get sent down. How he got a *first*, I'll never know!" said Barnabus.

"I suppose he's just *very intelligent*," said Elodea, in a way that she knew would annoy Barnabus, who was very clever himself but had had to work very hard to achieve his own first. Elodea was most annoyed at her youngest son's intolerance. The poor man had seemed quite harmless, in fact very sweet, there were many reasons why people might slip into alcoholism, it was sad not bad.

Barnabus ignored her and continued his tirade. "And as for the way he treated the *Whale*…"

"The *Whale*?" asked Elodea, who could not remember anyone called that either.

"Second Eight's cox. Pretty useless cox, to be honest. Would never have done for the Firsts. *Name's* a *joke, see*. Very small, so called 'the Whale'!" explained Barnabus, with a patient air.

"Yes, I got *that* bit of it. I'm not senile yet, dear," said Elodea. "But what did Andy *do* to the Whale?"

"The Walrus had an *affair two weeks* after their marriage, the Whale told everyone about it. So upset! Almost *instant divorce*. Shocker!" said Barnabus. "Well, if you aren't ringing for any more important or urgent reason than this social chat I am just off to eat dinner at the Bear with Walls, and I'll say cheerio for now."

"I'm glad you're going out with Walls," Elodea said. "That's what he needs: a few jolly social evenings to get his head straight. He's been working much too hard;

that's what's wrong with him. If he gets away from his studies a bit more his mind will strengthen up again."

"Bye!" said Barnabus in a final and dismissive tone, and rang off.

Elodea thought, in a pleased way, that now she knew something about Andy's partner, and she knew their nickname if not their proper name. Andy had married 'the Whale', who was a Kings' student and a female cox! Then Elodea corrected herself, realising that she herself had added the feminine details. 'The Whale' might just as well be *male*. A cox could be either sex after all and she seemed to remember that Kings was biased towards having male coxes when Barnabus was there, and she also recollected that Barnabus had blithely explained to her that this was because men could *steer straight*. She did hope he had never voiced this opinion to Angel who had been a Coromandel cox herself. Barnabus had also said the Whale was *small* but that was pretty likely if you were a cox and anyway Barnabus and his rower friends described most of the rest of the world population as 'small' in comparison to themselves. She did not want to ring Barnabus back to ask him, as he would be aggravated if she rang him again this evening unless she was in the throes of a bona fide emergency. It somehow didn't seem an appropriate question for a text message either. How could one word such an awkward query?

Then Elodea told herself that she didn't need to know the answer as it didn't matter *in the slightest* whether the Whale was female or male. But she found she was still unreasonably curious about this point. She should have asked Barnabus what the Whale's real first name was. *De Ville* didn't ring any bells in Elodea's memory at all. Walls would know what it was. She would ask Walls the next time she saw him. Walls must surely like Andy because Walls liked *everyone*. He wouldn't mind telling Elodea all he knew about Andy's marriage and also all about Andy's partner. But Barnabus also *usually* liked everyone. So perhaps there *was* something unpleasant about Andy that she herself hadn't noticed. After all, she had only spoken to him for a short time. But Elodea remained convinced that Barnabus was misjudging Andy. She had enjoyed her little outing with Andy, aka the Walrus, very much and she would like to have *another* conversation with him sometime.

* * *

Under the circumstances Elodea was more than a little surprised when Barnabus rang her after work on the *following* day to transmit some exciting information about an old acquaintance.

"You'll *never* guess who Walls and I met in the Bear last night!" said Barnabus.

"No, I won't," Elodea replied, "so to save time I'm not going to try and guess, just *tell* me! Who was it?"

"The *Walrus*!" said Barnabus, as if they had never discussed him yesterday. "You remember him: *Andy Heaven* as was, *Andy de Ville* as he is now."

"I could hardly *forge*t who he is; I met him at *lunchtime* yesterday, *remember*!" said Elodea.

"Oh yes, so you *did*," said Barnabus, in an offhand sort of way.

"Honestly, I don't think any of you children listen to a word I say on the phone; you just answer on some form of automated response system without the information passing through your brains!" exploded Elodea, thinking how sad it was that her children seemed to file all her phone conversations in the memory equivalent of the 'waste bin'.

"No, no of course I remembered," Barnabus protested. "Anyways *we* had a *great chat* with him. *Great guy*, you know. He's working for Médecin sans Frontières. *Great job* to have."

"You told me yesterday that he was *an evil drunkard!*" protested Elodea, wondering whether to point out that there were more adjectives than 'great' in the English language.

"Oh well, *that*, yes….long time ago though. He's changed *a lot* since college. He is a *teetotaller* these days. Said being thrown out of the first eight made him come to his senses," said Barnabus.

"And *what about the Whale*?" demanded Elodea.

"The Whale?" asked Barnabus, sounding puzzled.

"You said he had an affair just after he and the Whale got married!" Elodea yelled down the phone. "You said he was a shocking person! You must remember that! Men! One minute someone is a villain, the next minute he is your best friend. Women *never* change their minds all the time like this!"

"Oh yes, well, *two sides to every story, you know*," said Barnabus, in a manner that suggested he was tolerant and his mama was not.

"Men!" screamed Elodea, again, losing her temper entirely. "You are *all the same*! Rude about someone one moment and next moment he's *your best mate*! Inconsistent and Insincere! Women either *like* people or we *don't*, and we *stick* to that! And another thing….."

Barnabus held his phone at arm's length and rubbed his ear while she continued raving about the opposite sex for several minutes.

"Yes, yes, Mama!" he said soothingly, when he judged she had finished her speech by the lack of squeaking noises coming out of his phone. "Anyway I am going to meet *Finn* this evening so I'll ring off for now. Love you very much! Kisses!"

He cut the call off. Elodea was left staring furiously at her phone. She jumped up and down on the spot a few times. Then she went into the kitchen and threw a few cups into the stone sink. They broke in a satisfactory way. Suddenly her temper receded as fast as it had arisen.

For she had thought a very bright thought. She had been feeling *so* guilty about enjoying her little lunch and Ashmolean trip with someone who Barnabus had told her was a villain, but now if she happened to meet the Walrus *again* she could enjoy *another* conversation with him. That would be *pleasant*. It had been such a treat to meet a charming and sophisticated man who liked art as much as she did. She might even find out if the Whale was male or female, for while it did not matter in the slightest she still wanted to know, in fact she was beginning to feel that she really *must* find out. Even if this was purely due to *'satiable curtiosity*. She could ask Barnabus but she feared he might think that her desire to know was founded in politically incorrect intolerance and explaining that actually her need to know was just idle curiosity didn't really seem much better. Maybe she would never find out, which, she told herself, *very* firmly, would not matter in the slightest.

"It's OK," said Barnabus to Walls, who was standing just beside him. "I didn't say a *thing* about what happened yesterday other than about meeting the Walrus, although I had to fend off a bit of surprise because I had told her that I didn't like him at college just before. But I feel I carried that bit off very well, *very* well, she only squawked a *bit* about it. Also she *thinks* I'm going for dinner with Finn tonight so that's all covered. Angel won't find out I am dabbling in detection again provided I don't tell Mama. So, all fixed, all possible loopholes of escaping information are closed. Our investigation can continue! First of all we must make that list!"

To explain this conversation it is necessary to return to the previous evening at the point at which Walls met Barnabus outside his office.

* * *

Chapter 6

On the previous day Barnabus had left work in the company of several of his workmates. Consequently he was not at all pleased to discover Walls sitting on a low wall nearby, strumming an acoustic guitar and singing 'Old Man River' to an appreciative group of Far Eastern tourists who were singing along with him. Barnabus cast his eyes in the opposite direction from his friend, said a few words of farewell to his colleagues and waved them on their way to the bus stops and train station before looking at Walls again. He hoped against hope that his work acquaintances had *not* recognised Walls. It was worse than having an embarrassing parent meet you outside secondary school, he thought bitterly to himself.

He looked all around, carefully, to make sure no one else he knew was in the area and then sped over, seized Walls' guitar from his surprised hands, hauled his friend up off the wall and said to the startled tourists, "Show's over for today. Move on! Move on!"

"What the ****?" asked Walls, as the tourists hastily dispersed. "We were all *enjoying* ourselves! You are *such* a grinch!"

"*Walls*!" Barnabus expostulated, "Why, *why*, **why** do I ever meet you after work? Or rather, why can I never meet you after work without discovering you have discombobulatingly turned yourself into some form of sideshow? The usual physical jerks are bad enough, but *busk*ing!"

"What an ace word! Discombobulatingly! I just love your vocabulary, Buffy! But keep your hair on, old pal," soothed Walls, "I wasn't *busking*! I had simply brought my guitar with me to take it down to my college room. Yvette doesn't like me practising it at home. She says the twanging disturbs her thought train. I haven't played the thing for *aeons* in consequence, so when I stumbled across it just before I left I thought I would take the opportunity of moving it down to college. I can practise it there without bothering Yvette."

"But you didn't have to play it *in public*, Walls, old chap! In the *street*!" protested Barnabus.

"How *very* trying it must be to be *upper-middle class English*!" said Walls. "I'm surprised you ever get through your days when they are so full of mortified embarrassment. I am amazed that you do not expire with horror whenever you breach a tiddly little social protocol. Tell me, what would you do if you, *say*, belched loudly in public? Go and shoot yourself?"

"Such an event, Walls, *would simply not occur*," said Barnabus severely. "But to get back to you, *busking*, Walls, unless you are desperately short of money, is not just committing a *small* solecism, it is, it is…"

Words failed him.

"Sympathies old man! Your mortification must be extreme if it actually stopped you speaking," said Walls. "I had no idea I was so far from socially correct that your usual verbosity would fail you. But I wasn't *busking*, Buffy, you *clown*, I was just sitting on a wall singing along with my new-found friends. Plus I have to inform you that this was all your responsibility. *You shouldn't come out of work so late*."

"I don't really care what you were *actually* doing," cried Barnabus, bitterly, recovering his fluency, "I don't even care if you *were* busking. What I care about is what you *looked* like, so, so *ostentatious*, so *noticeable*! Please, Walls, please, next time I meet you out of work could you just be standing there, doing *absolutely nothing*?"

"You shouldn't care so much about your stuffed-up work colleagues. You aren't going to get refused promotion for *knowing a busker*, are you? That would be just loops. You ought to come back into academia! None of us give a toss what eccentric little habits all the other fellows have and I guess that's good as they all have plenty and to spare. Yes, I *could* try waiting in the manner that you suggest but you don't think I might look a little sinister to the local populace? Tall muscular black man, leaning on wall, doing *absolutely nothing*?" asked Walls.

"It's nothing to do with being tall and black and muscular, Walls, it's to do with being *you*!" said his exasperated friend. "Even if you did *absolutely nothing* you would still stick out like a sore thumb. It's your *character*. It's not your physical appearance, it's your demeanour, you are simply too, too…" Barnabus paused while trying to think of the right word and finally finished his sentence, "*too flamboyant*!"

"*Flamboyant*!" retorted Walls. "I am *so* not! I am apparelled in a perfectly quiet black tracksuit. Naturally my extraordinarily good looks and muscle resolution are hard to conceal but I wouldn't call them *flamboyant* either!"

"It's a very expensive designer tracksuit and it sticks out a mile," said Barnabus, "but that *wasn't* what I meant. You don't understand, Walls, you just aren't, aren't…" He finished in a dolorous tone, "You aren't *English* enough."

"I'm not *English* enough!" exclaimed Walls. "Why would I be? I'm *American*. How the heck could I be *English* enough!"

"No, I didn't mean your nationality, I meant your *behaviour*. Your *behaviour* is not *English*. That's why you stick out. Let me explain. When you are standing waiting somewhere for whatever reason you have to *merge*. You don't even *attempt* to *merge*," said Barnabus.

"*Merge*, Buffy?" asked Walls.

"Yes, *merge*," said Barnabus. "Now, *Flipper*, say, if he was standing against that wall he would *merge*. You would *never* notice him! And yet he is very tall and muscular and good-looking."

"Obvs! Of course *Flipper* can *merge*, Buffy; he's *trained* to *merge*! He would be fairly useless in his career otherwise. Come to that it must be simple for him! He can probably press a button on his suit and make himself vanish by looking exactly like the wall!" replied Walls.

"Shhh!" said Barnabus, glancing round in case anyone was listening, "You *mustn't* talk of things like that! You know that!"

"*No one* is listening," said Walls, helpfully, "but while we are compiling this list of *merging people* please don't give me *Finn* as an example either, for the same reason which I am now not allowed to mention. Who else is there? Angel won't do because her rainbow-coloured hair *never* merges, and your hair doesn't either. Red hair always sticks out a mile, don't try and tell me that you merge yourself!"

"Of course I do, Walls, it's nothing to do with *hair*! It's not to do with what you *look* like. It's your inner demeanour! You see, Angel *would* merge because she…because…. It's so hard to explain! But Angel *would* merge just as I would. Not to do with the hair or the hairstyle. It's….You see, Walls, you have to….OK, you are never going to merge. Let's think of another method that doesn't require you to lean on a wall doing nothing. I know! What you *should* do is you should see if I am outside work yet, then if I'm *not*, you should just pop into a nearby shop and *look at some things,* maybe *buy* something *small,* then you come back and see if I am there again and then if not pop into another shop and…"

"I thought you said it was my *inner demeanour* which made no sense at all! So glad you explained that my inner demeanour had *methodology*, this sounds *simple*! I wish you had told me before!" said Walls, sounding humbled and instructed. "I can do *that*. No probs in future!"

Walls had a wicked gleam in his eye as he said this, but Barnabus failed to see it and was pleased with his apparent compliance. Walls was now allowed to retrieve his guitar from Barnabus and they set off together towards Kings College, that venerable establishment which they had both attended and where Walls was now a don.

But Walls was becoming increasingly nervous as they continued on their route.

"You will come *right* to the door of my room with me, Buffy, won't you?" he said. "No nipping off to talk to someone else on the way and leaving me to go there alone? *I'm not going there alone* in case, in case *it's* there."

"There's no point in me coming with you *unless* I come to the door with you, is there?" asked Barnabus. "But, *no*, hang about! Suppose it's a *ghost*. It won't appear if *I'm* there, will it? And supposing it's a prankster? The same applies. Whoever it is will be listening to see if you are coming up the stairs alone. So, if I'm there as well nothing will happen. You *have* to be alone. What to do? What to do? *I know*: you go up from the Lodge *on your own* and I'll come along about two hundred yards behind, but we can be in phone contact all the time. Then if you open the door and there *is* anything there you can take a photo of it on your phone and also I'll be quite close behind you in case they make a run for it. But I must be a *reasonable* distance behind you as whoever it is won't want another witness to their appearance."

"But if it's a *ghost,* Buffy, or a *figment of my imagination*, say, it *won't be on the photo!*" protested Walls.

"*Precisely!*" said Barnabus, in a triumphant tone. "So we'll *know!*"

"We'll know *what?*" demanded Walls. "We still won't know if it's a ghost or if I have gone loopy."

"Yes, but we'll know it's not a mortal playing tricks," pronounced Barnabus. "One option closed!"

"True!" said Walls. "But I would rather you came all the way with me to make sure it wasn't there at all, or that if it was there you could help me grab it or whatever you want to do. Or we could find out if you *could* see it and neither of us could grab it and then we would know it was a ghost and not a figment. However, if you insist on *playing detective games*, I *suppose* that is OK."

"You are making less and less sense with your babbling" said Barnabus, "So let's just assume that I am right, due to the fact that your brain is clearly not operating as well as it might, and follow *my* plan. But, to make quite sure whoever it is doesn't know I am with you, we'll split *here*. Phones on, *you* ring *me*! You can afford the phone call, I can't! Almost no credit left this month and I can't afford the over-fees…. Right, all dialled up? I've answered *mine*! Phones *connected*. Your phone in your pocket! Mine in my hand! I shall go into this sweet shop and buy a few treats for Amadeus and Theo and some for us for now. Angel doesn't like the kids having sweets but I'll give them to her while she's out at work. I mean to say, Walls, what is childhood without sweets?"

"Nothing, Buffy, old man, nothing at all!" agreed Walls, who wasn't really listening to Barnabus or thinking about what he was saying because of his forthcoming ordeal. Otherwise Walls would have not only lectured Barnabus on the evils of too much sugar for children but also berated him about the evils of too much sugar in a training regime for anyone who wished to be truly fit, and added that it was time that Barnabus took up training seriously again as Walls feared that Barnabus was becoming positively *podgy*.

So Barnabus went into the shop and Walls, his phone connected to that of Barnabus but concealed in his pocket for now, headed towards Kings. Then Walls thought of a flaw. How long was it going to take Barnabus to choose his sweets? It could be hours. He fished the phone out.

"Buffy!" he yelled at it.

Barnabus, his hands laden with lollies and sherbet as well as his phone, heard the cry, balanced them all awkwardly on one hand, and extracted his own phone from beneath the pile. "Are you there already?" he asked, dropping two lollies as he spoke.

The shop assistant rushed to rescue him, picked up the lollies and made a neat pile on the counter.

"No, but you *must* tell me when you *leave* the shop," said Walls. "I'll wait where I am till you do. Otherwise you will be too far behind me."

"Good point!" said Barnabus, staring in disbelief at the astronomical running total for his sweets that was appearing on the till, putting his loose change away and getting his credit card out. "I am just paying."

"Great!" said Walls. "I'll sit down here and sing another chorus of 'Old Man River'."

"No!" cried Barnabus loudly and suddenly, to the shop assistant's surprise.

Barnabus kept his phone to his ear once he had left the shop so he could hear Walls' progress. He heard Walls entering the lodge and exchanging a few pleasantries with the porters. He heard his feet trotting through the first big quadrangle. Barnabus had now reached the lodge himself and put his phone into his pocket. It was a while since he had been into college and he stopped to exchange pleasantries with the porters as they enquired after his family and he told them of some of the wonders of Amadeus and Theodora.

Walls, meanwhile, continued through the quadrangles, where the stone was drowsing pleasantly in the late afternoon sunshine, and up the stairs to his room.

What a dork I've been, Walls thought to himself. It was all just a fluke of my imagination. Everything is all fine and there is nothing to worry about!

He put his key into his room door and turned it.

Barnabus jumped slightly as a loud scream resounded inside his coat pocket. The porters also looked a little surprised.

"It's my ringtone!" announced Barnabus, pleased at his own quick thinking. "I do apologise. Expecting important call. Must take it. Popping in to visit Walls next. I'll carry on!"

He seized his phone from his pocket and pretended to answer it as he dashed out of the lodge. The call to Walls had been cut off. Assuming that Walls was still alive and functional Barnabus wondered if it was it too much to hope that the call had been cut off because Walls was using his phone to take photographs?

He tried ringing Walls but the call switched straight to voicemail. He must have dropped his mobile in a panic. But, and Barnabus felt a twinge of fear, what if this should be because it had fallen from Walls' cold dead fingers? He found himself saying aloud "No, his fingers wouldn't be cold yet even if he is dead." Barnabus pulled himself together. Walls was such a panicker, perhaps he had screamed because he had dropped his phone down the staircase by mistake, just a simple fumble, nothing to do with his stalker. Walls would be fine, he must be fine!

Barnabus paced round the first quadrangle as fast as a man can without drawing undue attention to himself. But when he reached the empty second quadrangle, out of view of the porters, he started to run. He finally puffed up the stairs to Walls' room to find Walls slumped on the floor outside it, leaning against his door.

"What is it? What happened? Where are you hurt? I never thought you would be attacked! I wouldn't have left you alone if I had known? I'll call an ambulance at once!" Barnabus whispered, clutching his friend's hand.

"No, no, no medics required! I am not *hurt*. No *physical* damage. Buffy! But it was there *again*. It was there *again*," hissed Walls, weakly, in reply.

"Where?" demanded Barnabus.

"Just inside the door, just inside the door," said Walls, "like before, like before, only here not there, here not there."

Hmm, thought Barnabus. Seems to be in shock. I had better try and remain calm and not scream at him.

"So," said Barnabus, *sotto voce*, as gently as he could, "*where is the photograph*? Show it to me!"

"Photograph? *Photograph*?" asked Walls.

"The *photograph that you took with your phone!*" hissed Barnabus. "The photograph of *it*!"

"*No* photograph!" Walls responded, in a hushed but firm tone.

"For ****'s sake, Walls, not again! No! Don't tell me, let me guess. You unlocked the door, feeling full of the joys of spring; 'it' was behind the door again; you dropped your phone, which," looking around the floor, "is over *here*, by the way, I don't think these flagstones have improved its health at all. Then you slammed the door shut; and then you slid to the floor," said Barnabus in sibilant tones.

"Buffy, Buffy, you know me so well. You know me so well," answered Walls.

"Do keep your voice down, Walls! Whoever it is might be able to hear us. And could you please try to stop repeating everything? I thought you'd quit doing that, and now you've started again. It's so annoying. Like talking to a parrot! I can't think when you do that. Just let me think!" said Barnabus.

There was a short silence. Then Barnabus spoke again. "Ah ha!" he said.

"What?" said Walls.

"Ah ha!" Barnabus repeated.

"*You've* caught the repeating problem now," giggled Walls.

"Your windows are small, medieval and barred, are they not?" asked Barnabus.

"Yes, you *know they are*, you fool!" said Walls.

"Therefore 'it' *cannot* have left your room You have been here all the time. 'It' was on the other side of the firmly closed door. It cannot have managed to get out through your window. Ergo 'it' is, *still in there*. Unless it is a figment of your imagination or it is supernatural, in which case the closed door and tiny barred windows would not stop its dematerialisation. So we will still be able to prove whether it is real or not. Proceed!"

"*Proceed? Proceed?*" quavered Walls.

"*Open* the door again!" commanded Barnabus.

Walls waved the key at him. "*No*," he said, in a voice that suggested he was about to expire. "*You* open the door!"

"I'll *open* it but you are coming in *with me*," said Barnabus, firmly. "It might take two of us to hold whoever this is, if a mortal person it be!"

Barnabus turned the key and flung the door back and they both sprang in, or to be more accurate, Barnabus sprang in, pulling Walls behind him by his collar.

The room was completely empty.

"Under the table?" quavered Walls.

"Don't be silly, Walls," whispered Barnabus. "We'd be able to see it. It must be in the bedroom. *Quick!*"

Now that there was no longer a dead body *just* inside his door Walls felt brave again. They both rushed across the room, opened the bedroom door and bounced in.

There was no one there either.

"Under the bed!" shouted Barnabus.

They flung themselves to the floor on each side of the bed.

There was nothing under the bed except stray pieces of fluff.

But Barnabus had heard a small sound from the other room.

He leapt to his feet and dashed back in time to see the door quivering slightly. There was a faint sound of fleeing soft-shoed feet rushing down the stairs.

Barnabus flew towards the door and down the stairs himself, but he was too late. There was no one on the staircase. There was no one in the quad. Whoever had been there was very fit and very fleet of foot. He dashed on to the next quad and ran on all the way to the main quadrangle but there was no one there either.

He entered the porter's lodge.

"In training for a race, are we, Dr Smith?" asked Bainbridge, who never forgot his ex-residents full academic titles.

"Yes, hoping to get an entry for the London Marathon, got to keep myself fit for that" said Barnabus, congratulating himself on his own quick wit, "Er, did anyone else just leave college, Bainbridge? A few of us were thinking of going on a training run together but I think I might have missed the others leaving and Walls and I haven't even got our running things on yet."

"No, Dr Smith," said Mr Bainbridge. "*No one* has left or come in for the last ten minutes if not longer."

"I'll ring them on my mobile," said Barnabus, "Perhaps we got the time completely wrong. The others all seem to be out of their rooms."

"Very good, Sir," said Bainbridge.

Barnabus wandered back to Walls' room feeling dejected. His mystery person had evidently exited without using the official lodge entrance. There were plenty of other routes in and out of the college provided you didn't mind scaling a few drainpipes and running over the odd roof. Barnabus knew that himself. He had to accept that he had entirely lost his quarry. There was no hope of catching whoever it was now.

Barnabus returned to Walls, who was sitting on the bed, immobile. He had returned to fearfulness.

"Why didn't you come *with* me?" demanded Barnabus. "You can *run* faster than me!"

"I'm glad you finally admit that I can run faster than you. But as for not coming with you *I* thought you were chasing a *spectre* and I'm really not a phantom-ologist myself. But you realise, don't you," said Walls, "what this *means*. If this is a *real* person this means someone was *following* me for certain. They knew I was coming here. They didn't just know that but they managed to get to my room first, *before me. They have a copy of my key*! They know how to get in and out of college and they know exactly where my room is."

"*Paranormal investigator*" Barnabus corrected, "But you *didn't* think it was a ghost. You just freaked out and turned into a heap of jelly again. You are a *wuss*! But there is no need to think they have your key. They don't *need* to have a *key*, Walls, I expect they just picked the lock with a bit of wire. Takes *seconds*!" said Barnabus, airily.

"You *know* how to pick locks, Buffy?" asked Walls, admiringly, ignoring the aspersions on his bravery as he would have had to agree with them.

"No, not *me* personally, but I understand that it *can* be done both easily and swiftly," admitted Barnabus.

"OK, so even if this guy doesn't have a copy of my keys whoever it is can still open my doors *easily and swiftly*. That's not much comfort. And 'mystery man' is stalking me to see where I go!"

"But at least it isn't a ghost or a figment, Walls; I heard their footsteps and they sounded jolly mortal to me. Look on the bright side! You *aren't mad after all!*" suggested his friend.

"So true, Buffy, so true. I am not mad. That is very important. And I haven't even gone as mad as *you*; I do not yet believe that I have *ever* seen a ghost. But surely *people* report *hearing* ghosts don't they? Phantom hoof beats from ghostly riders and whatnot? Maybe you *heard* the *ghost* running down the stairs? Just a thought!" teased Walls.

"Touché!" said Barnabus, "But I don't think so. You see when you hear or see a phantom there is something *about* it. You just *know* it's not mortal, see, however real it looks and sounds at the time?"

Walls made a very rude reply about his friend's dictates on how to detect if something is a phantom. Then he sighed and said "I suppose I'd better ring the police"

"No, Walls, *not on any account!*" cried Barnabus, ignoring the slight on his sanity. "We must *never* tell *anyone* about this episode!"

"Why ever not?" asked Walls. "This person is *seriously loops, one fry short of a happy meal, bizarre!* My life might be in danger."

"Nonsense! If this nutter, whoever they might be, had been going to kill you I'm sure they would have done it by now," said Barnabus, exhibiting a somewhat cavalier attitude towards his friend's safety, "and we can't tell *anyone* about this, *ever.* If we let people know we were both caught by the old 'standing behind the door as it is opened' trick then we will absolutely never live this down!"

"This guy might be just torturing me first so they can kill me later when I am a total gibbering wreck," said Walls.

"No, no, would anyone go to all this bother to dress up and appear in your room and then *not* kill you *at the time*," quoth Barnabus, blithely.

"Very reassuring suggestion, I *don't* think!" said Walls.

"Anyway, there will be no further opportunity to kill you," said Barnabus, stoutly, "You frightened me stiff screaming down the phone like that. You have taken years off my life this afternoon. I can't risk that much shock to my heart again. I am going to stick to you like glue except when I am at work or when you are with Yvette."

"That's a *big* comfort! That can't leave more than seven or eight spare hours of each day for him to kill me in! I think we *should* tell the police."

"Nonsense! But I tell you what – I'm *hungry*!" announced Barnabus. " I can't think properly when I'm this hungry! *I* think we should *go to the Bear*, order dinner and *then* consider who our stalking suspect might be once I have some food for my brain cells inside me! We must make a list of possible reasons, and possible suspects once we have thought of the possible reasons."

But no sooner had they ordered their meal at the Bear than the Walrus reappeared there too and instead of having any sensible discussion about facts about suspects the three of them had a happy evening of camaraderie, or rather Barnabus and Andy did. Walls just sat there. It was only when the Walrus popped to the Gents prior to leaving that Walls managed to hiss to Barnabus, "What about that list of suspects?"

Barnabus hissed back, "*Tomorrow*! I'll meet you at the college lodge after I finish work."

"Tomorrow is far too late! This is *high priority urgent*! This is my *life* I am talking about here! And I am not never ever going to ever go into my room again, not never!" Walls replied.

"Double negatives, Walls, *double negatives*" said Barnabus in an instructive tone, "And we are not meeting in *your* room, we are going to meet in the *college lodge*!" he added, firmly. Barnabus was quite determined not to repeat the error of meeting Walls outside his own office, at least not on two consecutive days. Barnabus continued "You can chat to Bainbridge for half an hour while you wait."

Then Barnabus added, rather wickedly, "If you hadn't left your guitar in your room just now you could play it for *Bainbridge* while you were waiting. But now you can't go back and get it without me. It's too late for any more investigations now. I have to get home. I have work tomorrow."

"We should have left and gone somewhere else earlier," grumbled Walls. "I *needed* to talk about all this; it's important! I tried to catch your attention earlier but you and Andy were whooping it up too much. I suppose it *does* have to wait till…"

Walls never finished his sentence because the Walrus returned at that moment and they all left the Bear together.

Walls ran off at his top stalker-evading speed to the safe haven of his Yvette-inhabited apartment. Barnabus hurried west to catch a bus to the park-and-ride, and drive to Little Wychwell. The Walrus vanished from the Bear to wherever he was staying, and neither Walls nor Barnabus thought to enquire where that might be.

Chapter 7

Barnabus and Walls met in the lodge of Kings College on the following evening and wandered together, trying to look as much as possible as if they were idlers with no particular purpose to fulfil, into the main quadrangle, where they traversed one side. Then Walls stopped abruptly.

"Where are *we going to?*" asked Walls.

"*Your* room, naturally!" said Barnabus.

"*My room*? I told you I *never* want to go there again. What if the *stalker* is there?" said Walls.

"Clearly, if the stalker *is* there we have no further problems," said Barnabus cheerfully.

"Eh?" said Walls.

"Since we can both grab him, and then the whole problem is solved," said Barnabus.

"I suppose that's *true*," said Walls, "but what if he pulls out an automatic and guns us both down? Or knifes one of us? Or maybe he will have brought some friends with him this time?"

"I'll risk that," said Barnabus, dismissively.

"I don't see why," said Walls, "although I guess *you* aren't taking much of a risk, it's me who is taking the risk!"

"I just don't believe there is any danger from whoever it is.," said Barnabus, "More to the point, I am not expecting your stalker to be there *at all* since they must know that I pursued him down the stairs yesterday. Whoever it is must have only been expecting you and thought that you would slam the door and go away again just like you had when they appeared in your apartment. So when you *didn't* go away and then *two* of us suddenly burst *in*, they must have been completely put out. I should think they have entirely cold feet about this stalking business now."

"May I interpose to suggest whoever it is wasn't so put out that he didn't recollect that he needed to conceal himself behind the door?" said Walls.

"True. I wonder if he had changed back into more normal clothes before he left?" said Barnabus.

"Probably, possibly not. He could have had the army uniform on over his normal clothes. Whipped it off, stuffed it in a bag…Frankly though, who cares? What difference does it make?" asked Walls.

"Because someone might have noticed a blood-covered WWII soldier trotting around the streets of Oxford after they climbed out of college, *supposing* our suspect climbed out over the roofs and walls that is. On the other hand this is Oxford so maybe no would have registered it. You get weird people everywhere round here, and no one bats an eyelid. However supposing instead that our suspect went out through the main gate he would certainly have had to change back into ordinary clothes first. The porters would definitely have noticed a wounded WWII soldier leaving college. Did you hear any noises inside the room while you were sitting outside that might give us a clue as to whether he was getting changed in there?" asked Barnabus.

"No," said Walls, unhelpfully, "and I still don't see why it matters if my charming stalker who *you* say is *not* trying to kill me got changed before or after they left the room. He could have got changed while sitting on a college roof somewhere."

"It matters" said Barnabus, sounding superior, "Because if he changed in your room then he might have shaken some clothing threads onto the carpet, *muttonhead*. We must look!"

"And if we find some, Mr Clever?" demanded Walls.

"I don't know," admitted Barnabus. "Yes, I do. We could ring the police at that point and tell them you had seen the intruder again and we had some definite samples for them to analyse for DNA traces."

"I still think we should tell the police in any case," said Walls. "You are gambling with my life. Stalkers can be *dangerous*."

"Go on then," replied Barnabus. "Go and *tell* the police and see what happens."

He looked more closely at Walls' face.

"Walls!" he said. "You already *have*!"

"*Sure I have*," responded Walls. "I popped round this morning. And you are also quite right; it *was* a waste of time. I was not helped by the fact that the name of the other witness of these events was *you*. You are all over their files already, as you know, and, quite remarkably, they don't seem to see you as a reliable person. In fact the Inspector said something about 'Is that young fool still poking about in things that don't concern him' and I had to admit that you were."

Barnabus laughed. He was quite aware that the police thought he was some kind of mad nuisance.

"So," said Barnabus, "they didn't offer you a police guard then?"

"The only thing they offered was an atmosphere of barely polite disbelief," admitted Walls, "but they noted all the facts that I gave them down so, as a consequence, when I *am* murdered this means that Yvette, who you will have to fill in with all these details if such an event should occur, *will* be able to *sue* them."

"See, the police don't think there is any danger either," said Barnabus, in a soothing voice.

"No, Buffy, the police don't think there is any *stalker*. They still think the body is a product of my imagination. And that I have somehow infected you with my hysteria so that you are also imagining the same things. Although, as I said, from their previous encounters with you I don't get the impression you are very high up in their standing with respect to inbuilt intelligence and they also believe that you have a most fertile imagination. Maybe they think you are making me imagine these wild events, instead of the other way round."

Barnabus started to laugh.

"Have I missed something humorous?" demanded Walls.

"I was just imagining your interview with the police. Let me guess; I bet it ended something like this:

Inspector Bryant: So, let us summarise your account. You saw the same body behind a door but this time behind the door of your room in college, not your permanent domicile?

You: Sure thing, I did!

Inspector Bryant: And how did you know it was the same body?

You: It bore a very strong resemblance. In point of fact it was identical.

Inspector Bryant: In what sense?

You: It was a body, behind a door, in Second World War uniform.

Inspector Bryant: So, did you observe its features this time?

You, starting to gabble: No, no, I saw it, so I slammed the door at once. I don't like dead bodies! I told you that before!

Inspector Bryant: So, in fact, you don't know if it was dead and you don't know what it looked like.

You: It looked like it was dead.

Inspector Bryant, sighing: And it was only there when you were there alone. When you re-opened the door with a witness with you it was no longer there. Just like last time.

You: Indeedy!

Inspector Bryant: And this aforementioned witness was your friend, Barnabus Smith, the son of Elodea Smith, both of Little Wychwell, Elodea being the witness of the disappearing body having disappeared on the previous occasion.

You: Yes, but Buffy heard it on the stairs this time. It was using the old 'hiding behind the door' trick, like I told you. Buffy pursued it down the stairs.

Inspector Bryant: But he failed to catch 'it'.

You: Yes, I mean, no, I mean, yes. He didn't find the person or body or whatever you like to call it.

Inspector Bryant: But he saw *the person?*

You (flustered): No, he didn't see anybody. He just thought he heard someone running down the stairs.

Inspector Bryant: The college stairway is a public place?

You: Not public. You have to get inside the college first.

Inspector Bryant: But there are people inside the college? Many people?

You: Not so many as in term time but, yes, quite a lot still.

Inspector Bryant: And any of them might run down your stairs, in a perfectly legitimate way?

You: Yes, naturally. I do it myself, all the time.

Inspector Bryant: Well, thank you for coming in. We'll put the details in our records, and do call in if you see the body again. We will be waiting with bated breath. Good day, Mr, er – "

By now Barnabus was giggling so much he could hardly speak, but he stopped speaking at all very abruptly due to Walls slamming a large hand over his mouth.

"OK, Mr Clever Dick, maybe it *is* funny! And, sure, you are right! Going to the cops *was* a waste of time. But it's still good that I've reported it because they are going to be in such deep sh*t when I get murdered now!"

"You are *not*, repeat, *not*, going to get murdered!" said Barnabus. "I *won't* let that happen!"

"I'm glad *you* are so sure," said Walls. "It's easier for *you*. You aren't *me*. Anyway, the cops don't seem to be going to do anything, so what do *we* do next?"

"We have to work it out for ourselves. Just between the two of us. You are *not* to tell anyone else. Not under *any* circumstances. The police aren't likely to speak to our friends but if Finn and Paris and Dad and Elizabeth, oh yes, and even Aunt Pris, find out that I got caught by the 'hiding behind the door' trick I will be a laughing stock for ever and ever. It will be a favourite anecdote at every family gathering for years. You have no idea how awful it is being the youngest. They have all these terrible stories about me and it simply *isn't fair*! If Finn finds out then going out for a drink with him will be torture. He will never let me forget it either. Aunt Pris will most certainly laugh. Mama would not laugh, but she would take it all very seriously and worry about our safety. So we mustn't even tell her or she will get all worked up and anxious as *she* will think we are likely to be murdered as well. Angel simply mustn't find out about *any* of this; you know how she feels about me getting involved with murders, crimes, investigations or anything of that nature."

"Murders? I thought you said I *wasn't* going to get murdered! I thought you said you were *sure* of that!" squeaked Walls.

Barnabus laughed again.

"Don't get so wound up! You sound so funny when you panic and your voice goes so high that, honestly, you sound just like Mama! I didn't mean *you* getting *murdered*; I meant the dead body. I should have said 'bodies' not 'murders'. Slip of the tongue."

At that point Barnabus' mobile rang and he snatched it from his pocket, Grateful for the escape, he looked at the incoming number, said "Speak of angels and you hear the flutter of their wings" and had the conversation with his mama that has been already recounted at the end of the previous chapter.

"Now to make the list of possible reasons and suspects," he said, and despite Walls' protests he insisted on going to Walls' rooms to write it out. Walls handed his key to Barnabus and told him he could open the door and see what was inside this time, while Walls waited on the stairs.

But Walls need not have worried, for when Barnabus opened the door he discovered a silent and empty room. The evening light was streaming in through the windows. The silence of the cloistered quadrangle and the peace of centuries of ordered, studious lives filled the room. Walls smiled. His room was back to the way it always had been. He loved his college. He loved being an academic. His life was perfect. All was safe. Perhaps the police were right; perhaps he had imagined the bodies, but not because he was mad, but because his studies were overfilling his brain. Maybe he did need a little break from work, and then all would be well. He sat down in one of his antique armchairs, leant back and closed his eyes. The calm of the room enfolded him.

Barnabus did not feel peaceful. He was fully engaged with his investigation. Detective fever had seized him. He flung himself onto his hands and knees and crawled up and down across the carpet for five minutes, nose to the ground, backside in the air like a cartoon bloodhound.

Eventually Barnabus stood up.

"No trace of *anything* of any *use*," he announced, loudly.

Walls jumped slightly in the chair and opened his eyes. When he spoke it was in a leisurely and sarcastic way.

"You *surprise* me," he said, "especially as *my scout* will have been in this morning and *cleaned* the *whole carpet* with her usual thoroughness."

"Bother!" said Barnabus, bouncing up and down on the spot with agitation. "Should we interrogate *her*, do you think? Will she have emptied the vacuum cleaner? Where does she keep the vacuum cleaner? Can we get at it? Should we look in the college bins for vacuum cleaner contents?"

"No," said Walls. "Decidedly not! I don't mind making lists but I am not sifting through the contents of vacuum cleaners or bins as one of the activities of the final few days of my life."

"You are *not* going to get killed, Walls!" said Barnabus. "You *only* have a stalker. They don't *usually* murder people. Now, *please be serious*. What attributes do we know for *certain* that this stalker has? We must try and make a list of possible suspects, so let's start by trying to work out what we know must be absolutely true about this enigma. You know, Sherlock Holmes and all that, *When you have eliminated the impossible, whatever remains, however improbable, must be the truth*"

"I *was* being serious," said Walls. "It is you who is treating this so frivolously. You wouldn't be so happy-go-lucky if *you* had a stalker. It's no joke!"

"Right, let us think. *Attributes...*" continued Barnabus, completely ignoring Walls.

"Knows me," said Walls.

"Good, good. Good start," said Barnabus, seizing a pen and paper from the desk and starting a numbered list.

"Knows about college; knows where my room is, or has found out anyway; knows where I live," said Walls.

"All true. Excellent," said Barnabus.

"Knows exactly where I am about to be before manifesting himself because he has to get into my places before I do – I've been thinking about that. He has to either know when I am returning and then nip in quickly by a different route, or else be hanging around in my rooms for hours and hours. The hanging about for eons doesn't seem at all likely. So he doesn't just know where I *live*; he also knows exactly where I *am and* where I am going *nex*t. Also precisely how to get into both my apartment and my college room with the routes and timings all planned out in advance This person has done their research most carefully, Buffy; *that's what is freaking me out!*"

"OK," said Barnabus, scribbling furiously. "Just a minute while I get all that down!"

There was a pause while Barnabus caught up.

Then Barnabus said, "Next section – motives."

"My stalker doesn't like me," said Walls, "He doesn't seem like an *affectionate* stalker to me, they seem like a scare the pants off you stalker."

"But *why* don't they like you? Why do they dislike you enough to go to all this *effort*? Who have you *wronged* in the past?" demanded Barnabus.

There was a long silence.

"If it was one of your ex-girlfriends I could sort of understand it. But you say this is a soldier, a *man*?" checked Barnabus.

"As you know, Buffy, my ex-girlfriends all *adore* me! I always, always sent them roses or, if they were really mad at me, the odd diamond. These strategies have *never* been known not to work. In any case this is a man and I am quite, quite sure that none of my ex-girlfriends were men," said Walls.

"Why are you so sure about that?" asked Barnabus.

"Buffy! The answer is obvious, surely!" Walls rebuked him.

"Not your girlfriends, you fool, your *stalker*! How do you know it is a *man*?" Barnabus retorted, "You've had me thinking it was a man as well, but that is *one* of the other things *we simply don't know*. Together with all the other *small* unknowns such as whether it was a corpse or a dress dummy or someone pretending to be a corpse or…"

"I am *sure* it was a guy because it was wearing Second World War UK soldier guy's uniform. *Very* obvious which sort of uniform because the opposite sex wore *skirts* in those days," replied Walls.

"Walls, words fail me! I despair! It could have been a woman *in a man's uniform*, you idiot! How closely did you look at it *yesterday*?" asked Barnabus. "Any more closely than the time before?"

"Negative! *It* was *there* again, lying on my floor, *dead*. I slammed the door shut on the ghastly thing faster than a cat lapping chain lightning." replied Walls.

"While emitting a scream like a banshee," amplified Barnabus.

"Quite possibly," agreed Walls. "I was half scared out of my wits! Anyone would have been. Anyone!"

"I shall ignore that assertion. It is not even worth wasting my breath on it" replied Barnabus, "It might help if at least *one* of us indulged in some cerebral exercise. You try and remember anything that might be of any further help in identifying our mystery apparition and I will consider possible suspects."

There was silence for a few moments. Then

"*The Walrus!*" yelled Barnabus, suddenly and unexpectedly.

Walls jumped.

"What?" he said.

"*The Walrus* he's back in Oxford. He doesn't have any particular reason for being here. But, follow this sequence of events, *he* comes back, *you* start seeing dead bodies. ! But that isn't all, I've just remembered something. He has a *motive. You were the person who took his seat in the first eight*, when he got thrown out!"

"I *was*?" asked Walls.

"Yes! You *know* you were! Think! You moved *up the boat*!" said Barnabus. "It must have rankled for all these years. Now he is taking revenge!"

"But" protested Walls, " he works for Médecin sans Frontières, Buffy. He's one of the *good* guys! You said that yourself the other night! You said how well he has turned himself around and sobered up and become a decent citizen and whatever."

"What if he *doesn't*, though" said Barnabus.

"What if he doesn't what?" replied Walls.

"What if he *doesn't* work for Médecin sans Frontières? What if he just made that up to impress us both with what a good guy he was? Think, Walls, did he say *anything at all* about his work that he couldn't have just invented from things he saw on a news broadcast or a charity appeal or whatever?"

"How would I know?" demanded Walls. "I wasn't listening to any of the details about what he did."

"You *weren't listening!*" exclaimed Barnabus. "You are getting *just like Aunty Pris*! You really need a break from academia, old chap. It's not good for you to get stuck in ivory towers permanently."

"Yes it is," protested Walls. "It's *very* good for me. I *love* it. Leave my work alone! But I wasn't not-listening because I'm an absent-minded academic. I wasn't listening because, as you very well know, I am very squeamish about illness and death and corpses and all that sort of stuff that he was busy discussing, and I didn't want to hear about it, especially while eating my dinner!"

"And yet your specialist topic is twentieth-century warfare, is it not?" answered Barnabus.

"*And?*" retorted Walls.

"Don't your studies involve a bit of death, famine, disease and mutilation?" demanded Barnabus

"Yes and no, yes it does and no, it doesn't disturb me because I always skip the gory bits. Casualty *figures* are not at all gory, I assure you," replied Walls. "Quite dry, in fact. A set of clean, well behaved not at all gruesome numbers, on the whole. Also the military strategies and motives and meetings and politics. Not a drop of gore involved. But you have now set me thinking too. Why is the Walrus working for Médecin sans Frontières at all? *If* he is. Because I am quite certain that he definitely wasn't a *medic*. He studied Zoology, and that's hardly the same. Furthermore, he *isn't* French."

"I don't think the not-being-French bit matters. Especially not to the Walrus as he can speak it very fluently, always could – French parent or grandparent or something. He said he retrained as a nurse because he decided he wanted to serve others. I expect the truth is that he couldn't make a career out of zoology.

After all how many jobs are there in a subject like *that*? Not that he needs to work at all when I consider it – his family is loaded. So he might have made the whole nursing story up as well as the story about where he works. It could *all* be a load of lies. If he's mad enough to be a stalker he's mad enough to invent everything else to go with it," said Barnabus.

"Whereas," said Walls, drily, "unlike totally unemployable subjects like *Zoology*, there are millions of jobs for those with *History* degrees! Otherwise your logic is impeccable. I've just thought of something else though. It *can't* be the Walrus, because if he's *stalking* me then why would he have come over and openly greeted us both in the Bear at all?" asked Walls.

"Couldn't *resist* it, I suppose," replied Barnabus. "Sitting there revelling in the fact that he knew *everything* and you knew *nothing*. Yes, *and* he used to be a roof walker, so he would have had no trouble getting in and out of Kings, and naturally he knows the layout of the whole college since he came here himself."

"But I still don't think it's the Walrus because somehow I just don't" said Walls.

"And" continued Barnabus, ignoring him, "Andy's a *very* dodgy character. First the alcoholism, and then the way he treated the Whale."

"Oh, come on!" replied Walls. "What did you say about their break-up *yesterday*? *There are two sides to every argument.* Personally I don't know how he managed to stay married to the Whale for *two whole months*. Never known a cox who had so many disagreements and arguments with their eight in my life. Impossible person!"

"I thought it was two *weeks* before they split up , not two *months*. Come to that, didn't *he* say a *year* yesterday? Not that you can believe a word *he* says. OK then, have you got a better suggestion for who is stalking you?" asked Barnabus.

"No," admitted Walls.

"*Well* then," said Barnabus.

"Well *what* then?" asked Walls.

"There is only one thing to do," said Barnabus.

"And that is?" asked Walls.

"*You* will have to stalk *the Walrus*!" said Barnabus. "Find out what he's up to."

"*Great* idea," said Walls, unenthusiastically. "How do you suggest I do that?"

"Not *just* you. Naturally. I should have said *we* must stalk the Walrus! *I* will have to stalk him as well. You can't cover all twenty-four hours of the day on your own. We must work out the details of our stalking rota. Number one priority is that we have to *find* him again. We can't stalk him if we don't know where he is. Where is he staying?" asked Barnabus.

"I have no idea," said Walls, "and even if I did know I'm not going to stalk him. I absolutely refuse to do it. That is flat and final! Anyway it he is stalking me you just have to walk in the opposite direction to me and you should run straight into him."

"That is the most fatuous suggestion I have ever heard. He doesn't stalk you *all* the time. And even if he did he would stop stalking you if he saw me coming towards him. Really, Walls, you are simply not cut out to be a detective, not at all. Clearly. I don't see that we have any choice. Are you are just going to spend the rest of your life being harried and scared by this nutcase?" asked Barnabus

'I never said I was cut out to be a detective, it would be a perfectly awful career, you have to look at yucky things all the time. But I suppose I have to do something, when you put it to me like that, no," said Walls. "Are you quite sure that stalking *him* is the *only* option?"

"Yes. *So*, plan clear now, a) find him, b) stalk him!" said Barnabus, firmly.

"Not convinced about b) you know, not convinced at all. From my expert knowledge of similar military situations then If he is stalking me and I am stalking him I fear we may simply go round in circles? And how will I know if he is stalking me if I am stalking him? But a) should be *facile*. He is *somewhere in the whole of Oxford*. That narrows it down!" said Walls, sarcastically.

"At least we know he is in Oxford and not just in the entire country or the whole world or whatever. Oxford isn't *that* big, and the Walrus will probably be hanging around in the University bit in the centre, which makes things a lot simpler. I wonder if he's staying at the Randolph? He could afford that sort of place with his inherited income. But would he go for somewhere that grandiose, or somewhere a bit smaller where he can lie low? What do *you* think?" replied Barnabus, after waving an airy hand at Walls objections to part b).

Walls looked at his watch.

"I think I'm *hungry*," he said. "Being scared is *very* calorie consuming. My muscles may start shrinking if I don't fill up the tank soon. Come on – I'll treat you to dinner again. If we go back to the Bear maybe our friend the Walrus will turn up right there again, and then we can try quizzing him with some *leading questions* and see what he says. And then *you* can stalk him and I can let him get right on with stalking me in peace!"

But the Walrus did not appear in the Bear. Barnabus and Walls spent their dinner racking their brains for other possible suspects, people who might have a motive for frightening Walls, but they came up with no one at all. Barnabus agreed, however, that, due to Walls' objections to the idea of becoming a stalker himself, they would give themselves another day to think of possible people before they tried further investigating the Walrus.

"In the meantime, Walls," said Barnabus, "have a chat to the Kings College porters. They might have an idea where the Walrus is staying. They *always* know that sort of thing about ex-students, even if he hasn't been to college through any official route like the main entrance. They know when any of us are about, they hear about it somehow. Sixth sense I suppose. Or possibly because at least one of them will have met him wandering around the city somewhere. Or one of the other college staff will have and passed the info straight on."

"I'll *try*," replied Walls, "but I'm most definitely not going to go back my own rooms again on my own till this is sorted out. *No more dead bodies for me.*"

"But, Walls, we are absolutely sure it *isn't* a *dead* body now, so if you happened to see it again all you have to do is grab it and then find out who it is! And if it's the Walrus you can take him out to dinner again!" advised Barnabus.

"I would much rather not see it at all," said Walls. "Whoever it is. I've told you already enough times, seeing that sort of thing, real or invented, upsets my nerves! Yvette is back in our flat for now and whoever it is won't risk haunting me in the flat while *she* is there. So I am simply not going to use my college room by myself till it's all sorted and solved and fixed, and then I *can't* see any dead bodies."

"But whoever it is must know we rumbled them the other night. Bound to know that you and I must know that it's a person *pretending* to be a body because he or she or it must know we heard them run down the stairs. Surely they won't try to pull that same trick again?" said Barnabus.

"This is *true*," said Walls, "but not *reassuring*. What are they going to try instead? A new surprise tactic! Something much worse! Anything could happen to me! Stalkers move on from stalking to more heinous crimes. We might even be in the *final* stage of the stalking scenario: *actual murder*. I did a Google search and read up on the subject earlier today. Pretty fearful, I'll say."

"You can't believe everything you read on the Internet, Walls, as you know. I can't imagine the *Walrus* would actually *murder* anyone. Right, I'll see you after work tomorrow and in the meantime we must both keep thinking, and send each other any useful ideas we come up with," said Barnabus. "And if you see *any* sign of the *Walrus* or *any* dead bodies in World War II uniform you must ring me *straight away*, even if I am in work. I'll make some excuse and rush out to meet you. Ring *straight away*, even if it's the middle of the night."

"But he might have become completely hog-wild because of working in such traumatic conditions, you know, PTSD. And we don't even know it *is* the *Walrus*. *You* are jumping to *unvalidated conclusions* now! Personally *I* am going to stay in *close proximity to Yvette* till I rendezvous with you again tomorrow after work. If one of us must chat to the Lodge porters *you* can pop down there yourself in your lunch hour!" said Walls. "Right now I must *run* because Yvette will be in a flutter about where I am and I can easily outrun any stalker so they won't be just behind me in a few seconds even if they are lurking invisibly right now. I'll meet you outside your office at seventeen hundred hours tomorrow, prompt! I'm off!"

Suiting his actions to his word, he broke into a fast sprint, calling the final sentence back over his shoulder, and vanished towards North Oxford.

"No! No!" called Barnabus after his retreating figure. But it was too late and there was no hope of catching Walls up when he was moving at that speed.

Thus Barnabus was yet again doomed to meet Walls outside his offices on the following day. Barnabus considered sending him a text to change the venue, or ringing him to try to change it, but Walls would probably just be difficult if he did. Barnabus could only hope against hope that Walls had remembered his suggestions on how to wait *in a less embarrassing way.*

Unfortunately for Barnabus, Walls had remembered them only too well and decided to apply these rules to the letter while chuckling wickedly to himself. In consequence Walls was just as freakishly noticeable and Barnabus was heartily sorry that he had ever suggested the 'popping into shops to pass the time while he waited' scheme.

For at 5.00 pm on the following day mischievous Walls was almost invisible behind twenty brightly coloured carrier bags, all brimming over with miscellaneous junk.

"What a *time* you've been, Buffy," he said, addressing both Barnabus and a small crowd of Barnabus' work colleagues. "I must have visited *twenty* shops! I arrived *early* specially to try out your suggestion, and it's been *absolutely brilliant*! Here, I got *you* this gigantic pink *teddy*. You'll have to fish it out of my arms from underneath the rest yourself, for if I try to give it to you I will drop some of the other bags."

Barnabus opened and shut his mouth twice while glaring at his friend. He recovered slightly, removed two large handfuls of carrier bags forcibly from Walls' grip, straightened some of the others up and, regaining the power of speech, said, "Right, I'm not going anywhere else with you till we have deposited these impedimenta in your college room. That is flat and final. I don't care if you don't want to go there."

"OK. I'll be safe with *you* there, but we *have* to go to the room *together* at *exactly* the same time. I am *not*, repeat, *not*, doing any more experiments!" agreed Walls, amiably. He then added, apparently guilelessly, "I had *such* fun in the stores! I *so* wish you had suggested that method of waiting for you before!"

"Sometimes," said Barnabus, drily, "I wish I had *never* met you, *ever!*"

Walls laughed. "But it was *so* funny! You were so po-faced about my *exercises* and my *guitar playing* and anything else I ever do when I am waiting for you. And I followed your instructions exactly, I assure you. You can't deny that. I wish I had had a spare hand to video your reaction when you saw me. I could have made a fortune on YouTube. Face it, Buffy, a black good looking guy as big as me sticks out a mile in Oxford *whatever* I do. You are going to have to put up with the embarrassment."

"Walls!" protested Barnabus, "It isn't because you are *black*. I've explained that to you already. Any of my friends would stick out a mile if they behaved like you *whatever colour they were*. Can't you at least *try* to look a bit more run of the mill and normal when you meet me outside the office?"

"No I can't," said Walls, "for I *am* being normal; it is *you* who is being odd."

"Perhaps, perhaps you are right," sighed Barnabus. "OK, perhaps it *is* me being *oversensitive*. You can't help being who you are, and who you are is why you are my friend."

They gave each other a bear hug, somewhat hampered by all the shopping.

Then Barnabus continued, "But, I was just thinking, in future why don't we just meet at Carfax Tower instead of *right* outside my office because Carfax is *far* more convenient for you, much *closer to college* and all that."

Walls laughed again. "I do love you, Buffy," he said. "You give me more laughs than anyone else I know."

"I don't see anything funny in my last statement," said Barnabus, in an uptight voice.

Walls laughed more. "That, Buffy, is *exactly* why I love you!" he gurgled, as well as he could while guffawing.

"Anyway," said Barnabus, adopting a business-like tone and raising his voice slightly to cover Walls' noises, "to return to *strategy*! We are now engaged on a *Walrus hunt*."

This sentence had an even more disastrous effect on Walls. He laughed till he became so hysterical that he had to lean against the wall.

"Oh, oh, my belly," he wailed. "It's killing me. I can't stop! Please, *please* don't say *anything* at all before I have stopped laughing. I am going to *die* if you do."

"I am so pleased to find I amuse you quite this much," replied Barnabus, very stiffly.

Walls slid to the floor in a helpless heap of giggles. "I said, don't, *don't*, oh no, *don't* say anything else for *at least* half an hour," he gasped.

Barnabus reached down and hauled his companion to his feet.

"Very well," he concurred, "I will not utter another syllable until we reach the confines of your room."

'Nooooooo!" spluttered Walls, sliding back to the floor. "No, just can it, can it! Please, I am going to *die*!"

Barnabus glared at him. "Quite right, because I am going to *kill* you if you don't stop. Can you *listen* to me in that state?"

Walls, a shaking heap, managed to nod feebly.

"Right, well, while you are wasting time lolling around on the pavement let me explain our *Walrus hunting strategy!*"

There was a pitiful noise from Walls as he rolled over onto his left side and clutched his stomach. "No, no, Buffy, please, please! I beg of you! Stop speaking at all! You are *too too funny*! My *muscles*! I will *die*! I beg of you, stop! Let me at least recover before you say anything else!"

"I will," said Barnabus, pitilessly, "continue. We will deposit the excess baggages that we are currently carrying, in your room. Then we will depart on a route which I have already prepared that covers *every* public house and restaurant in the centre of Oxford. Clearly the Walrus does not eat wherever he is staying or else he would not have eaten dinner with us and lunch with Mama. Therefore he will be eating somewhere this evening. Therefore if we systematically comb *every* eating establishment, we are bound to encounter him."

This plan was sufficient to sober Walls up from his laughing fit and restore him to his feet.

"What? Do you know *how many pubs* there *are* in the centre of Oxford?" Walls demanded. "Even without the *restaurants*?"

"Obviously, for I have made a plan of our route. To be more accurate, *all* the public houses on my list are not in the *very* central area but they are all student frequented, or were when we were undergrads. There is no point in visiting non-student pubs since the Walrus is probably visiting all his old lairs in a sentimental way. Therefore most of them will be in Central Oxford and because time is limited we will not include the very outlying places like the Vicky Arms or the Trout. We will extend our tour from the central area to visit those on the Plain, those near the base of the Cowley Road, and also those in the north as far North Parade, and west to the pubs in Jericho and Botley."

"Am I allowed to wear my running gear in that case?" asked Walls. "That will give us some cover. We can pretend to be on a pub fun run!"

"Yes, certainly you can, for I have brought mine with me too. We will never finish our planned itinerary unless we run in between the pubs."

"I am looking forward to seeing *anyone* as out of condition as *you* running that far!" said Walls.

"I am *not* out of condition," said Barnabus, indignantly.

"Yes you are! Look at your waistline; it expands every time I see you. I hope you have got a separate route map to give to me and that the last pub serves decent food, because I will have to wait at the last one till you manage to turn up," said Walls.

"*Nonsense!*" said Barnabus. "In any event we must go together because if one of us finds the Walrus he might give a single person the slip." He then added, with a touch of malice, "And if you go ahead alone you might see another body or your *stalker* might *get to you* in some other way while you are running alone and unprotected."

"You are a cruel and heartless guy!" said Walls. "OK, I have to dolly-step along at your pace! Where do we start? Have you included the Arctic Ocean public house? That seems jolly likely to me."

"No. Why? Don't tell me you've finally remembered something useful. Did the Walrus mention that pub when we met him in the Bear? Or did he drop a receipt from it and you picked it up and read it> *Well done*, Walls! But I've never heard of it. How can there be a pub in Oxford that he knows about and I don't? I wonder where it is. Does it have rooms? Could he actually be staying there?" asked Barnabus, very seriously.

"No, no, it doesn't exist, it was a *joke*, Buffy. Where is your sense of humour? *Walrus*, Arctic Ocean. Get it? There is *no* Arctic Ocean public house in Oxford that I know of" said Walls.

"I don't think our senses of humour are in the same *universe* this evening," said Barnabus, rather ruefully. "You seem to be amused very easily by quite ridiculous and unfunny things. But then you haven't been at work all day, whereas I have."

"Your refusal to admit that what I do *is* work is really most distressing," protested Walls. In truth due to his desire to make sure his wife remained close to his side all day so that he was safe but at the same time being unable to tell her why, Walls had made sure Yvette did not wander off on her own academic pursuits and abandon him to a possible gruesome fate by using the simple expedient of spending the day taking his wife out shopping for a whole new set of stylish and very expensive outfits.

"But," added Barnabus, graciously, "you have an excellent point! You feel that the Walrus's nickname may have predisposed him to mimic his animal namesake in tastes and habitats. Unfortunately Oxford doesn't have any pubs named after seas, but perhaps we should concentrate on those with good fish menus?"

"Why don't we just look walruses up on Wikipedia while we are at it? We might get some clues," suggested Walls, sarcastically.

"A *splendid* idea," said Barnabus, not even noticing the sarcasm. He whipped out his phone, despite his carrier bag impedimenta, and did so.

"No, nothing much here," he said, a few seconds later, ignoring the fact that Walls was now pretending to bang his head against a wall, "but *this is* funny, Walls, listen: 'The Walrus has only two natural predators'! That's us, Walls, *you and me*; it's *written in Wikipedia*. We are *destined* to solve this case and bring the Walrus to justice!"

"Maybe you *have* been working too hard today. I think we had better get you a sandwich at the first pub. Your brain cells clearly need food. Time is rushing away. We must commence our task. We had better start by running to my room to put this stuff down and get my running gear, but you must, must, stick absolutely to my side" said Walls.

"Not in my *work* clothes," protested Barnabus, but he was speaking to thin air, for Walls had set off and Barnabus was forced to run after him.

By the end of the evening even Walls was flagging slightly, especially as they had felt constrained to at least buy a glass of coke each in many of the pubs that they passed through. Otherwise they felt the glares of the serving staff as they roamed round checking who was sitting at the tables. Thus Walls felt somewhat awash. Barnabus had avoided being so overfull by realising that they didn't have to *drink* the liquid they bought, but Walls told him that topping up with liquid during exercise was most important and then felt he must keep to his own words. However, despite all their efforts, Barnabus and Walls were not destined to meet the Walrus on that evening, their search was entirely fruitless. Yet if Barnabus had been less afraid of ridicule because he had been tricked by the 'behind the door' trick, if he had confided fully with his mama on the previous evening, if he had told her all about his and Walls' discussions and actions, he would have had a much more fruitful search, for Elodea had once again chanced to meet up with Andy earlier that day and had spent several pleasant hours in his company.

Chapter 8

The next day Elodea wondered where to go in celebration of her grandchild-free status. She thought of lots of places but she had been to all of them already and they all seemed like a very long drive for no particular reason to see something she could see so clearly in her imagination that it required no further reinforcement. . In fact she suddenly felt that going on a day out alone, a thing she often sighed to do when accompanied by two or more grandchildren, was an overrated activity. True, it was peaceful and you could look at the things you wanted to look at for as long as you wanted and you never had to worry about where the children were or what they were breaking, but it lacked something.

"No one else to talk to and show things, *see*," she said, to Pippy and the kettle, who, she felt, both agreed with her. They then both offered to accompany her but she explained to them that dogs were not allowed into places like museums and that the kettle would not really enjoy it even if he thought he would. She had already met Priscilla for coffee. She could go and visit one of her Little Wychwell friends but she could *always* do that and take one or both of the children with her if she wanted as none of them minded.

"*So*, shall we have a day In together instead? A bit of peace? Do what we like *in* the house?" she asked the two of them, and they, she felt, both agreed that this was a good plan.

Then her eye happened to catch the bright white corner of something poking out from the base of a pile of objects in the kitchen. At first she could not think what it was and then she realised that it was her old sketch pad. She pulled it out as gently as possible while balancing the load above it. But, despite her care, a ladle, a baking tin, a china plate, five magazines, two books, three biro pens, a pencil, a birthday card and two parish magazines crashed to the floor.

Pippy scuttled to a safe distance and then sat there, laughing up at her. The kettle clearly felt the incident was most amusing as well. Elodea felt it looked far more smug than it usually did.

"Maybe I should have pulled it out much *faster*," she said to Pippy and the kettle, "then everything else would have just jumped a little way and landed back in exactly the same place, like that tablecloth trick?"

They both seemed to nod.

"I suppose neither of you would have made such a mess of it!" she said to them. The kettle looked even more self-satisfied, whereas Pippy looked sympathetic.

"Well, next time I want something from the bottom of a pile, *you* can try getting it out, and *I'll* watch and laugh," Elodea said to the kettle.

Then she said to herself, "I really must go out at once, *immediately*, before I go *completely* mad."

She opened the sketch pad. Some of the drawings were really rather *good*, she told herself, even though she hadn't thought so at the time. She hadn't done any sketching for years and years and years. You couldn't do it with small children around the place. If would be fun to go out today and sketch something once again. But what if she couldn't sketch anymore? Then she came to a page with a sketch of a Triceratops' skull on it and decided where to go. She picked the pencil up off the floor and added it to the sketch pad.

'I'll tidy everything else up later," she said to the kettle and Pippy, "otherwise it will be too late to go out."

Then she added, "I am going out to the University Museum to do some sketching. You two will have to stay at home. *You* won't want to sit in the car for so long waiting for me, Pippy, angel, and I'm not going out with you, Kettle, even if you do keep me company when I'm in! I'm quite sure you wouldn't enjoy it at all. *Not* your sort of place. You would probably prefer the Science Museum."

"I must get out, *right now*, I am not losing it, I have lost it!" she then said to herself.

Elodea drove into Oxford, parked in Norham Gardens and walked across the University Parks to the University Museum.

It had been refurbished recently but it still looked pretty much as it had always done to her. It is not a big museum but makes up for this by being packed full of interesting exhibits. The building itself is also an exhibit in its own right, with different types of stone in the pillars, and fruit and flowers and plants in the ironwork of the ceiling beams.

Elodea found a stand full of folding stools, and collected one. She felt happy. It was such a relaxing place, positively restful, and the visitors were treated like guests rather than people to be controlled. There were other visitors, but not too many, so she did not feel oppressed by being in the middle of a crowd. All she had to do was decide what to sketch, and then she could spend some happy time here, all alone, making a detailed and leisurely sketch, being an untrammelled grown-up, just for once.

She trotted round the dinosaur aisles, looked at the models, skipped about feeling all the 'please touch' exhibits and wondered, as she always did, over the fossil wood. It was stone but it looked like wood and it always felt like wood to her fingers. She could not believe in her heart that it was not still wood. She was having such fun that she nearly forgot her original purpose. Then she went on to study minerals and popped into the dark to look at the glowing minerals. But then she decided she really must return to her original purpose and eventually after some more indecisive and distracted wandering through pre-history she decided to sketch the Iguanadon skeleton.

After a while she realised that someone else had joined her: a man on the far side of the Iguanadon, was sketching the same thing. She ignored him and worked away. She didn't want to look at him in case he waved his sketch book at her so they could compare their sketches. His would be much better than hers, she was sure. She wished he hadn't turned up; she had been so enjoying sketching alone. Then she told herself off for being mean. The man was perfectly entitled to sit there and draw if he wanted to do so. She wondered whether to move and start sketching something else but then she decided that she had started so she would finish. She bent to her work again, absorbed but not happy. Finally she finished her sketch to her own satisfaction, stood up and picked up her stool to put it away. To her horror he was doing exactly the same thing at the same time.

"I wish I had waited another minute," she said to herself. For now they *must* speak to each other, maybe even must compare their finished works, for otherwise it would look rude. She told herself off for being antisocial and looked towards him, exercising her devastating smile.

She was just beginning to say "Hi! Were you sketching too?" when she realised who it was.

"*Andy!*" she said, with a sudden feeling of pleasure. "Hello! I, I didn't *see* you there!"

"How stupid I am," she added to herself. "How ridiculous and over sensitive I have been! It was Andy all the time, not a stranger! We could have talked to one another all the time!"

Then she looked at him more attentively. He was wearing *another* red T-shirt and this time it had "667 – the neighbour of the Beast" written on it in black gothic letters with yellow flames surrounding them. She remembered Mrs Shipman's words. She knew he reminded her of someone else! Now she knew who it was! If she added a little pointed beard he would look awfully like Mephistopheles on her cover of her copy of Marlowe's Dr Faustus. Then she chided herself for her own stupidity, reminded herself that she had always found such T-shirt slogans merely amusing previously and that what Mrs Shipman said or wrote was simply complete nonsense.

"Hello!" he said. "I wondered when you would notice I was here! I didn't realise it was *you* at first either! *Ages* since I was last here. Naturally I used to come here a lot. *Zoology*, you know! Jolly good way to pass the time, eh?"

"Yes," said Elodea. She hoped he didn't think she was always so idle and self-indulgent, so she added, "A good way to spend a *holiday*, and I am on holiday, like you, because of not having to look after Amadeus and Theo this week."

She glanced at his finished work. It was, indeed, very professional. Zoology probably gave you a lot of practice at sketching animals and skeletons and things she told herself. Her own sketch was not nearly as good! She slammed the sketch book shut but he had already seen it.

"I do like your sketch," he said. "Mine is only a *technical* sketch, but yours looks full of *life!*"

"A *living* dinosaur fossil skeleton," she said, and laughed.

"Have you been round the museum already? Are you just leaving?" he asked.

"No" lied Elodea. "I'm just going to look round everything else. Have you done that yet? I mean, are you just leaving?"

"No, not leaving, I was also just going to take a tour of the other exhibits. Splendid! We can look round together" he said.

So she went round all the exhibits again. It wasn't difficult to pretend she had not already done so as she enjoyed looking at them so much. He smiled at her childish enthusiasm for the 'please touch' specimens but even though it seemed a bit silly he obligingly also felt the meteorites and the fossil wood and even poked the poor stuffed Shetland pony and the fox which she stroked so very gently so as not to hurt their stuffed feelings.

Andy told her lots of interesting things about all the animals, current and fossilized. She thought it would be hard to find a better museum companion than him: he liked exactly the same things as her and he knew so much about everything. They began by looking at ammonites, which he explained were once believed to be snakes turned to stone by the saints – snakes, those creatures of ill-omen and works of the Devil. She knew that much about ammonites already but was polite enough not to tell him so, and encouraged by her interest he continued and told her many more details about these fables which she had not known before. It reminded her, she thought, of happy outings she had enjoyed with Barnabus, before he grew up and got married and then got so tired from work and small children. Strange though, she couldn't help but notice that the *Devil* kept appearing in all his historical and mythological accounts – first the ammonites, then the dinosaur eggs, thought to be the eggs of dragons; the Devil's beasts and so on. She told herself to pull herself together, for the Devil and the works of darkness appeared in nearly all ancient mythological tales.

Then when they started to look at the fish aisle he stopped.

"I'm not so sure I want to look at the 'flying whales'," he said. "I'd rather not go up here. Things like that make me nervous in case they fall on our heads."

Elodea, for one mad millisecond, had a feeling that devils, or, no, was that witches perhaps, were allergic to water, and fish, after all, lived in water. Surely *that* was not the reason why he did not like them? Then she told herself to stop being so ludicrous as she remembered his unfortunate history with *his* Whale and believed she understood his distress. Her eyes filled with sympathetic tears at the thought of how much this must pain him.

"I had *entirely* forgotten about the Whale," she said, without the thought that this might be tactless even crossing her empathetically sympathetic mind. "I am so sorry. We can just omit this aisle and go on to Pitt Rivers or go to the café instead?" she suggested.

"Do you know, I hadn't even thought about that" he said, smiling, "Please don't trouble yourself about *the* Whale. My feelings are no longer so damaged as they were once. I *really* don't like things being suspended over my head like that, I wasn't making an excuse."

But she was convinced that he was just lying to cover up his distress.

He was continuing, "I'd vote for the café; I'm *hungry*. But *is* there a café? Are you sure? There never used to be."

'Oh *yes*," she said, pleased to be able to give him some information instead of him telling her everything. "They have one now, isn't that splendid? So handy with the grandchildren. It would have been lovely if it had been here when *my* children were young. It saves having to bring a picnic to eat outside."

So they went upstairs and then realised how late it was and how long they had been sketching, so instead of this being *morning coffee* they had wraps and cakes and coffee for *lunch*, and Elodea was delighted to find that the Walrus liked cake just as much as she did as they both had two slices. But he chose to have devil's food cake for both his slices of cake. Elodea wished he had chosen the *angel* cake instead, at least for *one* of the slices. She knew these satanic references were all just a ridiculous coincidence but she was beginning to become jumpy about so many of them happening in close succession.

She looked at his apparently guileless handsome face. Such a sweet young man, devoting an hour of his time to her, who was only one of his not very close friend's mother, yet again. But then wouldn't the *Devil* look *charming*, said a voice in the back of her mind. She told it to shut up. She was having such fun. She wished one of her own children would devote a whole morning to her like this but they were either far away or too busy or both – Elizabeth in Edinburgh with her husband and her two children and her medical work; Paris in the Army, even though he now had a high-level desk job and was no longer posted abroad , but he had his own wife and child as well; Tony still on his travels with his wife Flic; and Barnabus, so run off his feet with work and children and Angel and everything else.

After they had finished lunch Elodea decided she really must go home. She had a guilty feeling at the back of her mind about the large pile of debris on the kitchen floor, and Pippy would need taking out. In fact Elodea was now feeling guilty about many of the long list of undone jobs which she had left for a day when the children were not there. She had been amusing herself for far too long.

"I must get back now. I have so much to do at home. Also the kettle and Pippy miss me," she said absent-mindedly.

"Do you have a *cat* called the Kettle?" he guessed, having already heard about Pippy being the dog.

"No, I have a *kettle* called the Kettle," she admitted. "It's quite a good listener though."

"I have been rather alone while on leave too," he said. "I confess, I quite often talk to my suitcase when I get in at night. It has been very pleasant meeting you again. I enjoyed not lunching alone."

They smiled at each other. Then they walked through the Parks together back towards her car in Norham Gardens. Elodea felt young again. The years slipped away. The Parks always made her feel like a student again. The sunshine was bright. The day was charming. They looked at the ducks on the pond.

Elodea looked up at her tall companion. Such delightful curls, she thought, and beautiful blue eyes. She thought what a pleasant change it was from being with her family – what a luxury it was to have a companion who really paid attention to her, and to her alone, as though she was *someone* and not just Mama or Nonna.

"This pond is so much larger than it used to be!" he said. "I say, just a thought! Would you mind if we took a quick diversion before we continue to Norham Gardens? I would like to retrace our steps a little way and climb the Rainbow Bridge, if you can possibly manage to spare the time. It's so many years since I was last there, and so much has happened. I would like to go and stand there once again. I would like to travel back in time. Of course one can't, but just for a few moments, perhaps, I could feel that I had. Would you indulge me with this?"

Elodea thought she understood this. He had been in such terrible places with his work, seen such appalling atrocities, fought death in impossible conditions, he wanted to return to somewhere peaceful where he had once been happy.

So they walked back across the base of the park and climbed up the high curve of the Rainbow Bridge, and Elodea wondered if it had been less steep when she was younger and then remembered that it hadn't. They stood there, together, gazing at the Cherwell, and then he leant towards her, his head bent tenderly over hers... and just for a moment Elodea thought he was going to kiss her. The words that shot through her head in these few milliseconds were not "I shouldn't kiss him, I'm married to John" nor, in the confident assumption that this would be a *filial* kiss "Oh, how sweet, just like saying goodbye to one of my own sons". *No*, what popped into Elodea's head was the phrase "*Oh, so the Whale is a girl! Unless, of course, Andy is bisexual, then she or he might be either.*"

But it rapidly became clear that no affection was involved, he was only leaning closer towards her so that he could speak in a much quieter voice. She told herself, *very* firmly, that this was *such a relief*, except that it still gave her no clue at all on the Whale's gender.

Thus, having stooped over far enough to achieve a confidential distance between his mouth and her ear, the words that then emanated from the Walrus's mouth in a quiet, very confidential tone, were totally unexpected, "Tell me, Elodea, have *you* seen *the Whale*?"

Elodea was momentarily nonplussed. She did not want to tell him that she could not even remember if the Whale was male or female let alone what they looked like and so even if she had seen him or her, she wouldn't have known but that since the Whale was a member of the rowing fraternity at Kings it seemed extremely likely that she had sighted said person at some point in the past and then entirely forgotten them.

So Elodea's reply was rather confused, especially as she was unable to use a personal pronoun other than 'it' which she felt would be totally unacceptable under the circumstances. She offered up a silent prayer of thanks that English was not as gender specific as some other languages and plunged into muddled speech. "*The Whale?*" she asked. "Well, *yes*, that is, if you mean *your* whale, you know, *the Whale,* the one who was a cox, er, you know, when you were all at Kings, *years* ago, yes, indeed, when you were undergraduates, you know, yes, um…"

"Yes, there may be *other* whales but I meant *my* Whale, naturally: *Alex*," he interrupted her, not sounding at all ruffled, and laughing lightly to show that her tangled reply didn't matter, "But I didn't mean when we were at Kings. I mean *recently*, here in *Oxford*. Have you by any chance seen Alex *in the last couple of weeks*?"

"*No*," said Elodea, more emphatically than was necessary to cover up the fact that she had no idea who Alex might be. Then she added, for after all she *might* have seen the Whale for all she knew, "Not to *the best of my knowledge*, I mean, you know, *people in a crowd*, don't always see individuals even if they are there. *Yes*, I mean, *no!*"

Meanwhile she told herself that she might have *expected* that the Whale's name would be a *gender neutral name*, Alex. Typical! Furthermore it could be *just* Alex, or it could be short for many other names, Alexander or Alexandra or Alexis or…

Elodea jerked herself back from her own thoughts. Had she *finally*, after all these years of knowing Priscilla, caught the inattentive listening virus from her? What was Andy saying now?

"I proposed to Alex," he said, "standing here, on this bridge, just at this point. The world seemed so beautiful that day."

Elodea looked at him. He had tears in his eyes. She felt empathetic tears rise to her own eyes. The poor man! It was so sad! Andy still loved this Alex – that was perfectly clear, whoever Alex might be.

"But I thought, I *thought*..." she said, before she could stop herself.

"That *I* left the marriage. That I walked out by my own choice. Perfectly true. I did. Alex took revenge on me after that, claimed the marriage ended because I had an affair. I didn't, I mean, I hadn't, had an affair that is. But there were *reasons* why I left... Never mind what they were!" he said.

There was a rather awkward silence. Elodea tried hard not to look as if she was dying to know what actually happened. Why, she wondered, was scandal about other people's lives so very fascinating? She told herself off for her curiosity. Then she remembered that this human attribute kept a lot of media workers employed so it did have some useful purpose. Finally Elodea realised that the reason the silence between them was so prolonged was because Andy was waiting for her to talk to him, to offer a sympathetic comment on his last tragic speech.

"I'm so very sorry to hear that" she rushed to say, "And *of course* you don't have to tell me the reasons. I believe you without them!"

He sighed and changed his mind, "No, I *trust* you, I'll tell you exactly why I left. I'm *so* tired of having to defend myself, my Whale retaliated in such a toxic way after I left. I lost a lot of friends. I get so weary of being cast as the bad guy, and trying to explain and no one believing me. If I don't tell you what happened you'll only wonder and then someone else is bound to tell you an untrue version. *Alcohol* was at the base of it all – very bad stuff in large quantities. I know that only too well, I used to drink too much, far, far too much, even ruined my rowing with it. I daresay you'll remember that. Buffy must have told you all about it at great length. I remember how angry he was with me for almost getting us bumped because I was too p*****d to row properly. But I'm clean now, haven't touched a drop for years. Never will. Can't risk it. So I had sympathies with Alex's drinking problems. I tried to help, I understood. But things got worse after we graduated. I hoped that once we were married things would steady down. I was wrong. The end was brought about because, while under the influence, Alex attacked me with one of our wedding presents."

"With a *wedding present?*" Elodea gasped.

"It wasn't still boxed and wrapped; it was in use, naturally. Would have been safer if it hadn't been" he said, then added quickly, "*Lovely* present from someone or other, careless of me, entirely forget who it was from now" just in case the gift had been from someone Elodea knew, Walls or Barnabus, say.

Andy put in a little cough to cover this awkwardness and then resumed his story, "Anyway it was an *electric carving knife*. I'd just been using it to carve a joint of beef. I had to have stitches. If I hadn't leapt to one side and run out of the house I'd probably be dead," he said.

"I'm, I'm so *sorry!*" said Elodea, feeling gladness in her heart that he had *not* been the villain, that he had had *reasons*. Such a nice young man would *never* have left without a *good* reason; she was quite sure of that. Really, he was an *angel:* the *work* he did, the fact he had spent *two days* of his own holiday going round Oxford with someone who was only the mother of an old. Besides he was not just good but also charming and good looking. If he was evil she was sure it would show on his face. Didn't grumpy and angry and unjust and bad people always finish up with faces to match?

Then the words of Aunt Jamesina from L.M. Montgomery's *Anne of the Island* shot into her brain: *I don't believe Old Nick can be so very ugly. He wouldn't do so much harm if he was. I always think of him as a rather handsome gentleman.*

Bother Mrs Shipman! Bother Barnabus! Above all bother L.M. Montgomery! They were all *spoiling her afternoon*. Inside her mind she made a very rude gesture at all of them. They were all wrong! Andy was a *very sweet person*.

"I discovered Alex, the Whale, you know, was also visiting Oxford right now from, er… from one of the college porters and this is why I stayed on, I *must* find, I mean, not *must*, I would *like* to find, I mean, I would *quite* like to, er, *meet up*, er…" His speech trailed off in a muddle.

"Andy, Andy, dear, it's not my business, but don't, *don't* look for Alex. You might be exposing yourself to more *pain*," said Elodea, her heart aching for the man. So much in love, she thought, *still* so in love.

"I was surprised to hear Alex was here," he said, as if talking to himself. "Don at Cambridge these days. You know that, I expect – the Other Place. So not expected to be here in Oxford but…Funny thing, both of us chancing to be here at once again…it was here, you know, just *here*, on this bridge, on a day just like this, exactly like this, that I proposed, right here, not really expecting to have the joy of being accepted but…"

"Well, I think Oxford and Cambridge are sort of friends these days, don't you? Old rivalries – very silly, don't you think?" gabbled Elodea, who was becoming worried about his mental state. "I think, I think the dons *do* talk to each other now and er, visit, collaborate, you know. So perhaps the Whale is here frequently, er, more frequently than you might think, er…"

"Yes, yes, I suppose cross faculty collaboration is encouraged. I tell you what, give me your mobile and I'll put my number in it for you, then if you *should* see Alex around in Oxford, you know, if you just happened to, I mean we keep meeting so you might just as well meet Alex too, er, can you ring me, straight away, at once, and say where it was, or is, or whatever?. I am worried about what...I mean, I miss, I mean, I..."

He trailed off again.

"I suppose I should tell you the truth," he added. "I didn't find out from a college porter; I know Alex is here because of Facebook. I check Alex's FB and Twitter pages every day... I like to keep an eye on them, for..., in case..., just to see..."

He stopped again.

Oh dear, thought Elodea, the perils of social media when it came to broken relationships. You could fool yourself so easily, feel like you were still near to someone who was really far away from you.

Elodea obediently handed him her phone and he fiddled with it for a while.

"Can't work these touch screen phones," he said, ruefully. "Should have given you my number and got you to put it in yourself. My fingers – much too big for these tiddly little keys on the touch screens... There, I think I've done it now!"

"I'll check you put it in the right place!" said Elodea.

She looked in her contact numbers. Yes, there he was, under 'A'.

"It's in the directory but your name's not come out quite right," she said, with a giggle.

He glanced at it and laughed himself, and then said, "Oh, just leave it like that. I think my huge sausage fingers and autocorrect must have got at me."

For what the name in Elodea's contact list was not Andy de Ville or even the Walrus, but simply A Devil.

"Why," he said, "that's quite *humorous*, don't you think?"

"I'd better ring the number to see if you got that part right!" she said, and did so.

There was the sound of a brass band playing a fanfare in Andy's pocket. He retrieved his phone and solemnly answered it.

"Hello!" he said.

"Hi!" said Elodea into her own phone, smiling at the silliness.

"I've had a thought. The Whale used to love the Vicky Arms. Might be there. I'm going to plunge down the other side of this bridge and trot up there. Be seeing you! Cheerio!" he said.

"Bye!" said Elodea, switching her phone off.

Then she watched him go, down the very steep bridge at a rush and then striding off alone up the towpath. She felt anxious about him, wandering alone, searching for a lost love who wasn't worth such devotion. Then she told herself off. Even if this Alex was an extreme alcoholic many people recovered from this state. Yes, surely could not be too bad now, after all Alex was a don now and could have already been to rehabilitation and be completely well again but now too ashamed of earlier violent attacks to seek Andy out again. So if Andy found her or him they could get back together and be *perfectly happy*, just as she herself and John were. Elodea's eyes grew misty with emotion. She had to find a handkerchief and blow her own nose at the beautiful vision of reunion that she had created. But, she thought, the phone number was a waste of time as she couldn't aid Andy in his desire for reunion even if she spent the whole of tomorrow searching the streets of Oxford, for even with a full name, Alex de Ville, she still had absolutely no idea who Alex might be. The only certain description she had was 'short'. Not even necessarily all *that* short either, for Barnabus and his friends were all so tall that they thought anyone under six feet tall was undersized.

Elodea looked at Andy's phone entry of 'A Devil' again. She chuckled to herself. What *would* Mrs Shipman say if she saw *that* in Elodea's phone contacts? Then Elodea skipped off alone across the Parks, enjoying the sunshine, getting back to Norham Gardens only just in time, for her ticket for parking was about to run out of time and a parking attendant was rapidly approaching.

Mrs Shipman might have been *amazed* to have seen the phone entry but she would not have been as staggered and as angry with Elodea as Barnabus was when he rang her at a very late hour that evening. He was just giving his Mama a very quick ring to make sure she was OK when he returned home following his totally fruitless pub and restaurant search with Walls. But when Barnabus discovered that his Mama had not only met the Walrus earlier but could also have told Barnabus exactly where he might have been found that evening, Barnabus was, quite unjustifiably, furious.

"You *met* the *Walrus* and *you didn't ring and tell me straight away?*" he yelled at his very surprised mama when she mentioned that she had had a lovely day out and she had just *happened* to meet the Walrus again in *another* museum – the University Museum this time.

"What?" she shouted back, "Why should I do that? I only met him by chance, and you were in *work* when I met him. You don't *like* me ringing you at work. Besides which, you didn't *tell* me to ring you if I *happened* to see him – you said, only yesterday, that he was a *good guy!*"

"You *met him by chance*," he said, making the phrase sound most sinister. "Well, *don't do it again*! Or if you do, *tell me* at once, *immediately*, whether I am at work or not! Now, tell me *exactly* what happened and everything single thing he said – every single word, every syllable!"

"Well really, Barnabus! You are being most unreasonable!" she yelled, for she was thoroughly annoyed by his meteoric changes of opinion and the fact he seemed to think he had a right to know everything about her life, "There was nothing secretive about our meeting so I can quite happily tell you everything about it."

She took a gigantic intake of air and then plunged into a spectacularly long, angry, breath-free and entirely unpunctuated monologue. "I went to the University Museum and did some sketching and he appeared and he had done some sketching too so we looked at each other's sketches and then we went to the café for a coffee and some cake and we talked about coffee and cake and then we did a tour of the whole museum and the Pitt Rivers Museum and we talked about the exhibits and nothing else and then we set off across the Parks together for my car and he told me that he still misses Alex, you know the Whale and is only in Oxford because he heard Alex was there and he is sad and only left because Alex attacked him when drunk and he was in danger of his life and then he decided to go the Vicky Arms because he had suddenly thought Alex might be there and I got into my car and came home and I felt sad for him searching for a lost love who probably isn't worth looking for at all from what he said is that enough information for you?"

Elodea had omitted the part of the story where the Walrus had asked her to look out for the Whale for him, and also decided to not mention that she had his number in her list of contacts, she had the feeling that Barnabus might not approve.

Barnabus was, as always when his mama was angry, temporarily overcome with admiration at how many words she could emit in one breath. But he was still unfairly furious simply because his mama had *once again* met the Walrus by chance when he, Barnabus, couldn't find him *on purpose* and also because her judgement was so impaired that she seemed to find *such* a villain so *charming*.

"*Sad* for him?" cried Barnabus when she finished. "*Sad for him*? As for the Whale attacking him, that's *ludicrous* – he's four or five times the size of the Whale. Keep away from the man. He's *bonkers*! This just proves it. It *is* him! *He* is stalking Walls and pretending to be a dead body to freak him out And we now know that he is also stalking the Whale and, what's more, I have now realised that he's probably *stalking you as well*! Don't you think it's *odd* the way he keeps turning up in the same places? You should have rung me and told me you had met him again, *at once*. The man is completely and utterly off his head."

"Are you sure it's *him* who is bonkers? *You* are being quite ridiculous," said his mama, taking another gigantic breath. "There is no evidence for any of your assertions Andy meets me entirely by chance and you might as well say I am stalking him and he is looking for his lost partner and that is perfectly understandable even if sad and regrettable and you need to imagine how you would feel if it was you and Angel and whoever was in Walls' apartment could have been anyone at all and was most likely no one but just Walls' imagination and I know Walls is your close friend but the more I think about it the more I lean towards the view that it was a trick of Walls' imagination and I think that Walls needs to take a break from studying and the Whale used an electric carving knife so the size differential hardly mattered."

There was a short pause, in which Barnabus suddenly remembered that Elodea did not know about the second 'body' in Walls' room in Kings and that without telling her about that he could hardly explain his changed view of the Walrus. He couldn't tell her about that because she would tell Dad, and Dad would know he had been caught by the 'person behind the door' trick and tell Elizabeth and Paris and Tony, and he would never live it down. Being the youngest child *sucked*, he told himself. It was so annoying to be permanently seen as the stupid and incapable one even *without* making such an appalling *gaffe*. For now he must somehow find an exit from this conversation, get out of the enormous pit he had first dug and then fallen into. He must be more reasonable. He must pretend to be upset and hurt himself, so Mama would think that that was why he had spoken so strangely. The *sympathy vote*: that always worked on Mama's soft heart even when she was very angry and, she wasn't yet really enraged, not for *her* anyway, so far on the Mama-scale her behaviour was only registering *mildly annoyed*. She was not yet *screaming* at full volume or jumping up and down on the spot or throwing things.

"I'm so sorry, Mama," he said. "It's just the creepy way the Walrus, I mean Andy, keeps turning up wherever you go. It's unsettling me. *I am worried about you*! You know, after Fran kidnapping you and everything, I worry about you, you might not be looking after your own safety properly. Andy isn't the most stable person I know from university as you know. He might be drinking again himself. I feel *guilty* too. I never take you to places these days and now Andy is doing it instead. He isn't your son! I'll take you out the *very* next time I have a day off and Angel doesn't have one at the same time, I promise! Next bank holiday, say? We could go out for the whole day, take Pippy and everything."

"That would be *lovely*. We can all go together, the five of us, you and me and the children and Pippy. We could all go to Stratford or somewhere like that! It will be *wonderful*. But you are *busy*, my own baby son! I understand that. I don't expect you to take me out," said Elodea, now beaming and happy again, "The Walrus and I had nothing better to do today than trot round a museum together. But we *enjoyed* it too, I like his company, he is a very pleasant person!" she finished defiantly.

Elodea had forgiven Barnabus' irrational outburst. He was just feeling guilty about neglecting his mama, and he was *jealous* that she was going round with the *Walrus* instead of with *him*, that was all. Silly boy, how *funny* he was sometimes!

Then Elodea remembered that she must seize this opportunity. She could not carry on talking about the Whale and discussing him or her without even knowing their gender. "Barnabus! I have something to ask you. I know this is going to sound silly but I don't know the answer. Is Alex, you know, *the Whale*, a *boy* or a *girl*?"

"*What?*" asked Barnabus, "How old do you think we all are Mama? Boy or Girl? Don't you mean Man or Woman? In any case *why do you need to know?*"

Elodea glared at him, resisting the impulse to tell him that to her he would always be three years old, at least until he started acting like an adult. She succeeded in overcoming this desire and tried to explain matters.

"Because *I don't know who the Whale is*. I can't remember from when you were at Oxford. It's such a long time ago now, and I don't remember anything about Alex, not even which gender Alex is. The only things I know are that Alex is short and was a cox. So, I just *wondered*, it's simply so annoying not knowing!" she explained, "When I talk about people I usually have a picture of them in my mind and in this case – nothing at all."

"Does gender *matter*?" he asked in a superior 'the older generation are homophobic' tone. "And you *do* know who the Whale is."

"Are you *sure* I know Alex?" asked Elodea, so surprised by this fact that she decided not to try to defend herself against his completely unjustified implied insult by explaining that knowing the Whale's gender would halve the number of possible people the Whale could be.

"Absolutely you do! *Rowing Club Dinner*, my *first* year. You *must* remember! Love you! Good night!" he replied, and he rang off abruptly before he slipped up and told her something that would force him to tell her everything about the body's reappearance in Kings College.

"*Rowing Club Dinner, first* year? That makes no sense whatsoever to me!" she said to the phone. But the call was already dead. How very annoying Barnabus could be sometimes!

She decided to text him back to ask for more details. But she tried composing a suitable text three times, and failed to achieve anything that she felt he would bother to answer. She was now cross with him for being so aggravatingly cryptic. Then she decided to ignore the whole thing with dignity. After all, she told herself, she would probably never meet Andy again and would never know if she ever met the Whale again anyway, and so none of it mattered and she didn't need to know anything at all about *either* of them.

She nearly deleted Andy's number from her phone on the grounds that it was just stupid to have it there but then, smiling a little to herself, decided to leave it. After all, she just might, by chance, meet the Whale and if, as Barnabus said, she *did* know who the Whale was she might also recognise him or her and realise who they were, and then she could ring Andy and then he and the Whale could meet again and be reconciled. She was sure this would be wonderful and magical, and the world would be set right and everyone would be happy ever after.

But she was *not* going to ring Barnabus if she happened to meet Andy again, he was just being silly. There was absolutely no reason why he needed to know. In fact she wouldn't even tell Barnabus next time she chanced to meet Andy because, she told herself, she never knew if he would be pleased or horrified and she was getting tired of dealing with his irrational reactions. That would save him from feeling jealous too. Also it was, after all, none of Barnabus' business who she met when he was not there or even when he was.

Perhaps if she kept the words Rowing Club Dinner hovering in her mind she might even remember who on earth Alex, the Whale, could be.

Even if she had rung him straight back she would not have reached Barnabus for he had already rung Walls up to tell him the latest development in the Walrus Hunt.

Chapter 9

"No, Buffy," said Walls, in world-weary tones as he answered the phone and before Barnabus had a chance to speak, "I will not go out again round all the open-for-24-hour public houses that we have not yet visited this evening on the off chance that the Walrus has suddenly materialised in one."

"No, *no*, Walls, not that at all. *Listen to this*! I have been talking to *Mama*!" said Barnabus, so excited that he was bouncing up and down.

"Stand still, *mon ange*! You are upsetting the already fragile signal," said Walls.

"I didn't think you spoke French!" said Barnabus, ignoring him and still bouncing up and down with excitement.

"I don't," replied Walls. "But your persistence in contacting me is having a terrible effect on my brain. *Mon ange* is a phrase I often used on demanding girlfriends who insisted on ringing me up at odd hours. It calmed them down and it was easier to get them off the phone. If you carry on like this I may absent-mindedly send you a bunch of red roses next. What does it mean anyway?"

"What does *what* mean?" asked Barnabus, baffled.

"*Mon ange*," said Walls.

"My angel. Male angel, in fact, according to the article but I'm not sure that means anything in French really," replied Barnabus.

"I thought so. Just checking. Thank goodness," replied Walls. "I didn't accidentally say anything too *gay* then!"

"Walls!" scolded Barnabus. "Don't be homophobic!"

"I'm not! And I wasn't being. I just don't want *you* to get the *wrong idea*, like those girlfriends did after I used the phrase sometimes," replied Walls.

"Well if I do I can look forward to the diamond bracelet next presumably? I think that would be rather nice," replied Barnabus.

"OK, now we've finished flirting, you might as well tell me why you rang me," said Walls. "But for goodness sake stand still!"

"How do you know I'm not standing still?" asked Barnabus.

"I've told you once, your signal is already bad and every time you jump up and down it does even more terrible things to it," replied Walls.

"OK, OK, I'll perch on the edge of the table, then I'll keep more still. But you have to listen to this! All of this! This is important!" replied Barnabus.

"Don't tell me, let me guess, you will say it only once?" said Walls. "Er, don't you have chairs?"

"Yes, and yes," said Barnabus. "Too excited to sit on a chair, I can lean on the table, but sitting would be too restrictive! Yes, I will say it only once because it's so very long but it's also very involved, so you had better listen!"

"Buffy, old chap, calm down! Wikipedia *may* have produced another amazing fact about walruses but I doubt it is really the oracle that you think it is. How about putting your phone away and going to bed!" suggested Walls.

"Not Wikipedia, you moron, *Mama*! I said Mama!" said Barnabus.

"Ah, yes, now your mama is an oracle. I would agree with that assessment, a very far sighted woman. Very well, I will compose myself to hear what she had to say," replied Walls and listened accordingly. But once Barnabus had started his tale he became truly attentive, only punctuating Barnabus' account of his mama's encounter with the Walrus with the odd gasp.

"So," Walls said, when Barnabus finally ran down and stopped, "the Walrus, it would appear, is not just stalking *me* but also *the Whale*, who happens to be in Oxford, which is *why the Walrus is here*. And possibly stalking your mama as well but that seems unlikely to me because even Andy could not possibly have any reason whatsoever for doing that. Although possibly he is not stalking your Mama *as such* but only following her to get information about us because she is connected to you and thus to me. But the fact remains that it is not just me who is in danger. At least t*wo* of us are in danger, Buffy, *me and the Whale*!"

"Yes, and so we *have* to trace the Whale too, as soon as we can!" said Barnabus.

"We can't even find *Andy* and he is *enormous*. How on earth are we going to find a tiny little person like the Whale?" asked Walls.

"The Whale must be visiting Oxford for some *reaso*n. Probably staying in a college?" mused Barnabus.

"No, because your mama said Andy was *still* whale hunting and finding someone in a college – *surely* that would have been simple? You could ask at the Lodge. There aren't *that* many colleges!" objected Walls.

"There *are* that many colleges and the porters can be inscrutably evasive," objected Barnabus. "And if he doesn't know which one the Whale is visiting it could take…"

"Hang about, how did he know Alex was in Oxford at all? Did your Mama offer you information on that point?" asked Walls, "It could be vital!"

"Mama said he found out through social media pages," replied Barnabus. "You weren't listening, I'm sure I told you that. To be a good detective you really must listen more carefully!"

"I need a recording device for you. I'm absolutely positive you didn't say a *word* about that!" protested Walls. "You only said that he had *found out* that the Whale was in Oxford. But if *he* got his information from the Whale's social media pages then *we can read them as well*! Q.E.D. Honestly, *Sherlock*, I sometimes wonder if you have a brain. Why haven't you looked this up online already?"

"Touché, you are right. I am humbled. I bow to your superior conclusion. But we might not be *able* to read the pages," cautioned Barnabus "One might need to be a friend or follower or whatever first."

"We must be though," replied Walls. "I mean, the Whale was in the rowing club. Whale is bound to be on both our 'friends' lists, surely? In any case the Whale's pages must be open to public view as if anyone has been unfriended by Alex it must be *Andy*? While we are at this we must also look at *his* pages as well. They might be packed with clues. Morons, *both* of us! Completely overlooked the ****ing obvious!"

"I am not at all sure that *I* didn't unfriend, unfollow and delete Andy after he left the Whale. But I probably *am* still a friend of the Whale. I haven't really used Facebook or Twitter for *ages* – you know, children, work, watching cute cats on YouTube: it all fills all the time up," replied Barnabus.

"*I* didn't unfriend Andy," said Walls. "I *never* unfriend people! That's why I now have 2500 friends, or something like that. And that is on Facebook, I have thousands and thousands on Twitter, too many to be bothered ever looking at postings or tweets in fact. *Whatever!* We must both investigate this lead immediately. I tell you what: *don't* use your phone to do it. We are both at *home*, so we can use our computers. Then we don't have to interrupt this call, we can do the looking up and talk to each other simultaneously."

The sound of tapping keyboards clicked down the phone lines.

"I'm in Facebook already!" cried Barnabus.

"I'm *nearly* there," said Walls. "This connection is so slow sometimes."

"Oh *my*!" said Barnabus, getting out a neatly ironed handkerchief and wiping his brow. "Oh my! Walls, the Whale's Facebook page, look at it! Look at it!"

"Just getting to it," said Walls. "Why? Does Alex know that Andy is on a Whale Hunt…?"

Then there was a short silence and then Walls said, "****!"

"Precise-ment," said Barnabus. "Old chap, have we made a serious error! I feel one might even say that we have been hunting *entirely the wrong mammal!*"

Walls could tell how very agitated Barnabus must be, for his accent was getting progressively more plummily upper class – a sure sign of his nerves being entirely in disarray. Walls himself said nothing, he was still sitting there with his mouth open.

For in the last entry made on the Whale's Facebook page said "Going to Oxford to seek some long-overdue revenge on a very old acquaintance, for *revenge is a dish best served cold*."

"I say, old boy, no wonder the Walrus went into spasms when he read that. He must be desperate to find the Whale before something perfectly frightful occurs!

Andy's not stalking the Whale; he's trying to prevent a disaster," said Barnabus. He wiped his brow again.

"You are wiping your brow with a neatly ironed handkerchief, aren't you, Buffy?" asked Walls.

"How do you know that?" demanded Barnabus.

"Because the shock has put you into very posh Kings student mode," chuckled Walls.

"There is nothing even slightly humorous about this, nothing at all. We have to find Andy immediately. We must offer our sincerest apologies, tell him all that we know and offer to help him find the Whale," said Barnabus.

"I told you there was something I remembered about that body," said Walls.

"No you didn't," countered Barnabus

"Yes, I did. I said I was sure there was a reason it *couldn't be the Walrus*, but I simply *couldn't* think why that was right then. Just a moment while I gather my thoughts!" said Walls.

There was a rather prolonged silence at the other end of the line. Was his friend still there, was he OK? Barnabus began to panic.

"Where are you?" yelled Barnabus. "Don't leave the apartment! Don't step outside without having someone with you! Electric carving knife! *Electric carving knife!*"

I'm glad you are *finally* taking the danger seriously! But don't panic; I am still right here," answered Walls, rubbing his ear, "if slightly deaf. I like your new exclamation. I might use it myself sometime! 'Electric carving knife', very effective. Splendid thing to yell when exasperated. But please don't shout when I am holding the ****ing phone against my ear! I was just moving over to look at the space by the front door. Yes, yes, *as I thought*. Yes, the body must have been *about four foot six inches high*, maybe *five* feet, yes, *cox-sized, in fact*. You see, I *did* know something about it all the time, I *had* observed something! Even in that *moment of horror* I knew there was *something* about it something that I felt was familiar, something that I thought I had seen before! It was exceptionally short! It was the same size as a diddy little cox!"

"The *Eel* wasn't diddy," Barnabus pointed out.

"True, no, *he* wasn't *diddy*, but he wasn't *all* that tall, but no, he was *skinny* but not *diddy*..." Walls' eyes glazed. He had wandered off into romantic reminiscence. "*Most* of them were diddy though, especially the *girl* coxes. So sweet, like your *Angel*. So tiny and light when you picked them up off the floor to kiss them! Ah yes, but they only *looked* cute - when you picked them up they were all *wiry*, just like little piglets. Don't you just love girl coxes?"

"*No*! I mean, *yes*! I mean I *only* love *Angel* and she isn't a cox any more even if she was one once," said Barnabus.

"Once a cox, *always* a cox. Like you. You'll always be a rower even if you have got unfit and flabby these days," replied Walls.

"I am not unfit and flabby," protested Barnabus, "and Angel is nothing like a piglet, and anyway, when have you ever picked a piglet up?"

"Aw jeez!" said Walls. "Back on me old granfer's farm in the good old days, I used to lasso the hogs for him..."

Barnabus glared at the phone. "You," he said severely, "have never been on a farm in your life. So when have you ever picked a piglet up?"

"OK, it was at *your* wedding," admitted Walls. "If you recollect, your mama brought a baby hog with her. A real diddy one. It looked real *real* cute till it up and bit me."

"They *do* have sharp teeth," agreed Barnabus seriously, entirely missing Walls' ironic humour, and thinking that Walls was clearly very agitated as his English had become so very American. After so many years living in England Walls' normal speech had become far more anglicized. Barnabus felt smugly happy that his own speech *never* betrayed his feelings like that and that, indeed, he himself always managed to remain *perfectly calm*.

Then Barnabus bounced into being his efficient detecting self. "That's enough of all this banter! We have *work* to do. Congratulations on *finally* remembering how large said corpse was but as for *observant*, my boy, as a detective you score minus one hundred. *The body was very short*! This was clearly a *vital* piece of evidence which you should have conveyed to everyone else immediately! Under these circumstances it could not *possibly* have been the Walrus. For heaven's sake, man!"

'Buffy," said Walls, beginning to laugh hysterically, "I kept *telling* you it wasn't the Walrus. I had an underlying conviction that it could not possibly have been the Walrus. Mystery solved! My stalker is the Whale. The Whale, not the Walrus. Wrong W, wrong Arctic dweller. The Whale not the Walrus; the Whale not the Walrus!"

"OK, old chap, enough, get a grip! This is still an *emergency*! Nothing has changed at all. I agree that you said you didn't think it could be the Walrus, but you couldn't expect me to take any notice when you failed to produce a rational reason to refute the undeniable evidence that was pointing in the opposite direction!" answered Barnabus, without thinking to ask Walls why on earth the Whale might have decided to stalk him. Somehow in the excitement of identifying the mysterious stalker he had entirely forgotten that stalking usually required a motive. Walls acceptance of the fact without argument somehow prevented Barnabus from noticing that this was odd.

"*Buffy!*" said Walls changing to a very serious tone, having thought of something awful and becoming entirely sober in his demeanour.

"Yes?" replied Barnabus.

"*What* did your mama say about *the Whale attacking the Walrus*? Exactly and precisely, *all* the facts." asked Walls.

"I'm not sure I was paying much attention. It all seemed like a load of tosh at the time. The Whale is so small compared to the Walrus and…" answered Barnabus, regretting mentioning the electric carving knife earlier and hoping Walls still thought this was an outlandish exclamation. No point in panicking Walls entirely.

"*What did the Whale attack the Walrus with?*" demanded Walls.

"Let me think. I must be able to remember. Yes, a knife of some sort, a, er, yes, certainly, something sharp if I recollect correctly, quite probably a knife! But, dash it, no need to get yourself into a silly lather" pronounced Barnabus.

Walls' skin achieved an ashen tone.

"You sure didn't say just any old blade! Jeepers, that wasn't a plain exclamation. The weapon *was* an *electric carving knife*" he breathed. "*Electric carving knife*. You could really slice folks up!"

"Keep your hair on, toughen up Walls! Remember, and hold this most securely in your mind, the Walrus can't have sustained *much* damage," said Barnabus. "He is still most definitely and certainly in the land of the living."

"But the Walrus is four times as big as the diddy little Whale – you can't deny that for you said it!" replied Walls. "And Andy may be a hero in a fight-type situation, whereas I may be a lily livered coward. I've never been in a fight. You know well that I don't like blood and fighting and all that sort of s*it, but, listen well, I have concluded from my research that there is one certain and sure rule in a desperate fight – the candy assed always get killed! Heroes get killed too, for sure, but the cowards get slaughtered for sure and *certain*, every time."

"Oh, *pull yourself together*! Quench your despondency and trembling! For a start off, when we consider the question of size differential *you* should have no worries either," said Barnabus, heartlessly, "since you are even bigger than Andy and thus probably *five* times as big as a *diddy little* Whale."

Then the question of the motive finally occurred to Barnabus.

"What we *do* need to worry about" he continued, "Is what on earth you did to get stalked by the Whale. Without finding that out our investigation might yet founder. Come on, you must have done something!"

"With a sigh of gratitude I can cancel out sexual attraction or being dumped by me as a motive," said Walls "The Whale is not my type and never was."

Hardly!" agreed Barnabus. "So what *did* you do to cause this?"

There was a pause.

Then Walls answered, in an unusually hearty voice, "*Nothing*, Buffy, *nothing at all*. I can't *recall* doing *anything*! *Honest*!"

If Barnabus had not been on the phone so that he could see Walls' face or if he had been listening more attentively he might have been suspicious about this statement. As it was Barnabus was busy trying to make his own deductions about this puzzle and failed to register anything strange about Walls' voice. Barnabus was running back through his memory to find any incidents at Oxford when the Whale and Walls were in some way connected but failing to come up with anything that might provide a conceivable motive for such odd behaviour.

"*I* can't think of anything either" Barnabus sighed, "But if the Whale is mentally disturbed enough to go in for stalking then it might not have been anything very *much*, I suppose, stalkers have pretty odd motives sometimes I believe" replied Barnabus. He considered for a moment more. "Unless...it wasn't *you* who invented the *nickname* the *Whale*, was it?"

"No, definitely not. *Always* been called that, as far as I know. Nothing to do with me whatsoever. So, what do we do now?" asked Walls, *still* sounding rather *too* heartily convincing. Barnabus continued to concentrate on his own planning and failed to notice this.

"Right," said Barnabus, deciding to ignore the little hiccup of no apparent motive and putting himself firmly back in charge, "Motive unknown but there must be one. We must find out what it is, it could be most important in judging what will happen next. So, kindly spend the time till I join you in scouring your memory for any clues. As soon as I am located in the same place as you I can look after everything so that you don't need to be either distressed or nervous in the interim. Now, pay attention, this *is* the plan! Firstly, I am coming over *right away*. Secondly, you will stay right where you are *with* Yvette *in* the flat till I arrive; you will be perfectly safe with her, there will be no possible danger. Do not, I repeat, do *not* move, do *not* step outside before I rendezvous with you. Thirdly, when I *have* arrived we will both try to find Andy again and this time we will succeed because we *must*."

"Sir!" said Walls sarcastically, then he added "I wish you would stop referring to Yvette as if she was some kind of *pit bull terrier*. Furthermore she won't be at all keen on you and I going out *again*, especially at this time of night. She considers you to be a bad influence on me, as you know. But I will admit to being pleased that you *finally* agree that I am in *danger*. I have been in *vile peril* ever since I first saw that supposed corpse in the apartment. So while I am feeling superior because of this I will also inform you that the answer of how to get hold of Andy is now staring you in the face *obvious*."

"Well, if I'd known it was *the Whale* before, then *of course* I would have agreed that you were in *danger*. Andy is just an alcoholic but the Whale is, well, you know, a *completely bonkers alcoholic*, I mean to say, attacking Andy with a meat cleaver! As for Yvette, I'm sure you can invent some story about why you need to go out again, and then instead of meeting me in your apartment you can meet *me* downstairs at the entrance so she doesn't know that I have anything to do with it." replied Barnabus.

"You say *I* ignore details! Get it right! It wasn't a *meat cleaver*; it was an *electric carving knife*. It's true though, the Whale *was* always loops: legendary rows with the Second Eight, and then *that Rowing Club Dinner!*" corrected Walls.

"OK, OK" said Barnabus, "Now, enlighten me, what is this *so obvious* method to get hold of Andy?

"The answer is completely and utterly facile. I can't see how we have both been so stupid about it so far. Fortunately I am now in the plains of light even though you still rest in the dark vale of total idiocy. *We are friends with him on Facebook*, leastways I am even if you unfriended him. I'll simply send him a DM asking him to come round to my place immediately as I have something very important to tell him. That will be sufficient of a draw to get him straight round, and then we can explain everything, apologise for suspecting him and throw our lot in with his. It's quite likely he might even know where the Whale is boarding and then things will be simple." said Walls.

"Yes, but we don't have to explain *everything* to Andy," wailed Barnabus. "He will think it's bloody hilarious if we do and I will never hear the end of it. He will tell the whole rowing club. We can just tell him that we didn't tell him about the Whale stalking you *before* because we have only just seen that page and realised who it was who was doing it."

"Whatever. *Youngest children*! You are all so *sensitive* about being ragged! Such fragile little egos as you have" said Walls. "Now come on, Mr Youngest Child; get yourself organised and moving. Shouldn't you be already in that car and driving? *I've* already DM'ed Andy with my other hand."

"Yes, yes, I'm going or rather coming," replied Barnabus, "but, Walls, listen up, *this* is *so* funny. Wikipedia *is* an oracle after all. You know what the end of that sentence about walruses said?"

"No," said Walls. "Now get off your butt and get round here!"

"But you simply *have* to hear this first," replied Barnabus. "The *whole* sentence *actually* says '*The walrus only has two predators: the killer whale and the polar* bear'. So, you see, there it was, staring us in the face. The answer is *always* in Wikipedia! The *Whale*! Certain proof!"

"In that event which of us, may I ask, is the polar bear?" demanded Walls. "Running round Oxford after a day at work *has* absolutely been much too much for you. You are so unfit! Your brain has to be oxygen deprived due to over-exertion."

"I didn't catch those last sentences because I was walking down the path and it's completely dark here so if they were important you must repeat them. I'll assume they were just chit chat unless you say otherwise. Right, I'm at the car now, Walls. Now listen: this is most important. *Do not leave the flat till I get there*. You are safe with Yvette there. Nothing happens unless you are alone, remember, and also get Andy safely into the flat with you if he gets there before I do, and then I will sort everything out when I arrive," Barnabus commanded.

"Do not fret, *mon ange*," answered Walls, pulling a face at the phone because of the 'chit chat' insult and the air of command assumed by his friend, "We will simply wait here until you arrive bearing your superior skill and intelligence inside your charming personage. Andy and I are clearly quite incapable of acting alone."

This Whale stalker business is doing something terrible to my brain, Walls thought. *Mon ange again*! My reputation as the man of a thousand sweet endearments is being shattered as I descended to only one repeated multiple times. Even worse, I am saying it to *Buffy* again and not to a woman. It might not be long before I send Buffy a diamond bracelet for real. This is terrible. I do need a psychoanalyst after all.

"That's *right*," said Barnabus, without noticing any of Walls' irony, "Quite *correct*. You must *both* stay there and do *absolutely nothing* till I arrive. I'll ring you up from outside the flat so I don't aggravate Yvette by appearing. You must be able to think of some excuse for going out with Andy if he is already there and then meeting me outside. If he hasn't arrived we'll both wait for him outside until he does get there. Did he get your message? Has he replied? Now, I am leaving the village so I must get off the phone. Don't want to be pulled over by the police."

"I had no idea you were already driving the car and using your phone at the same time, you dangerous maniac," said Walls. "Goodbye; I am cutting you off." Walls hurriedly pressed 'end' on his phone and put it down and then checked his Facebook page again. Nothing from Andy yet but maybe he would rush round to the apartment without even replying.

Walls decided to tackle his next task: that of getting Yvette to believe his cover story for meeting Barnabus *again* when he had only just come home from meeting him last time.

"Yvette, *mon ange!*" he called.

ARRGGGGHHH! He had said *mon ange* again. He had to stop. Why couldn't he stop?

"What, *sweetest*?" Yvette called back from her little office.

"*Finn* just rang me. He fancies running a half-marathon right now because at night the streets are so clear. He wondered if I would care to join him and I said I would, so I'll be popping out shortly. Is that OK with you?" lied Walls glibly. "Oh yes, and another of the old Kings boat club might call in shortly too. Finn thought it might be fun to have a sort of reunion half-marathon run!"

"Don't worry, *honeybunches*; I have *more* than enough *work* to keep me busy till 6.00 am or even later," she called back, "so you just get out and enjoy yourself with your little friends. It will be much easier for me to work without you crashing around the place."

"I adore you, my piglet," he called, while being pleased to find he had managed an endearment that was not *mon ange*.

"And I you, Pooh Bear!" she replied.

Walls wandered into the lounge and dropped his phone down on a chair. He might as well fill in the gap by freshening himself up before going out again. He was still wearing his running clothes from the evening and if he was not going to bed after all, he would go and have a shower right now and put clean running things on so he looked ready for the supposed half-marathon with Finn. Running clothes would do fine for whatever he was actually going to do with Buffy and the Walrus. Surely neither Buffy nor the Walrus would arrive for at least ten minutes. He let the hot water soothe his agitated self, he put the radio on in the shower, and started singing loudly. Time passed.

The doorbell rang.

Andy, thought Walls, or maybe even Buffy. How long have I been in this shower? I might have missed Buffy ringing me up from downstairs. Being Buffy, he won't have waited there patiently; he will have rampaged up to make sure I am safe. Then he remembered that Barnabus was also one of the old rowers so his cover story to Yvette would do for either Buffy or the Walrus. However, she would not like being interrupted by having to answer the door while she was working.

Walls leapt out hastily and started to towel himself.

"It's OK, my *little bumble bee*," called Yvette through the door. "It's only one of your rowing mates. I knew you were in the bathroom. I'm just fixing myself a coffee so I'll pour another one out for our guest."

"Just coming!" said Walls, deciding that since things were under control he might as well brush and floss his teeth while he was in the bathroom. Yvette and Andy could have a little social chat. Walls had just realised that having to explain to Andy that his ex-partner had become a dangerous stalker might be a little socially awkward. What if Andy still loved the Whale enough not to believe a word of such an idea? He might become angry at the suggestion that his lost love was a dangerous criminal. Perhaps Andy wasn't looking for the Whale because he had read that posting and wished to save the victim, but because he was desperate to find his lost love.   Walls had to grab a tissue and blow his nose at the thought of the Walrus, wandering the streets of Oxford, searching, searching for his loved one. Perhaps, thought Walls, he could just stay right here, in the bathroom, till Buffy arrived. Buffy enjoyed explaining things and smoothing things over and whatever. Walls didn't feel the red roses and the diamond bracelet would work on a ruffled Walrus. Walls brushed his teeth carefully, gargled and then flossed each tooth with slow precision.

"Are you going to be much longer?" Yvette's voice floated through the door. "My work is going *cold*. It will be quite *arctic* if I leave it any longer. The *flow*! I am losing the *flow*!"

"Just coming, my *little fairy queen*. Hold the fort for a few more seconds," said Walls, who had now changed from worry about how to break the news to the Walrus to panic at the thought that he was annoying Yvette. He tried to put both his own legs through one leg of his running shorts and had to clutch the basin for support while he untangled himself. Then he put his running vest on backwards and had to redo it.

He finally emerged from the bathroom and crossed the tiny lobby to the lounge. He opened the door. There, sitting on the sofa opposite the door were a very cross looking Yvette and with her, oh sugar honey ice tea! Their visitor was not the Walrus. It was *the Whale*.

Even worse, the Whale was pulling out something made of silver-coloured metal from a pocket.

Walls flung himself sideways, just in time. There was a loud explosion and the sound of breaking glass falling.

"*My Louis Quatorze mirror!*" screeched Yvette.

Yvette was neither a keep fit fanatic nor a self-defence expert. She professed to be a pacifist and her physique was on the flabby end of normal. But as feminist discourse theorists went she was surprisingly pugilistic. Indeed even while screeching the above phrase she felled the Whale with a terrific left hook.

"It's OK. I'm OK. I'm *alive!*" said Walls as he levered himself off the floor, feeling himself all over. "*Or am I?* They always say shotgun wounds are *painless*. Have I got *blood* coming out anywhere, Yvette? Am I about to drop dead like they do in films?"

"You are A1 fine!" snapped Yvette. "No danger to you whatsoever. No aim. Must have missed you by a mile! But look at what this *vandal*, this *philistine*, has done to my *Louis Quatorze* mirror! A genuine *Louis Quatorze* mirror. *Unique!* And now *destroyed!*"

"Oh my sweetness, I am so sorry!" soothed Walls, feeling truly apologetic and guilty. "It might not be beyond restoration; they are so clever. See, mostly the glass broken, not the frame. I can buy another!" said Walls, glancing at the mirror casually and then turning back to survey the scene before him. The Whale was laid out on the sofa, with a large red mark on the chin and the gun safely held in Yvette's hand.

"*Mon ange!*" he cried, even at that moment wishing that he could stop saying that phrase. "You are my heroine, my saviour, my cute, diddy and so brilliant wife! You *rescued* me! You *never even thought of yourself*!"

He opened his arms and she ran across the room into them. He hugged her, and the gun promptly fired again.

Walls leapt back from his wife's arms as what remained of the mirror fell from the wall to the floor. Parts of the frame now also left their original setting, and distributed themselves among the scattered shards of glass.

"Oops!" said Walls. "You must have hit the hook holding it up, I guess!"

He removed the gun firmly from his wife's grasp and hastily put it on a very high shelf.

"What is wrong with you, my *tiddlypoms*? Are you such a *male chauvinist* that you cannot trust a *woman* with a *firearm*?" demanded Yvette, angrily.

Fortunately for Walls he was spared from answering because at that precise point the doorbell rang again.

Walls rushed to press the intercom.

"It's Andy!" said the Walrus's voice. "I got here as soon as I could!"

"Come straight up!" said Walls. "Third floor!"

Walls pressed the release button for the front door.

"Is that *Finn*?" asked Yvette.

"No," said Walls, "It's *Andy*. He's the rowing club friend I was *expecting*. Andy, the Walrus. I'm sure you've heard me speak about him."

"So who is *this* person?" asked Yvette, who had no idea who he was talking about but decided to pretend she did.

"*Another* rowing club friend," said Walls, "The Whale."

"I thought there was only *one* of them calling in. What cute tags you all have. I must analyse them sometime," said Yvette, rather absently, as she had just thought of exactly the right sentence with which to finish the current paragraph in her paper – succinct, and yet conveying all the meaning that was required. "Does the *other* one believe in carrying arms and shooting people's mirrors out *too*?" asked Yvette.

"I do hope not," replied Walls. "The Whale was aiming at me, not the mirror. What a good thing you are so brave and I am so superfit!"

"Don't be *silly*. Clearly 'the Whale' is a narcissist with exhibitionist tendencies. That was entirely apparent while we were conversing earlier. You had caused annoyance by remaining in the bathroom for so long. Result: perfectly predictable release of frustration by demonstrating sharp shooting ability. Really, Walls, you should have warned me that the Whale was a Republican, and I would have asked that small arms be left at the door. I must get back to my paper before it becomes entirely *glacial*. Try not to irritate this *other* one as well; we could have no *house* left."

"The Whale is English, not American, and the target was *me*." Walls faltered under Yvette's glare. "Er, never mind. I and Andy, the Walrus, you know, can deal with all this. Er, you go and get on with the important things in life," said Walls to her retreating back as she wandered back to her study.

"Nonsense, Walls, my *little bunny rabbit*! *All* rowers are *American*, on rowing *scholarships*, you know. Remember to ask the *gun-toting* one to pay the full cost of replacing that mirror before leaving…"

Yvette's voice faded out as she vanished into her study and shut the door firmly behind her.

She's so *cute*, thought Walls. I do love my wife. *Adorable*! Female academics, all the same: they don't wander off their aims like us males. Mind on their work *at all times*. Yvette is *so* like Priscilla, he thought to himself, and Priscilla is very cute in her own way too. Now, if Pris had been younger and thinner, when he was staying with her he might even have considered…

There was a loud banging on the front door of the flat – the sort of sound produced by a huge ex-rower who thought he was knocking quietly and politely. There was a loud cough from the study – the sort of cough that implies that if nothing is done the person behind the cough will be bursting back out herself to deal with the interruption.

Walls rushed to open the door.

"Shhhhhh!! Ssshhh! Walrus, old man, *don't disturb Yvette*!" he said. "She's *working*."

The Walrus surveyed the scene. His eyebrows rose. His mouth dropped open.

"What the f*** has been going on?" asked the Walrus.

"Whisper!" hissed Walls. "You must *whisper*... *Yvette! Working!*"

He pointed to the study door.

"But what have you been *doing*? Is Alex *alive*? What is *happening*?" answered Andy, *sotto voce* but in very puzzled tones.

He rushed over to the Whale and began a medical check.

He straightened up. "All OK. Bad bang on the chin but should be OK. Also as loaded with alcohol as the proverbial owl. Probably ought to call an ambulance but the casualty unit won't do anything other than observation overnight, and I can do that myself just as well."

"*Where am I?*" asked the Whale, suddenly coming to and sitting bolt upright but appearing quite unfocussed.

"With *friends*, Alex," said Walls, in his best soothing tone. "With *friends*!"

"I'm *tired*," said the Whale. "I think I'll go back to sleep."

"Good plan," said Walls. "Here, let's tuck you up on this sofa. I'll wrap this throw round you! There you go!"

The Whale curled up obediently and was soon fast asleep again.

"Is that OK, going back to sleep like that?" Walls whispered to the Walrus. "Do you think we do need a doctor? Should I ring 999?"

"No, I think it's OK. Not so much the blow, more the alcohol. Also probably not been sleeping much while planning whatever has been happening here, and now the adrenaline rush from the excitement has died down. I've seen this sort of thing with Alex before," the Walrus said. "No need to call the emergency services, eh? Might ask awkward questions, you know. We don't want the *law* involved, *do we?*"

"No, no!" said Walls, suddenly considering the fact that Yvette had knocked the Whale out, even if in self-defence, and that the Whale was a Cambridge don and Andy's ex-partner and a Kings Rowing Club member and an invited guest in his and Yvette's flat – *all very awkward*.

"No! Decidedly not!" Walls said, very firmly.

At that point the doorbell rang again.

"Hi!" said Walls to the intercom.

"Thank God! You're alive. Don't do anything till I get there! Don't move!" said Barnabus' voice over the intercom.

"Shhhh!" said Walls, as quietly as he could, his mouth almost against the intercom. "Keep your voice down! *Yvette is working.*" Then he added, a little louder, "I thought you were going to wait downstairs for me to join you, Finn."

"No, Walls, I am *not* going to wait downstairs," Barnabus whispered back into the intercom. "What the **** is going on up there! Let me up there at once! I had my phone lying on my front passenger seat and it was still connected to yours. You may have thought you had cut off the phone call but you hadn't. You must have put your phone down somewhere, so it could pick up loud noises but not clear conversation. *I heard the shots*! I nearly drove off the road when I heard the first shot! And the second! I very nearly swerved into a tree. But then I heard the sound of your voice each time it happened. *Are you OK?*"

"Yes, yes, everyone is absolutely fine. But if you really insist on coming up, in contravention of the pre-declared rules of this visit in which you said you would not do so, then do come and join the party! But let me repeat, and I cannot say this too often or too emphatically, we are all in a situation code red here, and nothing to do with the shots, my stalker or any similar occurrence. No, we are on a code red because *Yvette is working,* let me repeat, *working*" replied Walls.

Walls was thinking that this was most interesting, research-wise. Buffy was exhibiting typical 'sudden traumatic event' human behaviour. Buffy's conversation was now centred purely on his own experience, he wasn't really at all interested in what had happened in the room itself; he was too busy recounting what had happened in his own car.

"Is that *Finn* making all that disturbance?" Yvette's voice floated out from her study.

"No, *cherry bun with icing on the top,*" replied Walls, giving up any hope of concealing the fact that Barnabus was in fact here, and was about to meet him again for the second time in one evening, "it is *Buffy.*"

"Bing?" called Yvette's voice. "Is he going on the half-marathon run too?"

"Buffy," corrected Walls, automatically, thinking that it was fortunate that Yvette was so immersed in her work that she must have forgotten he had already met Buffy once that day. Yvette always called Buffy 'Bing', apparently by mistake but Walls was pretty sure that she did it on purpose. He had better not annoy her by attempting to correct it yet again. Walls felt sad, as he always did when Buffy and Yvette spoke about each other. It was so unfortunate that his own two favourite people, Yvette and Buffy, did not really like *each other*. He could never understand it, but there it was.

"Did you *hear* my question, blueberry muffin?" Yvette's strident voice demanded.

"Yes, he's going on the run as well, angel food cake! Just waiting for Finn now!" Walls called back.

"Can I *remind* you that while all your friends are crowding over the apartment it is essential that you *all* keep your voices *down*? I am *trying* to work. I do hope you are all *going out again* soon," Yvette answered, and then had another thought. "*Bing* doesn't *carry arms* these days, does he? If so please ask him to leave them outside the apartment. Otherwise we may have no furnishings left."

"No, *my adorable apple pie*, he doesn't" replied Walls.

He and the Walrus looked at each other, looked at the room again, looked at the sleeping Whale, and began to explain the whole situation to each other but very, very, very quietly.

When Barnabus bounced in a few moments later they both grabbed him and put their hands over his mouth until they were sure that he had managed to fully understand that he absolutely must achieve the same pianissimo tones.

They had to exchange a very long series of whispers. Andy had to hear about the stalking of Walls by the Whale, and Walls had to tell the other two about how Yvette had thought the Whale was the intended visitor, about the shots and about Yvette's heroism. Then they all had to worry about precisely what to do next.

They all kept glancing nervously toward the study but its inhabitant appeared to be still content. They felt they could move on to what to do next without having to vacate the apartment first.

So they anxiously discussed once more, with Barnabus added this time, whether the full force of the law must be involved and whether the Whale needed to go to

Casualty, and whether in this case, if the police had not been informed by them, the casualty unit staff would believe that the Whale had tripped over and been knocked out by the edge of the coffee table rather than being punched.

Finally they all agreed that they would all make all efforts to keep the entire sequence of events away from the official legal system and that they were confident that the Walrus was enough of a medical expert and carer unless the Whale's condition worsened, in which case they would be forced to use 'coffee table on chin' route.

A loud hinting sort of cough emanated from Yvette's study. They dropped their voices lower till they could barely hear one another even with their heads very close together. The evidence of the impressive force of an annoyed Yvette was lying on the sofa in front of them to remind them of the importance of keeping her happy.

"You know what I *still* don't see?" hissed Barnabus, "I *still* don't see *why* the Whale was stalking and attacking Walls. I have searched and searched my memory and I can't remember a single incident in the rowing club or college or anywhere else that could explain it."

"Oh, I understand that one," breathed Andy "This all makes sense now! The event concerned wasn't as long ago as you think. Only last year. It was a paper that you wrote, Walls. Received a furious email tirade about it myself. Alex must have still got me on some mailing list and clearly sent the message to everyone. I should have realised, I should have known why Alex was seeking revenge. I just didn't connect it. I'm so sorry!"

"A *paper that* I *wrote?*" gasped Walls, but with a very suspiciously innocent look.

He *sounded* surprised but Barnabus was looking at him at the time. Walls looked innocent but also *furtive*. Had Walls completely omitted to tell his friend something? Had Walls done something of which he was possibly a little bit ashamed?

"Indeed, yes. Don't you recollect? You must do! You *refuted Alex's opinion*," replied Andy, "somehow. Something to do with a *paper*. Can't say I even begin to understand the finer details of the issue. I read Zoology not History, you know."

"Ah!" said Walls, trying to sound surprised, "*That* paper! *I* thought that whole incident was *closed*, but I guess, yes, it's just possible that the Whale *didn't*. It was a glorious triumph for me – newly discovered irrefutable evidence– but I suppose, yes, it was a *teeny* bit of a setback for the Whale's own theories. All the same, not my fault, the luck of the draw, you know, this sort of thing happens to everyone from time to time. You know, I was right, the Whale was wrong. I got the accolades, Alex got the brick bats. My sources were impeccable. So important with sources, check, check and check again as they say! I guess that very minor incident *might* provide some kind of explanation. Me, I'm a laid back sort , but, guys, some academics do over react, like their research was their kids. Even my own sweet Yvette, tends to get a bit wound up if anyone argues with her academic theories."

"Oh yes, *you're* laid back! You *never ever* spend *days* jumping up and down and getting all wound up about *some Australian academic*, do you, Walls?" said Barnabus, feeling satisfied that he had been entirely right about Walls having a furtive look, "Even so, Andy, you must agree, bit of an over-reaction from Alex, not safe, needs help., I mean, *actually trying to shoot* Walls. *Not* good form! Not *sporting*! Hardly the way to conduct an academic dispute."

"I'm not on *Alex's* side, Buffy," said Andy. "You mistake my intentions. I wasn't worried about *Alex*, I was worried about *whoever was about to suffer vengeance*. That is why I'm here in Oxford at all! It was just so stupid of me not to realise it was Walls. I had forgotten all about that damn paper till just now. I was just here because I was trying to save *at least one person*. I manage to save so few in my work. One person saved, that I knew *I* had saved, would be a little victory, a little success..."

The Walrus sat down abruptly and began to sob, but remembered to do so quietly.

"You know, Buffy," said Walls, "I know what to do to make up for all this. I can fix everything. What I think is I'll see if I can't get the Whale an immediate admittance to a private alcoholic rehabilitation clinic. I can afford it. Which is just as well as it *will* cost an absolute fortune. Do you think *Pay for Your Enemies* counts as *Love Your Enemies* in the sight of God? Can I get some remission from Purgatory for my other sins for this one? Like buying an indulgence? But we must all remember that the unconsciousness was *the result of falling over a rug* and hitting a coffee table corner head first. It is this injury, the fall being due to the drunkenness, that has moved us all to intervene and make the booking. There must be utterly no risk of getting my *dearest little butterfly* into trouble for assault and battery!"

Barnabus looked at Walls. Was he serious when he called overweight and clumpy 'vette his *dearest little butterfly*? His affectionate blandishments, and hers for him, *seemed* entirely sincere, but *were* they? Could his love for her really blind him that far? Or had their marriage already descended into blandishments that were a form of sarcasm?

Barnabus gave up pondering the strange relationship between Walls and Yvette, they both seemed happy enough after all. Then he thought how *very* good it was of Walls to pay for a private clinic for the Whale. *Naturally* Walls could *afford* it but that was hardly the point. The Whale had tried to kill him for a completely irrational reason. Barnabus wondered if he himself have been so munificent under the circumstances. Barnabus supposed Walls must be have a euphoric sense of relief at discovering who his stalker was and thus forgiving the Whale was not just a demonstration of his Christianity, for Walls was a sincere and devoted Catholic, but genuinely from his heart. Walls must, after all, be *so* relieved to know that his stalker was a comparatively harmless academic with a grudge, that he wouldn't be seeing any more bodies, that even what he had seen not only definitely existed but wasn't even dead and that there was a *reason* for the stalking

"You're a *good* guy, Walls," he hissed. "I'm sure you aren't headed for Purgatory, whether you pay for the Whale or not! But if it did all slip out I *don't* really see that Yvette could get into trouble for *self-defence*."

"I hope you don't think I am headed directly for Hell rather than Purgatory," Walls joked, in a sepulchral stage whisper and with a glance towards the study door, for another loud cough had just been heard from behind it, but he smiled at Barnabus to show he didn't really mean it.

Walls continued, "Whether there is any risk to Yvette from giving Alex a good knockout punch on the chin or not, I'd rather keep it all out of the public arena. Yvette would not like featuring in the local press for anything other than academic accolades I fear. Better get on so we can stop disturbing her work as soon as soon We need to make a push to get the Whale refloated from the alcoholic shore. No, that's the wrong way round! Dried out, not afloat. I'd better go and ring some rich alcoholic friends and ask their advice about clinics and then ring the clinics and then…"

"Don't you need a doctor's recommendation to get people admitted? Even for a private clinic?" asked the Walrus. "They all have such big waiting lists you'll never get an instant admission…"

"Don't fret yourself. I've not tried this before but I expect it's like everything else in life," Walls replied, confidently.

"In what sense?" asked the Walrus.

"Everything comes to those that have enough money to pay through the nose for it without them having to do any waiting first," answered Walls and grinned.

"But *you* don't have to pay! *I* can pay for it, just as well as you can. You *know* that. Let *me* pay!" said the Walrus, raising his head. "I feel it's more *my* responsibility."

"You do your charitable stuff when you are working. Let me do this bit. Besides I bet I can afford to pay better than you can afford to pay," said Walls, sounding like a child in a playground exercising one-upmanship, "I'm sure I can."

'Whatever! I can still afford it without even noticing" replied Andy, indignantly, also descending to playground level, "Any amount you might have more than me after that doesn't matter. I'm sure my family is as rich as your family anyway. Depending, naturally," he added, in a way that made Barnabus giggle, and got him glares from both of the others, "On the exact position of the pound with respect to the dollar."

"Keep your hair on! I said I'll take this one" said Walls, as if he was referring to picking up the tab for their evening drinks in the pub, "I might not even have to work out myself. I can probably get one of my mother's charities to donate towards the cost. Ma runs a lot of charitable foundations. There *must* be one for *academic alcoholics*, I would think. She's always making me fork out walloping contributions to them. I'll swear it was a foundation for heroin-addicted bunny rabbits last time Ma asked. Can it, Andy! Just forget the cost! Let's concentrate on Step One, find a clinic place. I'll go and start those calls."

Barnabus looked from one of them to the other and tried not to giggle again at the thought that he had forgotten that they both lived on a different planet to him when it came to money, and then scolded himself for, after all, he knew how very rich he was himself compared to so many people.

Walls crept off into the bedroom, where he could risk speaking a little louder without Yvette hearing him, as otherwise people would not be able to understand him on the phone.

Barnabus looked at Andy, who had got up from their huddle and was now slumped in a chair. Poor Andy: Andy the Good, Andy the Kind, Andy the Saviour of the Sick and Helpless. Barnabus felt overcome with guilt for the way he had misjudged the Walrus. He had had him down as Andy the Devil Incarnate when he was a Saint. Poor man too, still loving the Whale *so much*. Barnabus' eyes filled with water for a moment for he could now see clearly how very much the Walrus loved his Whale. He thought of how much he himself loved Angel and how glad he was that she would be back home so soon. He had missed her and the children so much this week, when they were away it was like a physical pain in his chest, always. Then he thought that actually it was a very good thing that Angel *was* away *this* week, for she would have been very cross about him getting involved in this investigation. Then he thought how wrong Angel was in this opinion. For Walls, his dear best friend, could have been *dead*. Walls had been quite right – the Whale was dangerous. Walls really had been in peril of his life, the maniac had tried to shoot Walls from close range! But poor Andy *still* loved his Whale, entirely, completely and for ever, till death us do part. How terrible; how truly terrible. The poor man! Such suffering!

Barnabus put his hand on the Walrus's shoulder.

"It's OK, old man," he said, "it's all good. Everything is good. And, and, if this clinic works out, and there is no reason why it shouldn't, you never know… the Whale will be better and stop doing such, er, such *silly* things and maybe, maybe *you and the Whale will have a second chance?*"

"*God forbid!*" said the Walrus, fervently. "Marrying Alex once was *stupid. Twice* would be *absolutely completely and utterly insane*! I am not in love any more, don't imagine that I am; I just feel sort of responsible. So relieved, so relieved nothing worse happened."

Then the Walrus sighed, "Funny kind of *holiday* I've had, reading that terrible Facebook posting, not being able to find the Whale, not being able to find out who it was that was under threat, not getting anywhere with any of it and being so afraid all the time that I was going to be too late! I have to go back to work *so* soon. I needed a *rest*. The funniest thing is, and this is really hilarious Buffy, after all that effort and bother from both of us, it wasn't me or you who saved Walls, it was *himself* and *Yvette!*"

"But it *was* you," comforted Barnabus. "If you hadn't said what you did to Mama about reading the Whale's Facebook page we would never have thought of doing so, which was really stupid of both of us, and we would never have twigged who the stalker was, and then Walls *would* have got shot because he wouldn't have been on his guard!"

"So it *was* me who saved him?" said the Walrus.

Barnabus nodded, *"Most definitely!"*

"One for me, nought for the Bear!" said Andy, joyfully. "I win *at last*! I lose *so* often, *so* often. When I am working, I lose far more times than I win. I almost never win. But today, today, I am the Victor Ludorum!"

"Absolutely, old chap" said Barnabus, who had been so excited by the opening phrase that he had not listened to the rest of Andy's speech, "*What* bear?"

"*The* Bear! The Enemy! When I'm working I have this image of the illness and suffering we are fighting. I see it as a real animal, a bear, floating above the patients trying to kill them," replied Andy.

"Real bears aren't *so* bad," said Barnabus, suddenly thinking that bears were beautiful and no better and no worse than any other animal, and also thinking fondly of his own much-loved teddy bear, Horatio Bear, who was now exiled to a high shelf in his and Angel's bedroom where the children could not get at it.

"But this is not a *real* bear! It is a *devil* bear! *Satan's bear* competing against me, against us, *the devil is loose and has great wrath because he has but a short time*!" said Andy, slightly misquoting the book of Revelations.

"Er, tell me," said Barnabus, wishing so much that Walls was still within earshot to hear this bit about the Bear and the Walrus, Walls would *have* to acknowledge the triumph of Wikipedia now, "I was just wondering...does your bear by any chance look like *a polar bear*?"

"No," replied Andy, "it's bright red with flames coming out of its mouth."

"Ah!" said Barnabus, disappointed. "So Wikipedia *isn't* a complete oracle after all."

"Beg pardon?" said the Walrus, surprised.

Barnabus was about to say "nothing important" but was saved from this because at that precise moment Yvette's study door opened and a magisterial figure stomped out through it.

They both quailed. Headmistresses from their past floated before their eyes.

"You are *disturbing* me!" Yvette said, each syllable enunciated very clearly. "I am in the process of writing a groundbreaking paper on the subject of the desire and love of material possessions, indeed the very existence of material possessions in the life of the human, having being entirely created as a construct of Western male discourse. Without the Western male voice we would still be living happy and untrammelled, free from these material millstones around our necks. And *you* are interrupting this *vital* work."

"I'm so sorry!" they both said, together, feeling the guilt of the world on their shoulders.

"Bing, it is *always* the same! *Whenever* you contact Walls *something of this nature* occurs. You have disturbed my Herculean labours on *multiple* occasions, so I judge this offence to be unquestionably *mainly* your responsibility, although *you...*" She looked at Andy, "...*whoever you are*, are also guilty. Why have you not yet all departed to participate in this *exercise fest*? I understood your presence here to be entirely temporary. And yet here is another one of you *lolling* about on my *specially designed* sofa! I do trust no *damage* is occurring to the *fabric*. It is *not* intended for use as a *bed*."

Yvette was staring at the sleeper as if the Whale had just materialised there and was someone whom she had never previously encountered.

"*Buffy*," said Barnabus, automatically, but without much hope of Yvette ever getting his name right. He was deeply impressed with the fact Yvette had clearly forgotten ever having seen the Whale before, let alone remembering having any part in the unconscious state of same. Yvette was not *like* Priscilla, he thought, she was *even worse* than Priscilla. She was completely and totally disconnected from the real world.

"*Bing!*" corrected Yvette, in a tone that suggested shock about his ignorance in not knowing his own name. "*Where is* Walls? *Why* has he not yet *taken you all out* to have your little run?"

"Walls is just in the bathroom, *Yvonne*," replied Barnabus, naughtily, as he did not want to risk her storming into the bedroom and interrupting Walls' phone calls, "And we have not yet left because *Finn* has not yet arrived. As soon as he *does* we will depart pronto!"

Not all lies, the bit about departing is *true*, Barnabus thought cheerfully to himself, because Finn is most unlikely to appear any time soon, although it would be unfortunate if he did decide to drop in for some other reason and they all had to decamp into the corridor.

"*Yvette* not *Yvonne!*" Yvette snapped, looking on the verge of fainting with the horror of Barnabus' error, "This is *typical* of a Western male, failing to make the *slightest* effort to get another person's name *correct*. A person's *name*, Bing, is the essence of their *being*, even though it is a *constructed* essence. Failing to remember it displays total selfish disregard for the rest of humanity!"

At that moment she caught sight of the blank space where the mirror had hung, and her memory of recent events was retriggered, "My unique, wonderful, amazing, beautiful mirror!" she wailed. "Destroyed by the despoiler on the sofa due to Walls' inability to leave a bathroom and take care of social niceties with his own comrades. Has he learnt from this disaster? No, he has not. Yet again he is *in the bathroom* leaving me, *me*, who is already so hard pressed and overcome with my gargantuan labours, to cease this vital quest in order to man the *trenches* of social intercourse. I must remonstrate with him immediately."

She stepped forward, evidently heading towards the totally empty bathroom.

"No, no, it's OK!" cried Andy, desperately, lest she find that Walls was not there. "Honestly, we can take care of our own social niceties, Buffy and I, all by ourselves. We'll manage. I beg you not to incommode yourself any further, Mrs Walls, please, please return to your most important work!"

Yvette's face now registered such deep shock that Barnabus and Andy wondered what was going to happen. Was she going to merely faint, actually drop dead from apoplexy, or go completely ballistic? Yvette selected the third option.

"Where *does* Walls find you all from?" she demanded. "*Rowers*! All the *same*! So lacking in *finesse*! So uncouth! I assume Walls has your email addresses, so I will send him a *most edifying paper* with instructions to forward it to all of you. I will send it via Walls because I do not *at all* wish to risk any of you gaining access to my own email address and sending me any form of group transmitted chauvinist junk. I am beyond shocked to discover that *anyone* could commit *so many felonies* against womankind in one *sentence*. Women are *not*, repeat *not*, under any circumstances whatsoever, the *property of their husband*. Bending to the social convention of taking his name should never occur. The Western male must not be allowed to force his partner into compliance with this abusive form of domestic slavery! And you should at least remember to use the right name construct! Walls' is not my angel heart's surname!"

She paused and swept them both with a withering look. She then turned this look upon the happily unaware and slumbering Whale.

"I cannot remain for one moment longer in the same room as the three of you. I *must* return to my *life's purpose*. Kindly refrain from making *any sounds whatsoever* in the interim before you *finally* leave the apartment," she said.

She gave a large sighing sob of self-pity and then slowly and dramatically turned away from them and went back into her study. The door slammed behind her.

Andy and Barnabus looked at each other and then both hastily grabbed a finely embroidered silk cushion each from the pile on the nearest chair and stuffed them into their mouths. They rolled around the pure wool carpet together, limbs flailing, the sound of their laughter only just suppressed by the cushions.

Barnabus recovered first and prodded Andy, who was still chortling. "Andy, please, *please*, stop! She *is* going to hear us if we don't."

At this sobering thought Andy stopped laughing and sat upright, staring nervously at the study door.

"Kind of boggles the brain, doesn't it," he whispered. "Walls, though, *why*? Why did he choose her? He could have married *any* woman on the planet and, er…"

Barnabus sighed. "Walls is my best friend and I'd like to pretend I don't know what you mean but… I think he finds it refreshing not to have a woman who simply falls at his feet, and when push comes to shove, he really, really does *love* her, you know! On top of which Walls probably *likes* the idea that he constructed the whole world with his male discourse – he's such an egotist, that sort of theory would appeal to him, you know! He's so naïve too, he's such an infant inside his big frame, he wouldn't see the insult; just the glory of the thought that he could construct a whole culture purely by speaking!"

Then Barnabus remembered that he had some real guilt to assuage. He held out his hand to Andy. "Andy, I've got to make a mega confession and offer you a mega apology. I know you are going to laugh at me, and everyone else is going to laugh at me for evermore too, but I have to say this because I hope we can be best mates from now on. I thought it was *you* stalking Walls. I, I'm so sorry!"

Andy took his hand and shook it enthusiastically and very solemnly and kindly.

"Thank you, thank you, Buffy. I won't laugh, not at all; anyone could have made that mistake. You know, me appearing like that so coincidentally. But I have to apologise too. I should have told you two the truth, when we had dinner at the Bear. I should have told you I was only in Oxford to try to stop Alex doing something stupid, and then we could have all joined forces. As it is, Walls nearly got murdered. That would have been my fault!"

The eyes of the Walrus filled with tears. Barnabus patted him on the back.

'Don't worry about it. Walls is fine. And you saved him too, remember. It was all OK. No damage done. Very understandable that you didn't tell us. Not a problem. Big hug!" Barnabus said, opening his arms.

They gave each other a bear hug. A *bear* hug, thought Barnabus, *more bears!* Perhaps it was he himself, Barnabus, who was the polar bear, but the polar bear was hugging the Walrus, not attacking him. The polar bear was the Walrus's friend, not his enemy. Wikipedia was wrong. Then Barnabus realised that it was very late indeed and that he was very tired and that nothing he was thinking was really making any sense at all anymore. The sofa looked very appealing, he could just lie down and... No, he had to stay awake, coffee, that was what he needed.

"I say" Barnabus whispered, "Do you think we could go and raid Walls and Yvette's kitchen? Or would that be an insult to feminism as well? No, it must be OK: men must be allowed to find that their place belongs in the kitchen, *surely*? See, I'm *really* thirsty and tired. We could see if we could construct some coffee with our Western male discourse. I seem to remember we would be aided by the fact that Walls and Yvette's kitchen is trammelled with a top of the range coffee machine."

"Good idea…" said Andy, in an unwisely loud voice. There was a very threatening cough from the study. Andy lowered his voice, "…provided our coffee-creating male discourse doesn't make *any noise whatsoever*," he finished, "I hope it's a very, very quiet operationally coffee machine. If not do you think there is any chance of finding some instant coffee and a kettle, or would that be an ideologically unsound male construct? At worst we can always chew some coffee beans and drink a glass of water with them."

They smiled at each other and tiptoed conspiratorially towards the kitchen.

Chapter 10

The following day Barnabus went straight to the Old Vicarage as soon as he had finished work so that he could give his mama the benefit of his own delightful company.

"I am *here*, Mama," he cried, "to give you *my full and complete and utterly undivided devoted attention* and also to eat some of that very delicious casserole which I can smell in the oven!"

"Lovely!" she said. "I'm so glad you are here. I've made far too much casserole and your father is working late again."

"Are you sure there is enough for me? Dad will need some when he gets in, won't he?" asked Barnabus.

"I made so much that there's plenty for about *five* of us; I got entirely carried away with the quantities," his mama replied, "So difficult to make meals just for two of us, I've never really get used to it."

Barnabus beamed. "We *never* have casseroles in our house, beautiful Mama. There isn't time to cook them after work!" he said.

"Don't get *too* excited yet," said his mama. "It has at least another half an hour of cooking to go yet."

"But I not just here to cadge dinner, although I will admit I did hope to achieve that aim, I am mainly here to give you my *devoted, full, utter and complete attention*," said Barnabus, "Therefore the half an hour will be a wonderful opportunity for me to do something for you by making you a cup of coffee and we can eat some of your cake to go with it and have a chat while we wait. You have got cake, haven't you? You *must* have!"

He started taking lids off tins and was delighted to find *three* cakes, he cut them both a slice of each one and then put the kettle on and started waving cups about with his mouth crammed full of one of the slices.

So it was Barnabus told Elodea the slightly crumb impeded story of Walls, the Whale and the Walrus, from the second discovery of a body in Walls college room' right up to the account of himself and Andy nervously trying to make coffee silently in Yvette and Walls' kitchen, which section made Elodea laugh very much.

Barnabus did, indeed, *beg* his mama *never* to mention that he and Walls had been fooled by the 'person behind the door' trick and she assured him that her lips were sealed. But his predictions that she would tell his father were totally justified as naturally she told John all about it as soon as he got in because she did count John as 'anyone' but as an extension of herself. Equally naturally John told Elizabeth who told Paris. Thus the story did, just as Barnabus had feared, appear regularly from then on as a family anecdote to be included in the embarrassing 'family story telling' which always occurred during the massed Smith family Christmas lunch. Barnabus, being the youngest, already featured in far too many of the *other* humiliating tales that his elder siblings recounted. Barnabus, at this dire discovery on its first retelling, comforted himself with the knowledge that this made things only slightly worse than they had been previously and that at least this was a *new* story. Then he wished that he drank alcohol so he could take several glasses full before Christmas Lunch each year. For now he contented himself with texting to Angel 'Please can we go abroad for a fortnight next

Christmas?" She ignored this as she knew perfectly well that he did not really mean it.

For now when Barnabus had finished his long, complicated and exciting account, Elodea, who was sitting on a backless kitchen stool and had been leaning forwards to listen more attentively, lolled back against the jumbled pile of objects on the nearest work surface and considered it all. An elastic band, a badge, three pens and a parish magazine all escaped and hit the floor but they both ignored them.

"I still don't quite understand all of it. How did the Whale get into Walls' apartment and college room?" she asked.

"It wasn't as hard as it seemed. The Whale already had full intimate geographic knowledge of Kings. The apartments were also much less of a bother than you might think because the caretaker happens by chance to be the widower of the Whales' scout at college. Very tragically Mrs Brown, that's the caretaker's wife, died of a heart attack while cleaning someone's room in college, and the Whale took the bother to go to the funeral – the only student who did so – which made a sort of bond between them. So, the Whale popped in to the apartments to see Mr Brown, switching the CCTV off on the way past it, and then slipped back in later knowing Walls was heading for home. Alex was pretty sure that Mr Brown would never have noticed that the CCTV was off and also, because of his track record at college and from the discussion with Mr Brown, that Walls would have left his apartment door unlocked and the security off. Walls is such a twit about remembering to lock things! Alex had also checked that Yvette was missing from the scene."

"Mr Brown said the CCTV was defective" said Elodea.

"Probably is. Might not have even needed to be tinkered with. But the Whale probably also bribed Mr Brown to keep him quiet on the whole subject," said Barnabus. "Anyway, the Whale having been to Kings knew where you could get in and out without using the Lodge, and Walls had left his room door unlocked. Alex knew he never locks things. Not really difficult to get into one of Walls' rooms. He is an idiot when it comes to things like that."

"See, I was *right*! I *told* you," she said, triumphantly, "You were so wrong about Andy. He is a good and well behaved hero and you were making an error."

"I know you did, Mama, and I admit it, I was entirely wrong about that. What's more Walls told me that his stalker was dangerous and I said 'rubbish' to that too. So I was completely wrong about that as well. Do you know that I am having to deal with the *crushing* sensation of having spent a *week* being *utterly wrong*. Do you know how that *feels*?"

"*Naturally* not, for, as you must know, *mothers are never wrong*. But, smallest son, I always think you are a wonderful person whether you are wrong or right!" she replied.

"Thank you, Mama," he said, "but I feel *lowered* all the same. I didn't do anything of any use in the entire investigation."

"But you *did*!" she protested. "Without you there would have been *no* investigation and Walls would *not* have been on his guard and he would have got *shot*!"

"Well, I'm not too sure about that, because…" said Barnabus.

"*Nonsense*! You were the most important person in the whole story. I am your mama and so I know how brilliant and wonderful and vital to any enterprise you are!" said his mama, meaning it too. Before Barnabus could protest about his lack of importance again, another thought struck her. "So, just to check this point, *Alex* is called *de Ville* as well, still, yes?"

"Yes! Obviously!" said Barnabus.

"Ah ha!" she said while thinking a*nother "A Devil"* among us!

"What?" asked Barnabus.

But she was already continuing "I meant to tell you this before. I was going to text you this afternoon as soon as I remembered but something distracted me: the onions were about to catch fire, I think. I remembered *who the Whale is*! I don't know how I could have *ever* forgotten. The *Rowing Club Dinner* when you were in the *first year*!"

"*Precisely*!" said Barnabus, "I told you that you knew! Finally I am *right* about something!"

They both giggled at their own recollections of the fateful event.

"Now tell me," said his mama, leaning forward and lowering her voice slightly, "as well as being called 'A de Ville' was Alex, the Whale *by any chance* wearing *red* yesterday? But maybe the red doesn't matter. Clearly a Cambridge don *is* a great *cader* so if that's what Mrs Shipman meant we are covered already."

"*Mrs Shipman*? You aren't about to tell me one of her off the wall prophecies has come *true*, are you? I guess it was about Satan and *that* bit is obvious, A Devil – the Whale and the Walrus were always getting twigged about being *two devils in collusion* when they *were* together. But wearing *red*? I suppose good old-fashioned devils *are* clothed in scarlet, aren't they? Oh yes, *very* Mrs Shipman *again.* I hate to satisfy these conditions, I really do, but if you must know the Whale *was* wearing a red T-shirt *as it happens.*"

"*My goodness,*" breathed his mama, in a satisfied way, "Mrs Shipman was *right* this time! Absolutely accurate to the last detail! Mrs Shipman *is* an oracle after all! But how did she know? How could she have known? *Wait till you hear this!*"

"*No*, Mama, there was an oracle in this case but it was not *Mrs Shipman*. The amazing oracle in this case is *Wikipedia*! *Wait till you hear this!*" countered her son.

"Age before beauty. You are the youngest; you can go first!" said his mama.

He stuck his tongue out at her but told her all about Wikipedia's omnificence.

Then Elodea told him all about Mrs Shipman's warning note and how it had all turned out to be true.

They were both sufficiently and also satisfactorily impressed with each other's tales.

"*Well!*" said Elodea when he reached the end of his.

"*My!*" said Barnabus, when she reached the end of hers.

Then they both agreed that it was a good thing that Angel and John were not listening to their silly conversation, for both Angel and John were very serious people with staid minds that would never admit to Wikipedia being oracular and definitely not to people being oracular and especially not Mrs Shipman. Fascinating and wonderful discussions about 'genuine' foretellings, that were not true unless the prophecies are bent carefully to the circumstances, can be completely ruined by the presence in the room of someone with a *really rational mind*.

"Does Wikipedia make any mention of a walrus *visiting Oxford*?" giggled Elodea. "That would top off the whole thing! I suppose the poor walrus would be a bit lost though. How far south do they live?"

"I expect the University Museum has at least one walrus in it. Didn't you notice the other day?" asked Barnabus.

"Not a *dead* one, silly, a *live* one! Has a live walrus ever swum up the Isis by mistake, do you think?" asked Elodea.

"What, zooming up it to escape from a killer whale that was charging along behind it?" asked Barnabus.

"No, just *swimming*, you know, exploring the Thames, wondering if Oxford would be a pleasant place to live. Do they only live in the Arctic Ocean or do they swim about *further south*?" demanded Elodea.

"Just in the Arctic; I'm *sure* of it!" said Barnabus, making the whole thing up.

"No, no, I'm sure they do occur further south, I seem to remember reading something about it. Hang on!" said Elodea.

By now they were both tapping away at the screens on their phones.

"I'm *right*! I'm *right*!" cried Elodea, triumphantly. "You didn't read the Wikipedia page very carefully, did you?"

"That's not *fair*!" said Barnabus. "They don't come *much* further south. Definitely no mention of Oxford!"

223

"They do come further south than the *Arctic* though. And they *used* to come down as far as Nova Scotia, and Nova Scotia is further south than Oxford; so there! And if a Walrus had been wandering around on this side of the Atlantic then it could have swum round the south coast and then it *could* have come steaming up the Thames!" crowed Elodea.

"Nova Scotia is *not* further south than Oxford!" said Barnabus. "I'm sure it isn't! It's in Canada, that must be further north…"

He tapped his phone again. Then…

"Oh no, that's *absolutely unfair*! How did *you* know *that*?" he demanded. "How many *more* times can I be wrong this week? I am becoming a useless and hopeless failure who knows nothing at all."

Elodea tried to soothe his hurt feelings. "Very strict geography teacher at my school. That's why. But isn't modern life wonderful? We can just stand here and look everything up on our phones whereas time was when we would have had to –"

"Walk all the way to *a computer* to find out!" said Barnabus finishing the sentence for her, "*Very* true! And the Internet used to be *so* much *slower*. It took *ages*."

"Stop making me feel so *old*," she groaned. "*I* was going to say, we would have had to go and get an encyclopaedia out to find out. One printed on paper that is. It was *dangerous* in the old days, you know, my child; Encyclopaedias were *dreadfully* heavy if you dropped them on your foot. Also if your parents didn't own a full-sized encyclopaedia then people had to go *all the way to the library* to look up things like this. We are all so much better informed now."

"Or worse informed. There's a lot of duff nonsense on the Internet and people always seem to read that in preference to proper research, and then plaster 'facts' all over Facebook," said Barnabus. "Must drive real experts and academics round the bend."

"Hang on! You aren't that young! *You* can also remember the days before the Internet was generally available. Or should be able to do so. Meanwhile, speaking of research, what *was* it in Walls' research that upset the Whale so much? He may have refuted Alex's ideas in a paper but surely that happens all the time. New evidence emerges, new ideas, new theories?" said Elodea.

"Oh, it was all nonsense really. You know how precious academics are about their research. However it was the *reason* why he was able to get hold of the evidence-busting material that totally unhinged the Whale," said Barnabus.

Barnabus stopped and showed no signs of saying any more on the subject.

"Come on; I am all agog, you *cannot* stop there! What was it *exactly* that Walls did?" demanded Elodea. "No casserole, otherwise!"

"OK, Mama, you win. It went like this. They were both researching who had really bankrolled a little revolution that happened in some tiny and insignificant country but subsequently had more far-reaching globally political consequences than anyone could have imagined. They both knew there was a vital letter about this in a private collection in the USA somewhere. But the Whale couldn't trace it. The Whale's theory on who had bank rolled the revolution was excellent and without this letter it had quite sufficient evidence to back it up. But Walls, who had the somewhat unfair advantage of being a very rich American himself, happened to be able to locate the private collector through a family connection of his. He also had enough money to persuade the owner to not just show him the letter but actually sell it to him so he could have it properly verified. This took a mound of money as the collector was very possessive. Walls refused to tell me who the collector actually was. He said he had promised to keep their identity secret. But what was inside the letter *completely* blew the Whale's theory out of the sky. Result: one very pleased Walls, who knew the evidence presented in his paper was unquestionably and undeniably true, and one very angry, disappointed and disgruntled Whale, whose brilliant piece of research had been destroyed for ever by Walls."

"But there is still something else I don't understand," said Elodea. "Why didn't Walls call the police? He is so *keen* on calling the police usually. Under these circumstances surely he *should* have? Shouldn't he?" she said.

Barnabus gave her a sideways look. Had she guessed the whole *truth*? Surely that was impossible?

"He was worried about Yvette, bless him. He thought Yvette might get arrested for punching the Whale, and he was prepared to keep the law out of the picture in order to save his wife. It's OK though; the Whale couldn't remember anything whatsoever about the previous evening so the 'tripping over the rug' story is quite safe," replied Barnabus, crossing his fingers behind his back.

"I do hope Alex never *remembers* exactly what happened. It *would* be terrible if Yvette *did* get arrested!" Elodea replied, but then added, "But she wouldn't. Would she? It was self-defence. She wouldn't have got charged for disarming someone who was carrying a live fire arm and had just fired it at her husband. Walls must *know* that. What if *Yvette* tells everyone else about it instead though?"

"It's OK. Yvette was in the throes of writing a paper. She didn't even seem to remember flooring the Whale only half an hour after she had done it." said Barnabus, "Although she isn't likely to ever forget about that mirror. I suppose she might tell someone about the mirror and then remember the rest. But her account would be quite incoherent to anyone normal anyway and if she tells other crazy academics it wouldn't matter. Yvette blamed Walls for the whole shooting event because she thought he had neglected his guest and felt that any resultant anger on the Whale's part was fully justified by Walls being such a shockingly bad host."

"But don't you think that Alex *should* have been arrested for trying to *murder* Walls, however sympathetic we all feel about the alcohol problems and the academic repudiation?" asked Elodea, who was still anxious about Walls' safety, "What if the Whale lapses back into alcoholism and *really* kills someone else?"

"Mama, if I tell you the *whole truth* please promise that you will *never, ever,* tell a living soul! Not even *Dad*." said Barnabus, solemnly.

"Ooh, yes, *do* tell!" said Elodea. "I won't breathe a *word*!"

Naturally she regaled John with this story too when he got in that evening and also swore him to secrecy about these particular facts. In this case it worked. John was quite happy to promise never to reveal *these* details because he had stopped listening to his wife's babbling, as he termed it, some time before and had no idea what she had been saying for at least fifteen minutes. He had been thinking deeply theoretically physical thoughts while making encouraging conversational noises whenever there seemed to be a silence.

"It wasn't a *real* gun, and there were *no* bullets. It was only a starting pistol loaded with blanks," said Barnabus. "Walls realised what it was the second he saw it in *Yvette*'s hand but he didn't want to tell Yvette."

"But if it wasn't a real gun, why did the mirror break and why didn't Walls want to tell Yvette?" demanded Elodea.

"The mirror broke, Mama, because Walls, being not only a gymnast but also a big headed show-off, did not simply throw himself sideways to miss the shot in the way that any normal person would. No, being Walls, he turned a beautiful cartwheel. Not only was that a singularly stupid way to throw oneself to the ground while trying to avoid a bullet but he hit the mirror with one of his gigantic cartwheeling feet. He knew he had kicked it but at first he thought the mirror had *been shot as well*. Until he saw the gun in Yvette's hand afterwards."

"But wouldn't a cartwheel risk putting some of yourself back in the way of the shot again?" asked Elodea.

"Precisely! And so I pointed out to him. He tried saying that he was too short of space for a simple fling to the ground and then when I told him that was nonsense he said he had been a little temporarily confused by being shot at. But the truth is that he is a shocking show-off who couldn't stop making an exhibition of himself even if it meant he got murdered."

Elodea laughed, then added, "I do hope he found your lecture funny, Barnabus, darling. Poor Walls! He must have been in a complete panic. He did well to do anything even *vaguely* sensible. Really, you are horrible to him sometimes!"

"Oh Mama! He didn't *mind*! He is just as bad; he is always telling me off too. He keeps telling me that I am unfit and flabby!" retorted Barnabus.

"That is quite possibly *true* in your case though," said Elodea, heartlessly, prodding him in the ribs. "Maybe I shouldn't feed you any casserole after all."

"Ouch!" protested Barnabus. "I am *not* flabby, Mama. You know that perfectly well without poking me about!"

"But that doesn't explain the *effect* of the *second* shot. Why did the mirror *fall off the wall* when the second shot was fired?" demanded Elodea.

"Well, Walls was by then already in the position of not wanting to tell Yvette that it wasn't a real gun, because she was so furious about the mirror being broken that he didn't want to tell her that he himself was responsible. So when the gun fired again he leapt backwards as if surprised by the shot, so he was able to give the mirror a good deliberate clout with his shoulder," explained Barnabus. "That made it fall off the wall, and then he pretended that the second shot had hit it."

"See, Walls is *very* resourceful in an emergency! But I don't see how he recognised that it wasn't a real gun. Starting pistols surely look much the same? *Don't* they?" asked Elodea.

"Well, yes, they do, but the reason that Walls recognised this one was because it *belonged to him*!" said Barnabus. "It's a quite distinctive one, with a teeny little Kings crest of arms emblazoned on one side, and also it's only half silver – the other half is bright blue to comply with firearm regulations. The Whale had opportunistically filched it while in the apartment pretending to be a corpse and then loaded it before returning there with every intention of scaring Walls stiff. Yvette didn't recognise it at all, but then I'm not sure Yvette would recognise Walls if she met him in a strange place. She's worse than Priscilla for that."

"But whatever was Walls doing owning a starting pistol that looked like that?" asked Elodea.

"A fitness fanatic like Walls? He probably fires it to start himself off on jogs!" said Barnabus glibly.

Elodea glared at him, "*And*? she said, "Why did he put a coat of arms on it then?"

"Oh, he's very loyal to our college, you know! Fond of the place. Why *not* have one looking like that?" asked Barnabus.

Her basilisk stare continued. His courage broke.

"OK, OK, he received it as a *special award* for his *brilliance at sport* for college. He didn't get it for *rowing* though, otherwise *obviously* I would own one myself in that case. Walls *runs* too, as you know, and he got awarded it by the Kings Athletics Club for winning some race or other" said Barnabus.

"So, the Whale *was* only intending to *frighten* Walls after all. What a relief! Not quite *so* psychotic as it appeared. You *have* told Andy that too, haven't you? You see, when the Whale comes out of rehab and is all better they can be reconciled and live happily ever after, and…" Elodea's eyes grew misty with the beauty of her own fantasy.

"Mama! *No!*" Barnabus interrupted. "Andy knows what the Whale *is* now. He doesn't *want* to get back together. He *told* me so! Also we can't tell him *either* because I *convinced* him he had *saved Walls' life*, and he loses so many patients when he is working that saving one person made him *really happy. Don't* tell him. *Please*!"

"OK. But you are yet again *wrong*, completely wrong; I am sure you are. I am quite positive that Andy *wasn't* just chasing Alex round Oxford because he was worried about the possible victim; he was hunting the Whale with deep love in his heart!" said Elodea. "I won't tell him though. In fact I won't tell *anyone* in case *Yvette* finds out. She might divorce Walls for his deceitful mirror-breaking, and Walls would be devastated because he really, really loves her even if she is a rather odd person. We must all be thankful that we don't all love the same people for it would be so awkward if we did. In any case I don't suppose I'll ever meet Andy again so I'm not *likely* to even have a chance to tell him as he's off abroad working again next week, isn't he?"

"By the way, I meant to say, I forgot entirely Andy sent *you* his *love* and said he'd tell you next time he is in Oxford and maybe you could go round a museum again, he said he had enjoyed it" said Barnabus, as she finally ran out of breath and he managed to get a sentence in.

"Oh, how *sweet* of him!" said Elodea, blushing just a little for no reason at all.

Luckily for Elodea a shrill peeping sound broke out right underneath Barnabus before he noticed the blush. Barnabus leapt up in surprise.

"Oh, *the casserole*!" cried Elodea. "It's *ready*! I forgot I had put the timer down on that stool! You were sitting on it."

"I thought it was just a *magazine* I was sitting on!" cried Barnabus.

His mama swept a current affairs magazine, a gardening catalogue, the morning's newspaper and a bank statement off the stool to reveal the kitchen timer lying beneath them.

"I was just reading a few things while I waited for the casserole to cook," she said. "I must have been putting them down on top of the timer. What a good thing we were in here when the timer went off, or it might have taken me weeks to find it the next time I wanted to use it. I would never have remembered putting it down on that stool."

"I do *love* you, Mama!" said Barnabus. "You are unique and perfect...! Just a minute though!"

"What now?" asked Elodea.

"*You* are calling the Whale '*Alex*', and you don't *like* abbreviated names or nicknames. You *never* use them unless their owner insists, like with *Walls* because he prefers that to Sebastian, and *Angel* because she doesn't like Holly... Ah ha! You can't *remember* what Alex is short for, *can* you?"

"I'm not sure I ever *knew*," she replied. "You probably always all called Alex 'the *Whale*', and anyway Alex can be an *entire* name! I was *assuming* it was! Like Andy, that *is* his entire name, *you* know that."

"But he was only named Andy because his father couldn't remember how to spell Andrusha when he went to register him and thought that would do as a short form of the originally intended name. Andy always says that his mother has never ever forgiven his father for that slip up. Alex *is* an abbreviation. And I'm *not* going to tell you! I'm *not* going to tell you!" he crowed, annoyingly. "Let's see if you can remember! Good for your brain at your age!"

"You are *so mean*, Barnabus! Not to say *very* rude! I am *not* that old!" she said. "You'll be lucky if I give you *any* casserole now!"

"But you *will*, *won't* you? Dearest sweetest little Mama!" he cajoled. "Rather than risk *that* I will *tell* you the answer immediately!"

"*No*, don't tell me! For you have set me a challenge and I am going to remember i *all by myself*!" she said. "Just go and lay the table, would you?"

She told herself that this was not going to be a problem, she would think about that Rowing Club Dinner again later, when he had gone home and stopped bouncing around distracting her. That dinner must be the clue to it all. Then she would remember.

They had a merry meal and talked of many things and Elodea felt happy because one of her family was giving her their full attention, and Barnabus felt secure and content and safe, wrapped in the special essence of 'home'.

But Barnabus had not had any sleep the night before, because, however Walls tried, the Whale could not be found a place in rehab before the following afternoon. So they had all had to vacate the apartment, carrying the little Whale between them, and pretending to go on their run. Instead of this they took a room at the nearest motel and watched over the Whale, who continued in deep intoxicated slumber all night. Andy had not slept properly for nights due to worry about what his Alex might be doing, and consequently as soon as he sat down he dozed off on the other motel bed. This left Walls and Barnabus to keep watch. These long slow sleepless hours were when Walls, whose ability to keep a secret was worse than Elodea's, had told Barnabus the full story, including the truth about the starting pistol.

In the morning Barnabus, as the one of the three who was least likely to be distasteful to the Whale for historic reasons, was given the task of breaking the news about the rehabilitation clinic to the potential patient. Fortunately the Whale acquiesced without much persuasion. So Walls and Andy and the Whale headed off to get breakfast and then travel together to the clinic.

"I'll better go too to keep an eye on things, otherwise Andy might let the Whale do a runner!" Walls had said. "And I've got to pay. Otherwise Andy will go and pay instead!"

But Barnabus had to leave them as he had to go to work.

So now, as he finished his second helping of casserole Barnabus, just as he sometimes had when he was a toddler, fell fast asleep, suddenly, quietly and unexpectedly, with his head on the dining table.

"My *dearest baby!*" said Elodea, lovingly, and left him there for half an hour before enticing him, still half asleep, to move to a drawing room sofa for the night. Elodea tucked Barnabus in tenderly with a duvet and thought how sweet and young he looked when he was sleeping.

***

The following week Elodea was taking Theodora for her morning buggy ride when she saw Mr Buttress, the local shepherd, in a field. He was fitting a tupping harness and a siring marker crayon on one of his rams.

"Just putting the redding bag on Herbert here, so as we know which of they ewes he has had relations with," he called out to her cheerfully. "Don't know how they used to manage without 'em! I allus use red in mine. You can get all colours these days, you know, but I likes red; it's a good clear colour. Stands out when you take a quick glance round the field."

"*Redding?*" said Elodea. "It's funny you should say '*redding*'. Mrs Shipman used the same word just the other day, and I didn't understand what she meant at all."

"Oh ay!" Mr Buttress replied. "Poor old lady. She gets fair wound up about the old redding of the ewes. She allus thinks my rams are the Devil in the first place. See, it's the horns and the wide spaced eyes and the cloven hoofs. Then having relations with they ewes out in the public view – she don't think that's right, especially when they aren't even decently married, see. Dear, dear, poor lady, what a cross Mr Shipman has to bear, eh?"

"Oh! I knew it couldn't really be true!" said Elodea, disappointed. She felt let down even though the rational section of her mind had always known perfectly well that it was impossible that Mrs Shipman could be an accurate seer of visions and dreamer of dreams.

"Eh?" said Herbert, thinking he must have misheard. "I didna quite catch that."

"I said what a pity it was that Mrs Shipman is how she is," Elodea replied, "I'd better carry on with this walk before Theodora gets fed up.

"Little un is being quiet today. Well, they allus gets grown-up and well behaved in the end, don't they. Like my lambs, bless them; soon stops frolicking around and grows into stolid old sheep! Cheerio then!" said Mr Buttress.

Elodea leaned over the pushchair back to look down on Theodora. Theodora's left cheek was bulging as she sucked furiously and happily on one of the giant barley sugars.

The little *darling*, she thought. So *good* and *well behaved*. All that was ever required was a lot of sugar combined with tartrazine and sunset orange! I don't think they are doing her any harm. To start with Theodora couldn't be much more hyperactive than she is naturally and secondly I really don't feed her *that* many.

Elodea leant further over and gave Theodora a kiss, earning a glare in return, and then said, "But what am I going to use to keep you quiet when you can talk well enough to tell Mummy about Granny's dark little sweetie secrets?"

Latin quotations included in A Walrus in Oxford

Tempus rerum imperator - Time, commander of all things

Lorem ipsum – Sorrow itself.

Quod erat demonstrandum – That proves it.

Nanos gigantum humeris insidentes – Dwarfs standing on the shoulders of giants.

Momento vivere – Remember to live.

Facta non verba – Acts not words.

Perfer et obdura; dolor hic tibi proderit olim – Be patient and tough; some day this pain will be useful to you.

Ut sementem feceris ita metes – As you sow so will you reap.

In vino veritas – In wine there is truth.

Deus ex machina – A god out of a machine; a sudden unexpected change. (Originates from Greek dramas where Zeus was lowered to the stage from a machine.)

Tempus volat hora fugit – Time flies; the hour flees.

Ecce panis angelorum – Behold the bread of angels.

Astra castra, numen lumen – The stars my camp, God my lamp.

Cura fugit multo diluiturque mero – Worry flees and is dissolved in much wine. [Ovid, *Ars Amatoria*]

Duas tantum res anxius optat, panem et circenses – Two things only do the people earnestly desire: bread and the circus. [Juvenal] (Priscilla has changed this quote from bread and circuses to bread and bacon – lardum.)

Auctoritas non veritas facit legem – Authority, not truth, makes law. [Hobbes, *Leviathan*]

Tarde venientibus ossa – For those who come late, only the bones.

Dum satur est venter, gaudet caput inde libenter – When the stomach is full the head is happy.

Vinum est dulcia venena – Wine is sweet venom.

Cuivis dolori remedium est patientia – Patience is the cure for all suffering.

Non semper erit aestas – It will not always be summer, i.e. enjoy good things while they are here before the hard time.

A diabolo, qui est simia dei – Where God has a church the Devil will have a chapel. (Priscilla is being very rude and is implying that Kings has copied Coromandel but in an inferior way.)

Corpora lente augescent cito extinguuntur: Bodies grow slowly and die quickly (Tacitus)

are pondus idonea fumo : fit only to give weight to smoke

Other quotations:

Revenge is a dish best served cold: appears to be a proverb with no definite source although there are several claimed sources.

When you have eliminated the impossible, whatever remains, however improbable, must be the truth: speech by Sherlock Holmes in Arthur Conan Doyle's, the Sign of Four

Revelations 12:12

quoted by Andy as *the devil is loose and has great wrath because he has but a short time*

The full verse version in King James' translation of the Bible reads

Therefore rejoice, ye heavens, and ye that dwell in them. Woe to the inhabiters of the earth and of the sea! For the devil Is come down unto you, having great wrath, because he knoweth that he hath but a short time

The land of the free and the home of the brave – The Star Spangle d Banner by Francis Scott Key

True and blushful Hippocrene – Keats, Ode to a Nightingale ('Full of the true, the blushful Hippocrene')

'satiable curtiosity - Rudyard Kipling, Just So Stories, The Elephant's Child